I0692037

The Pig Masters

by

Alexandria May Ausman

Copyright © 2025 by Alexandria May Ausman

All rights reserved, including the right to reproduce this book or portions thereof in any form whatsoever.

Book cover illustration by Alexandria May Ausman
Editor: Jon M. Ausman

Library of Congress Control Number: 2025927703

ISBN: 978-1-963335-59-0 (ebook)
ISBN: 978-1-963335-58-3 (paperback)

Published By:
Ausman & Cousins LLC
1700 North Monroe Street
Suite 11, Box 284
Tallahassee, Florida 32303-0501

For author interviews: ausman@embarqmail.com

Das Kaiser Haus Series

The Collar King Series

The Most Brutal Man in Europe Series

Claus's Revelations (Chapters 1 to 8)
Priceless Changes (Chapters 9 to 17)
Silver Well (Chapters 18 to 25)
Book Four (Coming soon)

The Psycho Series

Cemetery Kid Redux (Chapters 1 to 20)
Stop Calling Me Psycho (Chapters 21 to 33)
Motor-Psycho (Chapters 34 to 44)
Delusion of the Collar and the Key (Chapters 45 to 53)
Brutality's Prisoner (Chapters 54 to 64)
Aesthetic Akathisia (Chapters 65 to 74)
Metallic Burden (Chapters 75 to 83)

27 Masters Series

Anita the Benevolent (Chapters 1 to 7)
The Beast and the Witch (Chapters 8 to 16)
High Priestess of Schizophrenia (Chapters 17 to 24)
The Professional Dominatrix (Chapters 25 to 33)
Triangle of Trust (Chapters 34 to 41)

Minute Mistresses (Chapters 42 to 49)
A Secret 28th Master (Chapters 50 to 57)
A Touch Too Much (Chapters 58 to 65)
Bugs in the Wall, Turkeys in the Ditch (Chapters 66 to 73)
Death of a Psycho (Chapters 74 to 81)
A Harbor with a View (Chapters 82 to 89)
The Pig Masters (Chapters 90 to 97)
The White Room (Coming soon)

Stand Alone Books

The Grannybat's Weird Tales & Gothic Stories Volume 1

Book Twelve Characters: The Pig Masters

Alexandria: a schizophrenic trying to survive
Anita: a deceased former Master
Baker, Doctor: a clinical psychiatrist at Harbor View
Bastard: a shard of Boyd
Bob: married to Alexandria's maternal grandmother, a pedophile
Boswells: gypsies
Boyd: a deputy sheriff, a secret Master
Bradley: a Harbor View security officer
Carla: spouse of Dennis
Cathy: a deputy sheriff, dispatcher
Charles: a Harbor View security officer
Chipley: a Harbor View orderly
Christian Axel: secret husband of Psycho/Rachel, trainer and original Master
Christy: Henry's 'girlfriend'
Cindee: Rebecca's girlfriend
Commisso: a clinical psychiatrist
Daisy: Julia's mother, living in Baltimore
David: a schizophrenic patient at Harbor View
Debbie: Alexandria's psychopathic and sadistic mother
Dennis: the county sheriff
Douglas: a nurse's aide at Harbor View
Dude: a command hallucination, an aggressive anger shard of Alexandria
Earl: Julia's husband

Ginger: a former Master

Gothic Barbie: a vengeful, sexually sadist Dominant shard

Gretta: a high school classmate

Gus: a Master, psychopath, want to be serial killer

Heather: a local attorney, a former Master

Henry: a decease schizophrenic patient at Harbor View

Holcomb, Doctor James: a Ph.D. in Sociology

Huff, Doctor: a clinical psychiatrist

Jacinda: a high school classmate

Jake: Julia's and Earl's dog

Jon M. Ausman: the current Keyholder

Joppers: a nurse's aide

Joyce: a deceased pimp

Julia: a scheming friend of Sheryl and ex-foster mother

Julie: a former sadistic, abusive Master

Karrie: a deceased child

Keith: a deputy sheriff, a jailor

Kelly: a high school classmate and bully

Kick Start: a high school classmate; first name is Greg

Kyle: a deceased schizophrenic patient at River View

Leslie: a former Mistress

Linda: a deputy sheriff

Looper: a disembodied voice, Psycho's narrative hallucination

Ma Chère: Seine's partner

Maddie: a deceased friend of Boyd

Mary: a Maiden who takes care of Alexandria's children

Mary: Psycho's maternal grandmother

Matthew: a deceased submissive
Meeks, Officer: a Nashville police officer
Metcalf: a Harbor View wing supervisor
Michelle: a foster child who committed suicide, raped by Bob
Paula: a friend of Sheryl
Psycho: a schizophrenic trying to survive
Rachel: Alexandria's birth name, Simon is Rachel
Randell: a deputy sheriff, a bull
Rebecca: a cross dresser
Richard: a deceased schizophrenic patient at Harbor View
Ronnie: Maiden Mary's live in partner
Scruffy: a deceased fire dog
Seine: a fire dog
Sheryl: a DCFS area manager, the 17th Master
Simon Brag: a command hallucination shard of Alexandria, her lost inner self
Stephanie: a nosy high school classmate
The Chose One: a shard of Alexandria, Niemand
Timmy: Psycho's spouse
Tom: a high school classmate
Victoria: an abusive high school classmate
Williams, Doctor: a clinical psychiatrist
Wolff: a Harbor View orderly
Zeppelin: a fire dog

Preface

We all thought it was a new day dawning. Too bad it was just business as usual. Once again, we find ourselves on the run from some idiot with foul intensions. Where do we find these people? Ah, you see that is the secret. They find us. One would think we have sucker tattooed on our forehead.

The D/s couple have bonded tightly. Their metal is about to be tested by all those around them. Fingers and tongues are wagging. Everyone has an opinion about what is best for the diseased pair. Pulled in one direction, then into another, the Dominant and his submissive are coming apart at the seams.

The Alpha faces the pit of the Snake, and the submissive is in the crosshairs of the red-headed harpy. Things are looking grim in this battle for control. Simon has stepped into the fray to offer a simple solution. The fake collar. Too bad the one chosen is more of a lie than the circle she wants to wield.

Get ready to rumble. Okay, you can stretch your muscles and we will tag you in as soon as we are tired. This is one hell of a beast we are slated to try to pin down. For this book you will want to grab your bolt cutters (again and again), your thinking caps, and oh yeah, your glasses. What you thought you saw was not what you are about to get. Sometimes, truth is stranger than fiction.

Chapter 90: The Poacher
The Rise of Mistress Julia

Is it gonna be a nice day? Ah, with that title I think not. Where is Master Boyd? Well, he is going to be on a vacation for a few chapters. Things are about to go from horrible to fucking horror in the world behind the shattered looking glass. Just exactly what went wrong in this program and what were the disastrous results will astound, anger, and maybe even traumatize you. The trouble with living in the Real is that rarely is there a true happy ending. Can you dig it?

The submissive is lost. The human memory is the roadmap that all use to find their way in the realm of life. Alexandria has lost her way in her journey to where she is meant to be. Wandering, without understanding, she is an easy target for those who see profit in possessing one so vulnerable. There is much to gain by finding someone that won't be missed or traced.

Are we all ready to take our first steps out of the Harbor with a View as Alexandria? Wonderful. It is about time don't you think? We had been there for seven months. Well, part of us never did leave. We went into that horror hell hole as Psycho, but we came out as nobody at all. For this trip bring your crayons, your coloring box, a bag or two of Skittles, and don't forget our collar.

Never ever forget again what happened the last time we took that fucking thing off. Sheesh! We had thought we learned that lesson with the other trips we had taken to horrid places with white cells and no windows. This time, we messed up so badly. Shit we need to grow up. Hope we can do that super-fast, if we don't we will end up like Peter Pan in Never Never land.

"Bobbie always listened to you Psycho. She idolizes you. Maybe you can talk some sense into her. What Pat did, oh God. I will never forgive that man. Please, I know it is not right for me to ask you with all that I heard you have been through but could you just try?"
--Violet begging Alexandria for help, August 2000.

Chipley came into my room to find me in the floor coloring the last pages of the coloring books from the recreation room babbling to Simon.

"Okay kiddo, you have a visitor. She seems nice. I don't see her name on the list as a no. She says she is an old family friend of yours. Pretty lady too. Come on out and let's see if you can remember her." Chipley looked down at my work.

"It is a dog like Zeppelin. He is gold too. You will like him. I will bring him to see you when I have to go home." I said pointing at the picture while putting up the crayons into the beat-up box.

Chipley nodded. "Yes, it is a nice dog you have there. Look you even stayed in the lines. Very good Alex. I like that picture a lot."

I frowned. "I am out of pictures to color Chipley. What will I do now?" I had already colored all ten coloring books in the entire ward.

Chipley chuckled. "Well we will have to see if we can get new ones Alex. You colored them all in three days. I have never seen so much effort put into anything. I bet when you had a job you got a lot of work done."

I got up from the floor. "I had a job? When Chipley? I thought I was born here with you. Do you know who is my mom and dad? Is it Charlie and Missus Metcalf?"

She almost choked on her spit laughing. "Oh God no. I don't even want to imagine kids from those two. Honey I don't know who your parents are. You will have to ask Boyd."

I shook my head. "I don't know who that is. Please tell me who that is." I started to get upset over the fact that she was always talking about people I didn't know.

Chipley sighed. "He was just here Alex. You already forgot? He has Simon's key and the collar. Remember now?"

I just looked at her confused. "Simon has the Key. Chipley, why do you play tricks on me? I don't know what you are talking about."

She ran her hand through her hair. "Okay, you know what Alex? You are getting agitated again. I am not trying to trick you honey. You are forgetting. Just take a breath and let's go see your visitor."

I narrowed my eyes. "Visitor? Who? I don't have a visitor." I looked around the room unsure about what she was talking.

Chipley let out her breath loudly in frustration. "Honey, just come with me. It is like talking to the wall," she said under her breath.

I turned to look at the wall. "Why are you talking to the wall, Chipley?" I found that very weird. Does the wall speak? I never knew that.

Chipley walked over and took my hand. "Come on Alex. Forget about what I said."

That was not a problem. I already had. She walked me out to the recreational room. Sitting at the rec table was a woman about five foot six with medium length dyed blond hair. Her eyes were big and brown with a heart shaped face. This woman of near fifty had at one time been a real stunner. Her figure was still in decent shape, but the ravages of fried foods and sedentary lifestyle were starting to take their toll. Her face was still quite pleasant to look at.

She smiled at me standing up as Chipley and I arrived within earshot. "Wow, you are looking great Psycho. I don't think I have ever seen you weigh more than ninety pounds. You are much prettier with meat on your bones." She looked me up and down appearing pleased. I was 110 pounds thanks to regular feeding and not much exercise.

I furrowed my brow. "Who are you? I don't know any Psycho. I am Alexandria."

The woman's smile melted to that of concern. "What? You are kidding, right? Psycho, Alexandria, I am Julia. I am your best friend. We had coffee every morning for like the last year."

I shook my head. "Chipley, can I go color? I don't like all this light in here. it is too loud. Tell Simon to share the crayons too. He is stingy." I stomped my foot crossing my arms while pouting like a three-year-old. I already forgetting about the strange blond woman sitting at the table there to visit me.

Chipley looked at the now stunned woman appearing embarrassed. "I am sorry Julia. Alex is uhm, she had an accident. Her memory and mind are compromised."

Julia stared at me in disbelief. "No shit Sherlock. Holy cow. What the fuck did you guys do to her."

Chipley shook her head. "It was caused by a severe seizure, Ma'am. Look if you did know her as well as you say you did, could you help us out by seeing if you can get her to remember anything about you? I will have to ask you to be very careful. She has the mentality of a three-year-old child. If you upset her, I will stop the visit. Otherwise, I would really appreciate any help you can offer to her."

Julia sat down looking as if she was having difficulty wrapping her mind around my huge fall from grace. "Is she retarded? Is that what you are saying?"

Chipley looked at me appearing sad then to her feet. "Yeah, that is what I am saying. You have to be very careful what you say. She is easily upset. Talk to her in simple sentences and be nice. She will understand most of what you say. I can understand if you want to move on. Not many people can deal with this kind of tragedy."

The blond shifted in the chair then gazed at the table. "Is this permanent? I mean, will she get better?"

The sturdy aide patted my back as I stood there now interested in the cartoon playing on the television. "We hope so, but at this point it is unlikely she will even get close to who she used to be."

Julia nodded. "Okay, yeah that is horrible. I have worked with retarded children before. I can handle this. What was your name again?"

Chipley smiled while she directed me to sit down trying to break my attention from the Scooby Do cartoon playing. "Chipley, Ma'am. Alex, honey sit down and visit with Julia. She is your friend. Try to remember her okay?"

I snorted while I sat down. "I want to color and play with Simon. I don't know Julia. Can I have the crayons back please, Chipley," I whined.

"You know we are out of coloring books Alex. Settle down and be good. You don't want me to call Sally, do you?" She looked at me sternly.

I twirled my wig hair. "No, I am sorry Chipley. I will be good." I looked at my fingers angry that I was stuck talking to some strange woman.

Julia looked at me with curiosity. "You like to color?"

I nodded keeping my eyes to the table. "Yes, but the color books are all gone. I wanted to color. I can't talk about this or Chipley will call Sally." I remembered the threat of Chipley calling in the nurse to sedate me. I didn't like shots.

The woman chuckled. "I can bring you my coloring books. Then you will have a lot more."

I looked up eagerly. "You want to trade? I only have three packs of smokes. How many can I get for that?" I was excited that this lady could get me more lines to fill in with the colors they liked the best.

Julia smiled sweetly. "I will give them to you for nothing. What pictures do you like?"

I smiled back at her. "I like dogs. I have a dog. His name is Zeppelin. He is the color of gold. Simon and I are taking care of him. He is at home though."

Julia nodded. "Ah Simon. I know him. He is the railroad man."

That made my eyes wide, (and Chipley's too. "You know Simon?" I was now interested in this woman.

She nodded. "Yes I do. He has been to my house. I made him mashed potatoes. He loves those."

That made me smile wide. "He does. You do know him. He said he couldn't remember anything because they hit his head. He is blind and deaf you know. It is very sad. He cries a lot."

Julia made a sad face. "That is awful. Well, we will bring him coloring books too. One of trains. That will make him happy won't it?"

I nodded feeling incredibly happy that this lady seemed to know how to help Simon stop crying so much.

After we had 'the accident' he wailed and screamed a lot. He told me he was trapped in the tapestry. He could hear me and see me, but nothing else. The electricity had broken his connection to the outside world. This caused him a lot of terror, loneliness, and pain. It was extremely hard to listen to his chronic weeping and pleas every night and day.

I felt bad for Simon but didn't know how to help. It was slowly driving me mad. If only I could remember how to fix this mess. It seemed I used to know how to, but I was unable to focus my thoughts.

Julia spent the rest of the visit appearing interested while I showed her the pictures I had colored. I told her confabulated stories about each one. She used child-like excitement, clapping, baby-talk, and spoke softly. Chipley watched the woman closely appearing impressed by Julia's grasp on knowing how to handle a patient with significant intellectual issues.

At the end of the thirty minutes Chipley told Julia her time was up. "Okay sorry girls but this visit has to end. Julia, I wonder if you would mind coming back maybe around eleven in the next few days? I want you to meet her Guardian, Boyd. Alex seems to have taken to you and since you had a connection to her before, well, I think Boyd would love to pick your brain on techniques he could use to deal with her. He has a very heavy cross to bear. Alex is to be released back into his care in six days." Chipley said while starting to collect the numerous coloring books I had pulled out to show to Julia.

I was fawning over a photo Julia had let me see of her little dog, Jake. She had taken it out of her wallet and had been telling me about his antics. Jake's story made me giggle. I already decided he and Zeppelin would be friends. I liked Julia. She was a nice lady with a cool dog.

Julia looked up from the photo. "Uhm I can try. Will you be around Chipley?"

She laughed. "I am around every day but Saturdays and Sundays from eleven to eleven."

Julia nodded. "Is eleven the only time I could ever catch this Boyd? I mean I live all the way in Wells."

Chipley nodded. "Yeah he is here every day like clockwork from eleven till noon. If you could swing it, I am sure it would help him out and Alex too."

She smiled and looked at me with kindness. "Anything to help out my best friend. I want to see her well. I miss our coffee talks."

I smiled back. "I want to see Jake. Can you bring him too?"

Julia chuckled. "I would love to, but the hospital doesn't allow pets. Tell you what. I will let you keep that photo of him. When you are better you can come visit Jake all you want. Simon and Zeppelin can come too."

I gripped the photo in glee. "Chipley look, I get to keep Jake. Can Richard, Henry and Kyle come too? They would want to meet Jake." I was staring at the picture of her pug dog named Jake longingly having forgotten that my schizophrenic brothers were all dead now.

Julia shot a look of bewilderment at Chipley. "Uhm, sure. They can all come. Jake will love it. Are they your friends?"

I nodded. "I am going to marry Richard. I am his girl. Kyle is buying me a car. Henry is going to marry Christy. He doesn't like broccoli or eggs." I confabulated wildly.

She smiled as if she understood. "Well then no broccoli or eggs in my house. You can bring Richard, Kyle, and Henry. We can all color when you visit."

I frowned. "Okay, but keep the crayons away from Kyle. He eats them sometimes."

Chipley and Julia chuckled at that as the nurse's aide guided me back to my room. She reminded me to wave goodbye to Julia. I did one quickly but scurried off to hide in my cell with my new Jake treasure. I couldn't wait to show Simon.

The next morning right after breakfast the morning aide called Douglas told me I had a visitor. She then brought a blond woman into my cell. I was in the floor still yapping to

Simon about Jake when Julia came in carrying two plastic bags.

"Hi Alex. Do you remember me? I am Jake's mommy, Julia?" She looked at me curious to see if I recalled her.

I shook my head. "No I don't know you. You know Jake?"

She smiled appearing satisfied. "Yeah, I know him. Look what I brought for you." She sat on the floor rapidly frightening me a bit.

I began to back up cowering afraid she was going to hit me. "I am sorry. I was only looking at the picture. Douglas, help."

Douglas was not as vigilant as Chipley. She had gone down the hall to check on the laundry. I was alone with Julia in my room.

Julia frowned. "I didn't mean to scare you Alex. Here let me show you what is in the bags." She poured them out into the floor.

At least twenty-five coloring books about dogs and butterflies were in the bag. Then she emptied the other bag and out fell new boxes of crayons, markers, and even colored pencils.

I forgot about calling out for help from Douglas, entranced by the pleasure items laying in my room floor. I came forward to grab them forgetting all about Julia sitting right there watching me with a sinister smile on her face.

"Well? Do you like them," Julia chuckled out.

"Yes. Yes. Can I color in a few? Just a few? I will give them back, I promise." I couldn't believe how many cool pictures were in the books as I ripped through them trying to decide on just a few I wanted, in case she said I could only have one or two you know.

Julia laughed. "Alex, I brought these all for you. You can have them all."

I gasped. "What? But I don't have enough to trade for all of them." I was stunned into silence as I tried to think of what I could give her to keep them all.

She shook her head. "No Alex. Try to remember. I told you yesterday. I am your friend Julia. I brought all this for you for free. We are best friends."

I nodded. "Yes best friends. You are giving me all these to me for free?"

Julia smiled. "Okay I want a hug for them. Can I have a hug for them?"

I furrowed my brow trying to decide if this was a fair trade. Finally, I nodded that a hug was fair.

She came forward and wrapped her arms around my neck and hugged tightly. I held still tolerating the shocking sensation keeping my eyes on the shiny new books that this trade just bought me. I couldn't wait to get started on filling them all in.

Julia let me go but looked into my eyes appearing concerned. "Where is your collar Alex? Do you remember you are supposed to have a collar?"

My eyes went wide. "Simon's collar? I have lost it."

She sat next to me so she could speak without being heard. "You didn't lose it. I have it. It is at my house with Jake. You left it there. Simon told you to leave it with me. He must have forgotten."

I sat up straight. "Simon told me he left it with me, and I lost it." I was in shock that at last I had found my collar. I had left it with Julia.

Julia nodded making a knowing face, "It is okay. When you get out you can come get it or maybe I should bring it to you? Would you want it now?"

I nodded my head excitedly. "Yes, I need it now Julia. I need my collar. Simon says I have to have it and find my Master."

She smiled evilly. "I have your collar. That means you have found your Master. I am your Master, Alex. Simon will tell you if you ask him. He was hit in the head and forgot. I have been looking for you. Now I have found you."

I looked at the floor. "You are the Master? You have my collar? Where is it?"

Julia looked at the door to make sure we were alone. She reached into her purse. She pulled out a circle of silver that was like the one I saw sinking in the water in my fleeting memories.

My eyes went wide unable to look away. "Yes. This is the collar. I have seen it." I tried to reach for it.

Julia pulled it away. "Wait a minute. Alex, if you take it Chipley will make you give it back."

I narrowed my eyes looking at the door too., "No, I will hide it, I promise. I won't let them take it away from me."

She giggled. "Okay let's do this. I am going to make this official so you will know I am the Master. I will let you keep it by showing you how to hide it. Then you will come with me to be with Jake, Richard, Henry, Kyle and Simon."

I shook my head. "I don't understand Julia."

Julia frowned.. "Of course you don't, but you will soon enough. Now I am going to put this on you, and you will call me Master from now on. You will keep me and this collar a secret from Chipley. If you tell anyone they will take the collar away and I won't come, see you anymore. Simon will be mad at you for losing the collar and Master again, won't he?"

I nodded looking at the floor in distress. "Yes, he would be mad."

She grinned then unlocked the collar and put it around my neck. I felt tears falling down my checks as despair washed over me suddenly. This was strange. Julia smiled while she finished her collaring.

"Now you will do what I tell you. You will call me Master. You will protect your collar, and keep it hidden. Do your job. Do you understand?" He looked at me sternly.

I continued to weep silently. "Yes I do, Master."

Julia smiled happily. "Ah, see how easy that was? Now let's take off the collar and hide it. You can show it to Simon and no one else."

I nodded. "Master, do I still get to keep the coloring books?"

She laughed. "Yes Alex, the books and the other stuff are yours. When anyone asks where you got them what do you say?"

I looked at the floor feeling strangely despondent. "That I don't remember, right Master?"

Julia nodded then took off the collar. She took a roll of tape from her purse then told me to follow her. She walked over to a one of the pictures I had drawn that was taped there. Julia lifted the paper and taped the lightweight collar to the wall. When she allowed the paper to fall back into place, unless you were looking, you would never know.

Julia turned around to smile at me. "See, now my collar is with my submissive. You belong to me. I will come and get you out of here soon. Then you can be home with me."

I winced, "What about Zeppelin, Master? Can I get him first?"

She laughed. "Alex he is already at home waiting for you. You just forgot. It is okay. Your Master is here now. You just do what I tell you and everything will be fine. A Master helps you and Simon find your way. Do you remember that?"

I thought for a moment. "Yes Master, you are right. Simon says that the Master helps us in the world of the real. You are the Master. I am sorry I forgot you."

She patted my shoulder/ "I forgive you this once. Don't do it again."

Douglas came into the room to tell Master Julia her time was up. She smiled at me making a button your lips motion, then she left me alone with my new coloring books, collar and a feeling of extreme loss.

Simon walked into the room after she left to find me sobbing and coloring on the floor. He raised an eyebrow.

"What is wrong?" He sat down in the desk chair.

I shook my head. "I found the collar and the Master Simon. I don't want to have a collar and a Master. It feels bad Simon."

He jumped up appearing startled. "You found the collar? Where is it."

I pointed at the picture on the wall. "Behind the picture Simon. I don't want it or the Master."

Simon huffed. "I can't see the fucking thing. Are you sure you have it? What picture?"

I sighed realizing I forgot he was blind now. "I will look it for a minute and you can see through my eyes but I must leave it where it is taped to the wall." I got up and lifted the paper.

He sat there focusing. "I don't know Alex. It looks different. I seem to remember it was bigger. This seems like, well it is the collar. But where is my Key?"

I went and sat back down. "You wanted me to find the collar and the Master. I did. I don't know about any key." I went back to coloring while Simon sat there crying because he couldn't see anything without my help anymore.

Chipley and Master Boyd arrived together that day after Master Julia had poached the collar. They both walked into my cell to find me surrounded by tons of new coloring books appearing agitated.

"Where the fuck did all this come from," asked Master Boyd as he stepped over the mountains of shiny child tools.

I shrugged. "I don't remember. Someone brought them."

Chipley looked around. "Well maybe one of the night nurse's aides brought them. She has been whining a lot about needing more."

Master Boyd shook his head. "Well, I guess that is okay but is it safe to have all those pencils and markers laying around. What if she, you know." He was recalling my wires and other self-injurious behaviors.

Chipley nodded. "Yeah, you are right. After your visit I will confiscate some of it."

I looked up in anger. "Keep your fucking hands off my stuff, Chipley. I know what confiscate means, you know."

They both appeared startled by my outburst but also happy for some reason.

"Baby, you got angry and you knew a big word," Master Boyd said appearing thrilled.

I growled. "Duh, these are mine. Who are you? I am not a baby."

Master Boyd went and sat down on the bed with a sigh. "Well, I suppose it is too soon to celebrate when you still don't know your own Master."

I turned to look at him. "I do too. Stop lying about me."

He smiled brightly. "Come here Alexandria. I am so pleased you do know your Master. Very good. Give me a hug."

I groaned. "I don't want a hug. I want to be left alone. Why is everyone always bothering me? I have work to do. Do you see all these books? I must finish them. I am going home in a few days. Who will finish them if I don't?" I went back to coloring my books while huffing in irritation.

Master Boyd looked at Chipley appearing very confused. She shrugged. The two watched me for several moments. I colored fast and furious, never going outside of the lines they sent me the color codes for each photo reminding me of the taboo colors of 'yellow, orange, and green.' I began to pull out all shades of those three to throw away when Master Boyd reached down and pulled me to my feet by my waist.

I struggled angrily. "Stop touching me." I was furious that this strange man kept interfering with my work.

He frowned but pulled me toward his unit ignoring my anger. "I want to hold you Alexandria. You will be home with me soon. I can hardly wait. We even have a party ready for your homecoming. Even Seine seems to understand. He excited to see you."

I went limp in his embrace. "Who is Seine?"

Master Boyd laid his head on my breasts. "Your dog, Alexandria. Don't you remember Seine?"

I moaned. "You are stupid. My dog is Zeppelin. He is made of gold."

Master Boyd jerked his head up appearing stunned. "Did you say Zeppelin? You remember him?"

Chipley walked over and sat down. "She was talking about that dog to that woman Julia yesterday. Is that really her dog?"

Master Boyd nodded. "Yeah, about twelve years ago. Honey, don't you remember giving Zeppelin to Kick Start? Zeppelin lives with Cody now."

I growled. "Greg, he hates being call Kick Start."

Master Boyd squeezed me hard making me gag. "She is remembering, Chipley. That is true. Greg is his real name. Zeppelin was gold in color."

Chipley smiled brightly. "Ah that is wonderful news Boyd. Soon she will be her old mean self again."

Master Boyd kissed me deeply and I tolerated it but felt furious about his advances. He noticed my lack of kissing back and raised an eyebrow.

"Something is wrong here Chipley. My girl is behaving strangely. Are they slipping her medication again?" He looked at the aide suspiciously.

She shook her head. "Other than the visit I told you about yesterday nothing new is going on with Alex, Boyd."

Master Boyd looked into my face sternly. "Alexandria, tell me what the problem is right now. I mean it. What is bothering you? Is this about that visitor Julia yesterday?"

I looked away trying to avoid eye contact. "Nothing. I don't remember."

He growled. "Chipley, put Julia on the do not allow to visit list. I seem to remember a Julia from the days before she and I got sick. The woman was a menace to Alexandria. I seem to recall she was a friend of that horrid Sheryl. Yeah, that is who that bitch is. She is not to visit anymore."

I looked at Master Boyd in shock. "What? You will keep her away from me?"

He narrowed his eyes. "You know who I am talking about?"

I nodded. "Julia, you won't let her see me anymore?"

Master Boyd's eyes went wide. "You remember her name? What the fuck? Okay, who am I? What is my name?"

I tried to focus. I had heard Chipley say it, but I couldn't recall it. I shook my head much to his anger.

"Fuck, you can remember Julia but not your fucking Master. That is bullshit," yelled Master Boyd.

I hugged my Master tightly. "Thank you for not letting Julia come back. I don't want her to come back." My sudden affection both startled and calmed his anger.

Chipley had been only listening, but my statement caused her curiosity, "Alex, honey why don't you want to see Julia anymore?"

I looked at the picture on the wall, "She is a liar. I remember Sheryl. I know Sheryl is trying to re-collar me. I saw Sheryl's collar behind the paper." I pointed.

Master Boyd's eyes about bugged out of his head. "What?" He jumped and ran to the spot I was claiming the old bitch's collar was hiding.

He saw the circle imprint immediately. His anger was epic when he tore away the paper to revel the taped submission device.

"How fucking low can you get. Look at this Chipley. Fuck, just fuck." Master Boyd ran his hands through his hair appearing agitated.

Chipley stared in disbelief as my Master tore the taped collar off the hospital wall. "Oh, my God. I don't understand how that got there. No one is allowed in Alex's room."

My Master turned around shaking the fake collar at Chipley. "From now on no more visitors for Alexandria. I told you that there are assholes out there just waiting to take advantage of her. Enough, keep that door locked and for God's sake, unless the hospital catches fire, don't let anyone but the staff in here," he screamed loudly.

I fell to my knees covering my head in a cower from all his noise. My Master continued to rail about poachers and the hospital's ineffectiveness at protection of the patients for quite a while. I was frightened by his anger but grateful that Sheryl would not be able to get me.

NOTE: I *had somehow mistaken Julia for Sheryl. I didn't understand they were two different people. In my shattered mind, Sheryl, not Julia had come into my room and recollared me.*

Simon had told me the collar was not the one he recalled. This made me sure that woman had lied about it being the one he was looking for.

Interestingly, while I had forgotten who Master Boyd and Julia were, I did remember the name of the hateful, pushy slave driving Sheryl.

I have never understood the exact reasons for my misidentification of Julia as Sheryl. I suspect that Master Boyd's discussion of Julia being a close associate of Sheryl coupled with my fleeting memory of her aiding Doctor Baker in forcing me to sign the paper that got me hurt had something to do with it.

Julia had obviously attempted to poach Master Boyd's collar. She was unsuccessful on her first attempt due to the severity of my cognitive damage. I have no idea what she must have thought when she returned the next day to find no one was permitted access to visit me. She likely panicked a bit figuring out her trick had been discovered.

However, that would not stop her from another second attempt to get what Sheryl had stupidly told her I was. Sheryl had become desperate to get her collar back around my neck. When her attempts to visit and work on me failed, she asked Julia to go and manipulate me in her place.

She nor Julia had any idea of my mental decline. When Julia decided to help her old buddy Sheryl out, she discovered the truth. I was never going to be DCFS material again. This stunning surprise only made Julia more determined, but not to aid Sheryl's bid to re-collar.

In a double-cross Julia turned on Sheryl trying to get the collar and make herself Master. Julia had dark designs in mind for such a rare, precious commodity: A mentally ill and incompetent, young, pretty girl who had almost no associations or support system. She had been waiting a long time for this kind of opportunity to come her way.

Julia would stop at nothing to make sure she didn't lose out on this unexpected bit of luck.

My Master finally realized his yelling was upsetting me. He took the false ring of silver and threw it on the desk, then took my real collar out of his bag and showed it to me. I immediately felt better as he locked it around my neck. He found me much more loving and compliant when he pulled my collared unit into his lap.

He spoke lovingly to me while I played with Simon's key around his neck. Master Boyd and Chipley talked about his party plans for my welcome home celebration. He even invited her if she wished to attend.

"I wouldn't miss it for the world, Boyd. Alex has been here so long I hate to say it, but I will even miss her. I am so glad to see her going home to such loving hands. Few of my patients ever have anyone who cares waiting for them. They go straight to a residential treatment center. You have to promise to keep me posted on how she is doing," Chipley said while she watched me tracing while holding Simon's key.

My Master laughed. "You bet. I will even have Alexandria write to you to prove she has improved. She just needs the peace and quiet of home. That will help so much, you'll see."

Chipley snorted. "I hope you plan to keep your peace until she is better if you catch my drift, Romeo. She has the mind of child. You saw how bad that shit with that dirty snake Holcomb upset her." She looked at the floor appearing a bit embarrassed.

Master Boyd scoffed. "Now you are overstepping your bounds just a tad there nurse Chipley. What me and my girl do when she is no longer your patient is not your affair, not anymore." He kissed the top of my head.

The nurse's aide shook her head. "You are right, Boyd. I have no business professionally to tell you what to do with your fiancé once she is discharged. I am warning you as your friend, and I think we are friends, Boyd, to let the girl ease into bedroom games. She has been traumatized enough. You don't want to be just another one of those monsters in her head, do you?"

He grabbed my face and forced it to his while he kissed me with his tongue deeply. I followed his behavior unsure of what was going on but assumed if it were wrong Chipley would stop him. When she just sat there watching and scowling, I mimicked his behaviors. He began to pant and wrapped his arms around my waist pulling my unit to his tightly.

Master Boyd broke free of the kiss, gasping for air while he looked at her. "I have waited to have my One and Only for more than half a year, Chipley. You don't see her screaming or panicking at my kiss now do you? She will be with me in every way when we get home without fear, just like before she came to this hellhole you call a hospital. These assholes have taken my wife's mind from me, but if you think you will take the rest of her by trying to guilt me out of it. You are sadly mistaken. In six more days, she will be back in my bed and in my arms where she belongs. It is all I have dreamed of forever." He growled while looking at me with yearning.

Chipley shook her head appearing frustrated. "Whatever you say Master Boyd. I wish you the best, and Alex too. Poor girl has been through enough shit for a couple of lifetimes. Try to remember that."

My Master left taking the false collar to dump off in the garage. Chipley and the hospital followed his orders to a fault. My room was locked for the next six days. No one was allowed in or out other than necessary staff.

I didn't care. I had all those coloring books to finish. I was happy to finally be left alone. My Master did come visit every day but my memory for him didn't. While he was there, I understood he had Simon's key and my collar. The moment he left, I forgot immediately. Why exactly I could not get his identity to imprint into my fried brain is beyond me. It would have prevented a lot of pain if I had. At that time, my memory was terribly random, and unpredictable. I had already forgotten Julia and her attempt to poach, the fake collar and my belief that Sheryl had tried to re-collar me.

Then at long last December 20th arrived. Chipley helped me pack up my things as Joppers signed me out of the ward for the last time. Joppers was going to walk me out to the admitting area to await Master Boyd. I was trembling in terror. I was more than a bit scared to leave the world I had come to know, the only one I could remember anyway.

Chipley smiled as she reached out adjusting my hair. "You be a good girl for Boyd, okay? I will miss you, but I am so happy to say goodbye the right way. I will come visit you soon and I will bring Wolff. Won't that be nice?"

I nodded as I looked at the floor trying not to cry. "Yes Chipley, it will. Please can I stay? I don't want to go home." I almost whispered knowing it was useless.

I had been pleading for days. No one was listening.

She chuckled then pulled me into a hug. "You will love it once you are home. You will never want to come back I promise. Don't be scared. It will be wonderful, you'll see."

I sniffed back my tears. "Okay Chipley if you say so."

Jopper's came to walk me out. The nurse's aide took a moment to speak to Chipley about another patient. I stood there holding my small bag of stuff while pulling at the clothes that Master Boyd had brought for me.

That morning I was told to put them on. I was dressed in a black long-sleeved shirt, black pants, and a pair of platform boots. I was told this is how I used to dress. I decided I liked the outfit, but it was weird to be wearing real clothes after, well after however long wearing hospital scrubs (seven months).

The ladies finished their conversation and Joppers motioned me to follow her out. I turned around and looked for the last time at the cell that Psycho died in. Chipley waved with tears in her eyes as Joppers and I approached the metal doors guarded by Charlie and Bradley.

Charlie smiled at me while Bradley spoke, "Goodbye kiddo. It has been a real pleasure. Good luck. We hope you have a wonderful life and hey, don't ever come back okay?" They both chuckled at that while Missus Metcalf pushed the button and the gates opened.

We walked in silence as the second set of metal doors opened like the first. Joppers turned right taking me down the long winding hallway back to the entrance that I had not seen in seven months. The grounds that Chipley took me too were in the back not front.

I had no memory of this place, not at that time. People were sitting in chairs looking at us while Joppers spoke to the guards in blue standing at the big glass doors.

The officers looked at me suspiciously then opened them so we could step out onto the covered entryway. Joppers thanked the guards and guided me to a bench on the sidewalk. She had me sit down while she lit a smoke.

"It is going to be a beautiful day, Alex. I bet you are super excited," Joppers said while taking a drag.

I shook my head. "No, I want to go back to my room Joppers. Can I go back to my room now," I whined.

She chuckled. "Damn. I have never heard a patient from our ward want to go back. They really fucked you up sweetie. Bastards! Well just calm down. You will forget this place in no time. Home will be great. You'll see."

I looked at the concrete walkway feeling my heart sinking. "Chipley says that too. Okay I will be good." I sighed trying not to cry over my despair at leaving.

Joppers smoked her cigarette, then another. My Master was late. She started to tap her foot appearing irritated.

"Where is Boyd? Damn it. He is never late once till I need his ass to be on time. Shit. Alex, sit here a minute. I am going to go make a phone call to see if the ward knows what is going on," Joppers said while she went back into the hospital.

I sat there singing a song about a cat named El Gato when a car pulled up in front of me. The passenger side window was down. A blond woman was sitting behind the wheel. She smiled at me then motioned me to come to her car. I looked around and didn't see Joppers, the guards or anyone. I got up and walked to her car to see what she wanted.

"Get in Alex. I am here to take you home to Zeppelin, Richard, Henry, and Kyle. Simon can come too. Hurry and grab your things. Kyle said to tell you he won't even eat your crayons if you can get there fast. I put all your new coloring book in your room. I hope Kyle doesn't color them all up before we can get home," the woman said excitedly while giving me a friendly smile.

I smiled back in thrill. "You have Zeppelin already? Everyone is waiting on me?" I ran back and got my little bag happy that I was getting to at least see my friends at home.

I rushed back and got into her car. The woman sped off while telling me to put on my seatbelt. I did what she told me feeling much better about going home now that I knew all my friends were there.

"I can't wait to pet Zeppelin. Richard will be so happy that I kept his car for him too." I said ecstatically glad I had packed his red hot wheels corvette instead of letting Chipley keep it.

The woman smiled diabolically. "Just sit back sweetie, this is going to be a long ride." She took off out of town hauling my idiot unit off to face my nightmarish destiny.

Master Boyd had been held up an extra thirty minutes at work, then got caught in heavy traffic. He had called the ward, but the new aide forgot to write down he would be an hour late. When Joppers came back finding me gone she assumed Master Boyd came and took me home. He had never cared much for the hospital protocol. She wrongly assumed he would be just the kind of guy to leave with his ward and thumb his nose at telling anyone.

I can't tell you what happened when he did arrive and went to the ward only to find his property, the One and Only, was missing. I was told he went fucking ballistic and nearly got arrested for the fit he threw demanding blood for allowing me to either wander off or be kidnapped right under their noses. No one had seen me leave. No one knew where I had gone.

Normally the police must wait twenty-four hours to file missing persons reports. I was an exception due to my compromised mental state and the probability that someone had absconded with me against my will. Foul play was immediately suspected. I was told not only did my Master nearly have a heart attack, but so did Dennis, Maiden Mary, and my children. They all knew the likelihood that I would be found dead or worse, never found at all, was astronomically high given the condition I was in at that time.

This was bad as it could get. I had the mentality of a three-year-old and would not have been able to defend myself or even call home if I were lost or got away from my captors. It was painfully clear to my Master that I didn't even remember where I lived, my children, or even more than my first name. The county wide manhunt began, and a nationwide APB was put out. Everyone knew if I was not found quickly, the odds of finding me alive were zilch. No one had any idea where to even start.

The situation surrounding my kidnapping that day was like most things in my life. Bad luck mixed with a comedy of errors. A Master who was always punctual got caught in traffic and by a late arrest. A newbie staffer forgot to take a message. An aide breached protocol thinking I was peaceful enough to mind orders, not considering others may not. A determined poacher was stalking and waiting in the weeds for a chance to steal a prize. My inability to recall even simple details made me a sitting duck for victimization. In the end if only one thing in this series of fubars had not occurred the next few chapters would never have been written. However, they did get written. On with the Nightmare…

Julia had been clever enough to learn all she could about how the hospital handled releasing their patients out of care. To her benefit she found out it was horridly lax compared to the amount of effort they put into keeping a patient from leaving once admitted. Patients were taken out front with little fanfare while a single aide made sure they got into the right car.

Julia had found out about my release date when Chipley breached confidentiality without thinking and told her. She had used her two visits with me wisely as well. Julia asked all the right questions to find out what words she could use to coax me into her car without having to drag me kicking and screaming while causing a scene.

She had come there that morning and sat quietly in the parking lot stalking the front door. Julia knew that it was a long shot that my Guardian would not show up almost immediately after the aide brought me out, but to her it was worth the shot.

To her utter amazement not only did the guardian not show up but the aide left me unguarded. She would tell me later she couldn't believe her luck. It was a breeze to just kidnap a retarded patient right off the property without a single person watching.

Julia was very clever. She didn't assume no one saw her. She also assumed eventually; someone may come by to ask her if she had seen the missing submissive. Julia had thought of every possible pitfall.

I sat in the passenger's seat humming happily totally unaware of the deadly situation that I was in. Julia turned on the radio to play music to keep me calm and passive. She smiled while she watched my near empty head rocking with the songs. I had always loved music of most types so the treat of hearing it once more kept me gentle as a kitten despite the three and half hour drive it took to arrive at our destination.

Besides, the house he shared with his wife, Julia's husband Earl owned a small farm on the outskirts of Cumberland. She and he rarely ever visited his family homestead now that his elderly parents had been taken to spend their final days in the local nursing home. He and she had planned to sell the place eventually, but Earl had been far too busy with his construction business to get around to repairing the house his parents had lived in all his life. Without some work the farm would likely have sold for less than the couple believed it was worth.

The farm had sat quietly, without occupants or visitors for over six months. It was secluded, with the closest neighbors being a mile away on either side. Best of all it had a large outbuilding behind the old farmhouse that had no windows and only one door in or out. It was the perfect place to park a mentally ill patient that had just been kidnapped right off the hospital grounds. No one would think to look in a shed, behind an empty house, on an abandoned farm, miles from anywhere. Especially, since no one would ever hear screams for assistance, if the daft girl ever realized that she really needed such a thing. She did need help, she just didn't know it.

Julia pulled into a long winding drive that led to a small white house with a green roof. I smiled when she parked in front of this little place and killed the motor. I started to tear off my seat belt suddenly feeling extremely excited that in moments I would be re-united with Zeppelin and my schizophrenic brothers at long last.

Julia laughed. "Whoa there Alex. You are a wiry cuss. I see that has not changed. Good you will need that energy in time. For now, I want you to follow me, bring your stuff." She got out of the car.

I grabbed my bag quickly practically flying out of the car as I followed behind her. I frowned when she passed by the house front door and began to walk around to the back door.

"We are not going inside to see everyone?" I looked longingly behind me hoping that Kyle would not eat all the crayons before I could get inside and stop him.

Julia laughed. "They are back here Alex, just follow me. I know right where they are. Keep up now. Don't lag behind."

I smiled while making sure to get right up behind her as she walked to the shed and pulled out her keys. She unlocked the padded lock while I looked over the metal storage shed. I wondered why everyone was in this weird building instead of inside the house.

Julia turned around smiling. "You first. Go ahead, Zeppelin is waiting."

I strained my eyes to try to see into the darkness. "I don't see him. Is this a trick," I asked feeling suddenly very frightened.

She chuckled. "Not at all Alex. Here we can go inside together." She grabbed my upper arm and pulled me inside with her.

Once inside she turned on the single light that dimly lit the interior. Nothing was in the shed but empty storage shelves, dust, cobwebs, a large yellow bucket, and a long chain attached to a hook in the back wall. I wildly looked around for Zeppelin, Richard, Kyle, Henry or even Simon. No one was in here.

I looked at Julia. "Where is everyone? Did they leave?"

She shook her head. "At first I thought maybe you were faking this retardation thing to get out of the hospital. I see you really are one dumb motherfucker now." She began to laugh.

I felt fear race down my spine. "I don't like being here. I want to go back to my room. Can you call Chipley and tell her to let me come back? I am scared." I began to tear up realizing on some level that this woman was not taking me anywhere. I was home, this was it.

Julia shut the door still laughing as she reached into her purse and took out a collar like the one Master Boyd threw away. "I figured they may find the one I gave you. I got two of them. Now you will submit to me and wait here until I am ready for you to serve me. Get on your knees, Alex. I am going to collar you. I am your Master remember?"

I reached up and tugged at my wig hair nervously. "No, please, I want to go back to see Chipley. I don't remember you. I don't like it here. I want to go back to my room." I whimpered crying even harder.

Julia reared back her hand and slapped me. "I said get on your knees Alex. You will do what I tell you or I will make you fucking sorry you stupid bitch." I let out a yell then cowered to my knees before she could slap me again now wailing loudly.

She glared at me. "Cry all you want, Alex. If you don't do what you are told I will give you plenty to cry about. Now hold still. I don't like that word Master. You will call me Mistress. You got that dipshit?" She roughly forced her collar around my blubbering unit locking it into place.

I nodded terrified of this woman and unable to understand what was even happening. I couldn't remember how I had gotten there or why Chipley wasn't coming to help me, or Bradley or anyone.

"Say it stupid. Say, yes Mistress," she yelled after getting the circle of silver around my neck.

"Yes Mistress. Please, I want to go to my room. Where am I?" I sobbed while covering my eyes on the floor.

Julia laughed hard at that. "You are in your room until I say otherwise. Now get up and come with me. I am going to make sure you stay put till I come to get you."

I continued to cover my face still kneeling. Julia grabbed my collar. She pulled me roughly toward the chain. I instinctually understood that whatever she was going to do with it was not a good thing. I began to struggle to get away. She turned and punched me in the gut sending me right to the floor in spasms of pain.

"I told you to do what you are told. Don't fuck with me, Alex. I am not playing around here. I have no problem beating your ass if I have to. I have dealt with bitches since before you were fucking born. You know I used to turn tricks in Baltimore when I was a young woman. You must be tough to hook out there. I learned how to keep a woman in her place. I had to or it was my ass, you know. Girl, I have lived on the rough mean streets. So, guess what? I know all about schizophrenics. Met shit tons of your kind out there in alleys, parks, and the homeless shelters. Nothing but idiots if you ask me. Most were kind of like roaches, they were worthless shit. But you my little beauty, you have value. I intend to collect too. Until I can, you are going to stay put and shut your fucking mouth." She said while she pulled the chain to my collar and used a small padlock to lock it around my collar while I writhed on the floor gasping for air.

I wept in pure terror while she kicked my little bag at me and told me the bucket was for my potty needs. She told me she would return with food and to check on me.

"Make yourself at home loony toons. This is your new room. Hell, I would think by now you'd be used to this kind of living. I will see if I can find a cot laying around. Until then, sleep on the floor. Okay, that should do it. Next time I come here you better hope you remember who the Mistress is. If you don't, well I wouldn't want to be you. Bet you wish you had been nicer to me when we used to share coffee now don't you?" She laughed at that then left the shed.

I laid there in the floor where I had fallen afraid to move. I was leaking tears of misery as I heard her lock the door from the outside. A few moments passed then I heard her car pull out. I was utterly alone.

I finally sat up and pulled on the chain. It was in the wall tight. I couldn't budge it no matter how hard I pulled it. The length would not allow me to reach the door, but I could reach the bathroom bucket. I sat down and opened my bag taking out my coloring books and Richard's car. I couldn't understand what was happening, but I knew one thing, pissing off my Mistress was painful.

I began to color my pictures while waiting for Simon to come keep me company. I wished Chipley would come to visit me soon like she promised she would. I was unhappy that Zeppelin and the gang were not here yet, but I was sure they were coming. I just had to wait. I was used to waiting.

Julia came back the next day to find me playing with the toys I had and coloring. When she opened the door, I cowered into the wall recalling she had hit me a few times. I was afraid of her.

She just laughed at the pathetic scene as she tossed over a covered plastic dish of mashed potatoes, a few bottles of water and a bag of Skittles. I tore at the food and water like a wild animal eating it with my fingers.

"It is still impressive to see how retarded you are now. Not so high and mighty anymore, are you? I brought you a cot, so you don't have to sleep on the floor. You piss in it you are dead. It belongs to Earl, so it is a bit fucked up, so do you got that sweetheart?" Julia left for a moment and brought back a green cot and several blankets while telling me it was going to get cold soon, I would need them.

I kept my gaze down while wringing my hands as she set up the bed so I could reach it. She continued to tell me that everyone was looking for me, but no one was going to find me. Julia said that some police spoke to her asking if she seen me. She laughed while telling me she let them check all around her house. They left deciding she was telling the truth.

I looked at the floor starting to understand at some level that Julia taking me away from the hospital was a bad thing. "Will they come back to look for me Mistress," I asked feeling frightened that I would never see Zeppelin again.

She sat down on the cot smiling at me. "You remembered I am the Mistress. Very good, Alex. That means I don't have to hit you to get that through your thick skull. It doesn't matter if they do. You are mine now. You understand that don't you?"

I nodded. "Yes, you said you are the Mistress. I am wearing your collar." I wrung my hands anxiously.

She laughed. "Ah, so the moron can learn. Good. Now you keep coloring your books. I will see you tomorrow." She left again locking the door behind her.

I pulled my knees to my chest and began to cry again. Simon came through the door and sat down on the cot.

I saw him sitting there crying himself over his own pain. "Simon, I think something bad is happening. I can't remember what. Can you help me? I have to remember what is going on."

Simon put his head into his hands. "I don't know if I can anymore, Alexandria. This is as bad as when Debbie poisoned the oatmeal and we got schizophrenia."

I stared at him stunned into silence as suddenly I saw a woman called Debbie telling me the black leather outfit looked great on me while demanding I finish my oatmeal. She had tricked us into eating poison. She had been selling me to bad people so they could torture me in her basement hell since I was a little girl. My arms began to burn where she carved her name into them the day the man raped me on my eighth birthday.

A sudden storm of images flashed into my head: I could see Tom walking away after Gretta and Jacinda kicked me in the cemetery. I was dying. The police came with Anubis. I was reading the note from Michelle. She killed herself because Bob molested her. I saw the pills in my hand. I could feel the foam pour out of my mouth as the void took me away from my suicide attempt. The cold water of the river washed over me. Dude pushed me from the bridge. I could see the static, hear the cicadas, and see the transmissions rising. Doctor Huff told me I have schizophrenia. Doctor Commisso said there was no discount radar in my arm.

My trance ended with the memory of Doctor Commisso telling me the Sloans were my new guardians.

"Simon, oh my God. This cannot be right. Do you remember this? No, no, it is a lie. Oh God, no." I began to wail loudly realizing the only thing worse than having no memory of who we are was remembering who we are.

He stopped crying and looked at me. "You remember Debbie, Mary, Bob, Doctors Huff and Commisso too? Alexandria this is good, not bad." He stood up and came over to my weeping unit.

"Simon, I don't want to remember this. I can see the faces of those bad people. Oh, the pain Simon. We are sick. Our mother made us sick. I want to go home. Please let's go home now." I was in a full-on crying jag as I tried to deal with the trauma of my first sixteen years of life all at one time as if it were the very first time.

I felt my chest aching with the realization that I was an abused abuse and a torture survivor. I could not recall anything past age sixteen, but I now remembered every single blow, terror, loss, and horror to that age. I now understood the random images in my mind was my past.

Looper grabbed the voices, statements, and descriptions of my childhood. His many voices began to plague my heartbroken ears. There was no escaping it. I had not come from a good place. If this was what my mother and father were like what other horrific truth that were hidden in the darkness of my damaged mind? I knew right then and there I no longer wanted to find out.

QUICK NOTE: *I still did not recall the terror of Master Julie, the evil clique and much more. I could only recall five years old to 1987 and some of 1988. The memory of Debbie, Bob and Mary was enough to make me, or anyone to be honest, want to die immediately just so I would not have to live with those images in my head anymore.*

I am not sure why my memory suddenly started to return that day. It started to flood back in spurts, and in order by age and year, little by little each day for the next several weeks. It abruptly ended this flow back into consciousness with the death of Matthew and abandonment of Ginger in 1996. Why it ended there and didn't pick up any memories from 1997 to 1999 for the next six months is also a mystery to me. The brain is a strange creature and a damaged, mentally ill one is even weirder. So, who knows?

Once again, had my Looper been able to pick up any memories of those three missing years, the next few chapters may not have happened. But like my accidental kidnapping, I was unlucky.

For the next month, I sat in the shed, coloring my books, wailing with each new series of horrific memories, and trying to come to terms with the nightmare that is me. Julia came every day with food, water and to clean out my bucket. I rarely spoke to her now that I realized she was one of them. A cruel Master that had forced me into a collar like the ones in my memories.

I didn't recall that she had kidnapped me from the hospital, not yet, and now I had forgotten the Harbor with a View just as Chipley and Joppers had predicted I would. That was also a bad thing. I now believed it was 1996, and I had just been abandoned by Mistress Ginger.

I could recall the red-headed Mistress had sold mine and Matthew's collar. Matthew killed himself over it finding out he was sold to the pimp Joyce. Mine went to Mistress Leslie. The strange woman had used me for two days, then as agreed told me to go and wait for her phone call. She was going to sell my collar to another to get her money back. I was grateful to be free of the assless chapped weirdo. It seemed to me that Mistress Leslie had found a new Keyholder. Looks like Mistress Julia must have bought me out. It made sense. I just couldn't understand why was she not having me provide any service?

The whole thing was just weird.

Chapter 91: Fantasy Girl
Mistress Julia & the Rise of Master Gus

Of all the chapters and segments of our long, weird story the one after this is the one we dreaded the most. You have read of terrors, abuses, crimes, and tragedies beyond the wildest nightmares of humankind so far. So, when you hear me say I feared the next the most, you know it is time to brace yourselves for the unthinkable.

The story of Mistress Julia and the five months after my release by kidnapping from Harbor View is a demonstration of just how demonic one person can be to another. Understand this was not driven by mental illness, drugs or alcohol, psychopathy, or revenge. Mistress Julia did what she did for purely selfish interests and greed.

She didn't care that I had helped her in her darkest hour. It didn't bother her a moment that my mind was deficient, and I had already suffered terrible injury. All she wanted was a life of leisure and comfort that she didn't have to work too hard to acquire. My collar was the answer to all her dreams come true. All she had to do was find just the right buyer, and she had…

Ready to take a dip right into the fiery lakes of Hades? What? You'd rather not? Ah, we can truly feel your pain. I mean we really can. These are our memories, so empathy is just a given. Pull up your big kid panties, grit your teeth, swallow your need to scream, and remember to say your prayers. See you below, we hope.

19th Master (collar- no key)
Mistress Julie – the Poacher
Reign December 20th, 1999, until May 5th, 2000

"I have never seen anything like this Alexandria. It is like you took a perfect picture with that paint brush. It is weird, but since your brain injury you seem to have amazing art skills. Hey, would you be willing to sell paintings on commissions? Mister Duncan said he was willing to pay 1,500 dollars for an oil of a lighthouse in a storm. Do you think you could do one like that?" **-- Master Boyd admiring Alexandria's oil painting of Darlin Cemetery, September 2000.**

It had been four full weeks since Mistress Julia had snatched my mindless unit off the grounds of Harbor View. Over that time my intellectual abilities had been recovering at only a snail's pace thanks to lack of my receiving any aid from professionals such as occupational or physical therapists. As January rolled into February, my three-year-old mentality had only reached the level of a six to seven-year-old.

My most horrific and traumatic memories in my early life to 1996 had returned. I still didn't remember whether I had children, went to college, or who Master Boyd was. I also didn't recall most of my life as Psycho other than fragments of confusing images and voices of the past.

My recall had improved from five minutes to a full ten to fifteen. The short-term memory damage was significant enough to keep me from learning anything new unless it was repeated many times. This allowed for the continued expression of severe intellectual disability (retardation).

Worst of all, the high level of ECT treatments coupled with the catastrophic seizure had effectively lobotomized my shattered brains. I lacked the ability to become aggressive in any way. Without understanding, lack of ability to remember details for very long and a recall of only trauma of the most heinous kind from my past, I had developed a type of terrified personality.

Since I was incapable of fighting back, I would merely cower, whimper, cry, and try to get away when attacked by any method. I was completely helpless to defend myself against Mistress Julia's cruel treatment and restraints of my unit. Thanks Doctor Baker, you motherfucker. Grrr!

Mistress Julia found it extremely easy to intimidate me into total compliance with her demands with extraordinarily little effort. All she had to do more is yell loudly, slap or kick when I didn't move fast enough. I was unimaginably afraid of her though she had done way less than any Master before her ever had.

Psycho would have beaten this bitch Mistress into the dust with her platforms while singing El Gato with a loony smile on her face. The brain damaged Alexandria could only cover her head and weep, begging for mercy. It was truly a sad sight to see I am sure.

Mistress Julia had been right, I had been leveled to a point of meekness never seen in my lifetime as a survivalist in all my twenty-eight years. She could do whatever she wanted without even breaking a sweat. I had gone from bad ass schizophrenic submissive to retarded psychotic slave thanks to the cruel experiments of the greedy psychiatrist Doctor Baker.

Meanwhile back in the world outside the shed hellhole my real Master was searching high and low for his missing One and Only. Each day brought fresh heartbreak for the schizophrenic Dominant. He would go to work, then barely clock out before heading out to turn over every stone for miles in total desperation.

Master Boyd had already started his cycle of prodromal right on time in late November 1999. Remember, he had always cycled from December 1996 to June 1998. Well, 1999 was no different. In December, he began showing the irritable symptoms of his fresh dip into psychotic schizophrenic hell. The added stress of my brain accident, kidnapping and his lack of sleep while searching in vain for his collar, had set off an early and violent acute cycle by mid-February. Everyone had missed the dangerous signs that my Master was slipping off the bend until it was nearly too late.

Dennis, Linda, Randell, and Carla kept trying to get Master Boyd to accept that after almost two months of not hearing a single word that it was probable they never would. The belief was universal that I was dead in some shallow grave or my bones were bleaching in the sun in a field. It was simply too farfetched to believe that I had survived long if I had wandered off exposed to the winter weather.

It was also certain that if I had been kidnapped, the offender would not have decided to keep me around after having their fun with my brainless unit. It was fantasy to believe a kidnapper had run off with me to have a buddy around to color and play with toys. It was assumed the culprit had enacted their disgusting desires, killed me, then had hidden my remains in a well secluded place to keep the crime from being discovered.

My Master continued to refuse to give up. He knew that somewhere out there I was still alive. He was holding on to hope with both hands and his feet. He could not face a life alone without his One and Only by his side and in his bed once more.

Master Boyd pushed himself to the limits ignoring his own mental and physical health in his discouraging efforts to bring me home safe and sound. Master Boyd had not slept a single peaceful night, nor eaten enough to keep a mouse alive during those dark days. His prodromal was now slipping rapidly into the dangerous acute phase of his cycle.

On February 14th, Valentine's Day, he stopped at a store to gas up to start his search that day for his missing lover. I had been missing for fifty-six days. As he replaced the gas nozzle into the pump, he saw a man giving his sweetheart a dozen red roses. She squealed in happiness, threw her arms around the lucky guy and they kissed deeply. Master Boyd was triggered by the red roses, hug, and kiss. He had been bringing me red roses since the tea party before the days of Master Anita when I was hospitalized.

I was told he promptly got into the black Chevelle and wrapped it around a tree in an effort to end his pain. His plan was to join his beloved in the Summerlands, so we would not miss the holiday in each other's arms. Apparently, he had finally accepted I was gone and was never coming back.

Luckily, my Master survived the crash with only a minor head injury and broken ribs. He was taken to the hospital patched up, then Dennis had him immediately moved to serve his own inpatient sentence in the Harbor with a View. Yeah, you read that right.

Despite what Harbor View had done to me, Master Boyd was treated there as well. For starters he had a different psychiatrist. Doctor Baker was now losing his license thanks to Mistress Heather and David's folks.

Secondly, he was not placed in the psycho ward as I had been. His schizophrenia was the treatable type. The hospital placed him in the psychotic lite ward with the bipolar and barely psychotic patients.

Last, with Dennis being the big man of the county, no one was going to fuck with Master Boyd. His treatment at Harbor View was five stars compared to my own tragic run-in with those assholes.

Master Boyd told me later that while he was not treated to experimental drugs and overzealous ECT treatment, he did suffer some of the same foul practices. He spent many weeks in a strait jacket, rubberized cells and was often locked in his room.

QUICK NOTE: *My Master's expression while lighter than my own was still just as violent at times. His anger at this hospital over taking his happiness by injuring me and then losing me, caused him to be a less than compliant patient. He would not see the lights of our home until April, effectively serving from Valentine's day until April 28th in his longest inpatient stay (seventy-three days) during his entire adult life to that point.*

A FINAL WORD ABOUT DOCTOR BAKER

To this day I refer to Doctor Baker as the slayer of schizophrenics. He had been solely responsible for the suicide of both David and Kyle. He had caused Henry to be murdered, and me to be catastrophically brain damaged. He had indirectly caused Richard to commit suicide, Matilda to become catatonic for life and the serious suicide attempt of Master Boyd.

Just think, he actions killed or seriously injured seven schizophrenics in seven months. I know serial killers who are less prolific in their number of murder victims. To think this criminal was able to do this in the USA with a license and a blessing from the American Psychological Association. I am sure Doctor Josef Mengele would have been proud of this asshole.

Mistress Julia had been keeping me stored in the shed on her husband's old farm while the hub bub of my disappearance cooled off. Master Boyd had tracked her down through Sheryl. He had come by her home twice demanding to look around her property for me.

My Mistress knew he didn't have a warrant therefor no right, but she was clever. She allowed my Master to search both times trying to appear genuinely concerned and helpful. This kind of behavior would likely have fooled a normal police officer. My Master was a paranoid schizophrenic. He didn't believe for even a second that she had nothing to do with my mysterious disappearance. Master Boyd was certain that my Mistress was working for Sheryl.

My Master began to stalk both her and Sheryl focusing all his attention on catching the two harpies when they tried to move my unit from wherever they had hidden me. It is probable this was wishful thinking on his part. If he were right, I would be kept alive for the reason of using me for DCFS work. It was horrible for him to face the possibility that the Sheryl women would be willing to snatch me with my daft brain to use as a mindless slave. Still the outcome was easier for him to tolerate than a stranger abduction where murder was the goal.

Amazingly he was right to a point. Sheryl had no idea what Mistress Julia had done. Believe it or not she too suspected my Mistress was involved somehow. She had sent my Mistress to try to re-collar me for her. When Sheryl found out of my traumatic brain injury and low adaptive functioning, she wondered why Mistress Julia had neglected to share that information. Sheryl had spoken to my Mistress at length after that first visit. Mistress Julia never mentioned it. Old Sheryl was not a dummy. There was some ulterior motive for keeping that to herself, right?

My Mistress played it cool and calm while the old power mad Master Sheryl and paranoid psychotic Master Boyd came at her repeatedly demanding she spill whatever information she had. Mistress Julia was an old Baltimore prostitute and ex-pimp. She knew how to handle the pressure of the authorities without cracking.

She was experienced in abducting and holding a girl hostage until the family or do good folks stopped looking. Mistress Julia had done it many times in your youth.

My Mistress would come to bring me my mashed potatoes, water, and skittles daily. During her visits she would tell me stories of waiting at Greyhound bus stops for wide-eyed, young, naive girls getting off to live in the city on their own for the first time. Mistress Julia would be there as the first friendly, helpful local ready to aid them in any way possible. The innocent females would often take the bait of a tour of the city or a warm bed for the night. After my Mistress had them secluded, she would drug them, chain them up and keep them high.

She would then sell the stoned girls to clients and break the youngster into her life as a hooker. Often the female was addicted to drugs so quickly she would give over to her new employment easily, unable to function with both the memories of the indignities and detox side effects of not having the drugs.

Mistress Julia told me sometimes the girls' families or friends would show up in town looking for their missing loved one. She was caught in her first attempt to build a stable and did a year in the State penitentiary for human trafficking and kidnapping. Now see that would have been good information to have, oh I don't know, right away. When she got out, she was much more careful.

She had learned that the usual time for a search to be called off was around three to five months. Mistress Julia was careful to never come to the shed at the same time of day, often would park her car down the road and walk to the farm. She always took a different route. More than that, she didn't plan to enact her plan for me until mid-April. Thanks to the vigilance of my Master Boyd, she decided she may have to wait longer until he suddenly disappeared himself mid-February.

Mistress Julia waited all of March and noticed not even Sheryl was showing up banging on her door any longer. She did a little snooping and to her delight found out Master Boyd's new address was Harbor View, room 3. He was effectively neutralized and no longer a threat to her plans.

When she poked around to see what was going on with her old red-head buddy, Sheryl told her that I was presumed dead. My Mistress learned from the Area Manager most no longer expected me to be found. If I were, it would require my dental records to prove my identity no doubt. My Mistress had successfully shaken off all challengers. Nothing stood in her way to collect what she had stolen my collar to obtain in the first fucking place.

On April 1st after holding me hostage chained to a wall in a shed for almost one hundred days, my Mistress finally decided it was time to start the second phase of her plan. She was ready to start the life of her dreams, and I was the key to that fantasy.

I had spent all those months coloring, playing with my few toys, weeping, trying to work with Simon to get our memory back, and wishing to go home without knowing where that even was to be honest. I didn't recall Mistress Julia despite the fact she kept saying we had known each other. I was unable to understand most of what she would say to me when she visited.

The only thing I could comprehend was that she liked to slap me around and would yell at me for stupid things like not calling her Mistress or sitting there drooling like a fool. I was still very sick when the horrid month of April arrived. Let's just say the wheel was turning but the hamster was nearly dead. Sad but true. There is not much I can say about that time other than one hundred days feels like one million. My mind was just too mixed up and slow functioning to have many private thoughts.

Since there were almost no interactions, I was not sparked to do much thinking either. I will say those coloring books were among the most used items on the planet by the end of my prison term in that shed hell hole. I had not had such a traumatic situation since the days of Debbie's basement torture chamber.

QUICK NOTE: *As luck would have it, my Mistress may have been experienced at holding someone hostage for months, but I was more experienced at handling months of* *seclusion while being restrained. From my childhood with Debbie to many years of inpatient treatment, being held captive without much stimulation was unfortunately a skill I had developed so deeply, even brain damage couldn't break it.*

Thankfully, my sanity was not seriously impacted by this extremely dangerous implementing of the cruelest of tortures, namely isolation. I was still holding in a residual of a type with the symptoms of my disease only expressed very mildly. This would eventually be one of my saving graces. If I had gone into my cycle during the reign of Julia, I would not be here to write these chapters today.

I was awaked in my cot by my Mistress. She told me to pick up my stuff and put it into my bag. I was groggy and slow.

"Get up, God dammit. Lazy shit. You have laid around for four months. Now it is time to serve me idiot, move." She slapped me across the face.

I let out a yelp then wildly crammed my things into the bag terrified she would hit me again.

She stood there tapping her foot, blowing out her breath angrily. "Hurry! Fuck me, you are a loony bitch. You move like a glacier."

I got my last toy into the bag then fell into a kneeling position waiting for further orders unsure what to do now.

My Mistress chuckled. "Ah, now that is what I like to see. You are not as retarded as you were when you first got here. You and I will get along a lot better now that you are understanding who the boss is."

I sniffed feeling I may cry. "Yes Mistress." I was very confused by her strange behaviors. She was scaring me a great deal.

My Mistress walked over to my collar took a key from her jeans and unlocked the chain. "Alright, time to go. Follow me idiot."

I felt the weight of the chain drop off while pure terror filled me. "Where are we going Mistress?"

She smiled brightly. "Home Alex. Finally, we are going home. Get up, we have a long trip ahead of us. The boys are asleep in the back seat. I intend them to stay asleep. You will not speak unless I tell you to. If you do, I will break your fucking teeth out, got that?"

I nodded fearful to say anything since she said she would hit me if I did.

My lack of speech made her laugh hard. "You do mind well. I think I will enjoy having you around this time. I can find plenty of shit to keep you busy while I work out the details of, oh never mind that. Now before we go, tell me what year is it? Where are you from? Do you know what state we are in?"

I looked at the floor while I stood up wringing my hands. "Uhm 1996? I am from here. What is a state," I answered feeling very frightened that I didn't know most of what she tended to ask me. Somehow that seemed like a very bad thing.

Mistress Julia snickered. "Perfect. Man, do you know how much money you saved me? I didn't even have to drug your dumb ass up. A few sedatives in your mashed potatoes and you were calm as kitten. This is beyond my lucky year. God must love me. Okay dummy follow me. Remember keep your fucking mouth shut. Not even a burp out of you." She walked out the door.

I followed behind her feeling the outside air on my face for the first time in months. It was dark, perhaps near midnight but I couldn't tell. My Mistress led me to her car. In the backseat were two boys with dark hair. Both appeared to be under ten years old. I was motioned to get into the passenger's seat. My Mistress got behind the wheel and drove off. I had served my final day of captivity in that God forsaken shed.

I was quietly relieved to be free at last, but I was confused by Mistress Julia's driving through the darkness never seeming to reach our destination. For three days we traveled with my Mistress only stopping for a few hours a night at rest stops to sleep or gas stations to get fuel. I didn't understand at that time we were traveling across the country. The destination was my Mistress's original home of Baltimore, Maryland.

During our trip, my Mistress told me she had left Earl while he was away on a job out of town. He would come home to find his home empty of his wife and two sons. She had been desirous of a divorce for years but in a fault state if she tried to leave him without a lot of money for a good lawyer she would lose custody of her sons and all the money from the many properties he held.

My Mistress had never worked the entire marriage and had brought nothing into it. She was sure to end up broke, middle aged and destitute. She yapped about how she was planning to take everything Earl had and leave him the shaft now that she had decided to go home to her mother.

Mistress Julia told me that she had met Earl when she was still a working girl at a bar. Earl was there to do some work for his company on an old opera house. She was there hunting for a man with a big wallet who was seeking entertainment. The kindhearted construction worker had never seen anything like my Mistress back in his small-town home of Cumberland. He was immediately smitten by her very experience charms and beautiful face.

She laughed while she told me the hillbilly idiot asked her to marry him the second day they had been dating. My Mistress said she was nearly thirty at the time and losing her appeal for street work. She feared becoming a skid row ho. Earl's proposal was accepted simply because he had the financial means to give her a life of luxury without her having to get a nine to five job, or so she thought.

It turned out that Cumberland was not what she thought it was going to be. Her deep-seated love of danger, partying, and wild late nights were over in that backwater nothing town. They rolled up the sidewalks by seven in the evening and the county was dry. She couldn't even get liquor to drown her sorrows in.

She met Sheryl during a trip to the local Dollar Tree, the one I nearly ran into with the car, one year after she married Earl. The tough, no nonsense woman immediately took to the suave, glamorous Mistress Julia. Sheryl worked hard but finally talked my Mistress into filing as a foster home so that my Mistress would have some excitement in her life. My Mistress said she did enjoy the job, but it was never enough to make up for her lost city nights.

My Mistress had dreamed day and night for over twenty years of the day she would get to go home to her beloved Baltimore. Her mother still lived there and was thrilled Mistress Julia was coming home at long last.

I listened to her stories not comprehending most of the information she gave me, not yet anyway. I was more interested in the boys that sat playing quietly in the back seat. I was not allowed to talk to them. They asked my Mistress about me. I listened as she told them I was Aunt Alex and coming to live with them in Maryland.

That made me happy. I liked the children and couldn't wait to get to play with them and their toys. I just assumed I would get to do that at some point. My Mistress obviously wanted a babysitter or maybe a housekeeper. Why else would she be my Master? I was not smart enough to have a job. She had already told me I was too damned stupid to work at more than scrubbing a floor.

I wondered if I had always been this useless. It seemed I could recall that in my past life I had even fed pet tigers and once preached in a church. But the police made me stop for some reason. I was starting to question why my memories indicated I had been someone else a long time ago. What happened? Why was I not like that anymore? Did I have an accident? Maybe I broke my head when I ran into that outhouse wall when those girls put that shock collar on my neck?

As the days of travel continued, the scenery, the boys talking in the backseat and my Mistress's constant yapping started to awaken my need to understand my situation, location, and identity. The interactive stimulation was sparking my synapses to rewire for the second time in my life. I was starting to comprehend everything around me more by the hour. The sleeper had finally started to awaken.

On the third day we arrived in the huge city of Baltimore, Maryland. My Mistress cursed while she fought her way through heavy traffic. Me and her boys were in awe. We had never seen so many cars or people in our lives. There were millions of them. I could smell a foulness in the air. My Mistress took a deep breath while smiling.

"Ah, the Atlantic. I have so missed the ocean," she yelled out.

I breathed in the smell and decided the ocean smelled of decay, rotten fish, and foot odor. Yuck! The air was strangely cold for the late spring. My Mistress told me this was the North, and Spring often was much colder than in the south.

I suddenly had memories flood in of Debbie taking me to places just like this when I was a child. We moved a lot. I had been to Maryland before, and to other states near this place. All over the country. I sat there in a trance as the visions of those places flooded into my memory filling in more and more blanks in the darkness of my brain damaged head.

My Mistress noticed my trancing. "You going loony on me, Alex? Well cut that shit out. You are going to be a good girl and mind me and mom or else. No trouble out of you."

I nodded. "Yes Mistress," I said in a monotone voice still fixated on the many sights and sounds of my past life.

After what seemed like hours we arrive in the suburbs of this huge city. My Mistress was smiling with joy as she pulled down a street lined with colonial styled homes. She drove the car into the driveway of a two-story old white home with a grey roof. It was on a street that dead ended, and her mother lived in the second to last house on the left side of the cul-de-sac. The homes were widely spaced all down the long side street with large yards.

I looked around at the neighboring houses. They were like the one we had come to visit. It was then I noticed the last house, on the left hand of this street, to the right of my Mistress's mom's home. It was a mansion type home. It was huge.

The home was positioned far back behind a ton of large trees. It had to be three stories or taller, built almost in an old plantation style. It was white with a green roof. It was so different from all the other modest home I couldn't help but stare in disbelief at it.

My Mistress noticed my wide-eyed gaze. "Oh yeah, you see that? That house belongs to the sheriff's kid. Lucky bastard is a trust fund baby you know? Has more money than anyone ever needs. He still works as a jailor at the penitentiary though. Can you believe that? All that money and the dumbass gets a job. Crazy if you ask me. Move your ass. Mom is waiting and I am starving."

I got out of the car following behind my Mistress wring my hands keeping my gaze to the ground. The boys followed behind me stretching and bitching that they were cold. My Mistress knocked on the door. A woman who appeared to be an older version of Mistress Julia came out screaming in excitement. The two women embraced both crying in joy.

Me and the boys looked at each other shrugging. The tallest boy rolled his eyes and pretended to rub away a tear while smiling at me. That made us both giggle when…

I saw my daughter smiling as she opened the present Matthew my brother and lover gave to her. My son was in diapers. Wait, I have children. What the holy fuck?

I looked up from my visions in a panic. "My children, where are my babies? Oh my God, what has happened to my kids, Julia?" I started to cry and pace suddenly realizing I was a mother myself.

The woman and children started at my now agitated self in shock for a moment when my Mistress finally looked at her mother putting up her hands in a motion of 'I got this.'

"Alex, stop acting stupid. You know that DCFS took your kids away. You are here to get a job, and clean up your life so you can get your kids back remember? I know it is hard since the car accident but that is what happened. Now if you want to see those kids again, you better get inside and get with the program." My Mistress said appearing sure of her information.

I was frightened by her words. "I was in a car accident? I lost my children? What? I don't understand. Where are they?"

She smiled. "Come inside, let's all settle down and we can talk about this. Your kids are safe Alex, trust me."

I glared at her. "Do I have a fucking choice? I don't even know where I am now, do I. Convenient isn't it?" I was surprised at the words that just popped out of my mouth. It was as if I didn't speak them.

My Mistress frowned. "Not nice Alex. I am trying to help you. Now either you come inside and stop making a scene or I will call the police and you can go back to a cell. You remember that I bet."

I nodded. "I do." I dropped my head looking at the ground understanding I had no choice but to do as she told me or things could get worse. Something was bad here and now I was slowly starting to realize it.

I sat on my Mistress's mother's couch while Mistress Julia told her mother Daisy that I was a best friend who had been involved in a horrendous car wreck. The head injury caused memory problems, retardation and I had my children taken by the unfair DCFS due to my limitations. She told Daisy she had taken pity on me. My Mistress lied by saying she had brought me along to offer me a chance to rebuild my life and eventually get my children back into my custody.

Daisy told my Mistress she was a saint to take in such a troubled friend. My Mistress smile while she pretended we were the best of friends and she couldn't just leave me there in that horrid land run by bubbas and small minds.

I glared at the floor angrily realizing my Mistress was a fucking liar. I was not sure what went wrong with my intellect but it sure as shit wasn't any car wreck. I had already examined my unit in the shed, when I had memories flood through, to check to see if I had evidence to prove injuries I recalled like the discounted radar for example. I had scars all over the place, but I recalled how most of them got there. I didn't have any I couldn't recall, but one. A 'B' on my left arm. Weird that one I couldn't recall how or why it was there.

I had a memory that I was a mother of a boy and a girl. My anger at not knowing where my kids were and hearing my Mistress telling her mother lies was rising within. I decided this bitch had better start talking about me to me for a change. I was done with hearing all about her shitty life. I wanted to know who the fuck I was and right fucking now.

65

My Mistress was showing her mother pictures of her boys while the children ran about the house checking out the room when my anger boiled over.

"You get your ass outside and answer my questions or so help me get to calling the cops, Julia. I have had enough of this bullshit." I stood up suddenly yelling at the top of my lungs beyond angry.

Everyone stared at me in utter shock, even the boys stopped rough housing.

My Mistress looked at her mother. "Okay mom, give us a few minutes alone please? Alex is prone to little temper tantrums. I know what to do, but I need some privacy. Can you take the boys upstairs and show them their rooms?"

Daisy never took her eyes off my now red-faced unit. "You sure she is not dangerous honey? I mean she seems pretty angry."

Mistress Julia snickered. "She is just confused momma. Take the boys please? I will be right up after I get her under control. It will be fine, promise."

Daisy nodded then got up and herded the boys up the steps as my Mistress had asked her to.

I watched them go then looked back at my Mistress,. "Well? Get to talking, I am listening. Who the fuck am I? Who the fuck are you? Why can't I remember shit? What really happened."

My Mistress leaned back smiling evilly at me. "You are awful froggy for a girl that is in a lot of trouble. Well sit down and let's talk about it shall we? Or do you really want me to call the cops?"

I growled as I sat down. "You aren't going to call the fucking cops. If you did, I have a feeling it is you they would be arresting. I think you took me from my home. That is why people were looking for me. You kidnapped me, Julia."

She laughed out loud. "Well you are right about that but trust me you wanted to be kidnapped, idiot."

I narrowed my eyes suspiciously. "Huh? Why the fuck would I want to be kidnapped? That is stupid."

Mistress Julia looked up at the ceiling. "Well you were being held inpatient in the mental hospital, loon bird. They were never going to let you out. They took your kids, your job, hell everything, idiot. Then they ran electricity through that brain of yours till they fried the fuck out of you. I was your best friend before you lost your shit. I couldn't just sit there and watch them lobotomize your ass like that. Thanks to you I had to run, though I was ready to go mind you. I had to get you out of there and me too. If I got caught jail for me, back to the rubber room for you. Now, you have a chance to get work, start over, and when you have a place, I will even help you get your kids back. Until then, baby we are both on the run from Johnny Law. You understand that I bet."

I sat there stunned into silence for a moment as the memory of Doctor Baker telling me I would soon have no fight left in me, not with the amount of, oh no. My Mistress was right. They were frying my brains as some mental institution. I had been there a long time.

I gasped. "I remember the nuthouse, Mistress. You took me away from there. I remember that too. Chipley and someone else were shit, I can't remember. Doctor Baker was riding me on the lightning. Henry and Richard told me about it, broccoli and eggs." I lost the memory, but I realized this time the blond ex-hooker was telling the truth sort of. Think idiot. Damn Alex, wake up.

My Mistress laughed. "Yeah I helped you out and got my own ass in a sling for it. I had to be rough because, well they fucked you up, you know. Since you remember now, we can be best friends again. I am your Mistress, and you can serve me in return for my helping you get your life back on track. Deal? Or do I just buy you a bus ticket home? I mean the Greyhound station is only a block away. I could walk there right now. Of course the second you show your face there they will lock you up, then it is back to the boiler for you sweetheart." She smiled knowingly.

I shook my head. "No. Of course not. I guess I should thank you for helping me escape. Could I at least call my kids you think? Make sure they are alright?"

My Mistress sighed. "We could if we knew the number. They put them in a foster home, Alex. I have no idea where. We need to get money for a lawyer and a house. If we both get jobs, we could afford one in no time. I need a divorce and you need custody of your kids. So, tomorrow I will start looking for work. You are still wanted, so I will see about getting you some housekeeping jobs. No one asks questions about a maid. I will try to get on with the jail. Gus next door works there. He is an old childhood friend of mine. I think he could pull some strings to get me all set up."

I nodded. "You seem to know all this. I am not completely sure I understand all of it, but if you know the way I will follow your lead." I began to wring my hands looking at the floor in extreme nervousness at my latest discovery.

Mistress Julia snorted, "Yeah I have a fool proof plan Alex. You just do what you are told and in no time, you will have nothing to worry about anymore. Mom is getting on up there. Tomorrow after we all get some rest, I will give you a list of chores. You can start to earn your keep and pay me back for all my help."

I looked up startled as tears filled my eyes. "Earn my keep? Debbie used to say that. Okay Mistress, whatever you say. I am tired. I would like to go to bed now."

She laughed. "We all are and that is the best fucking idea you have had in over a year. Up and at 'em. Let's go see your room."

Over the next four weeks I was told that I was not to leave the house. My Mistress convinced me that the authorities were still seeking the violent escaped mental patient. She feared someone would see me and alert the cops to my whereabouts.

My Mistress and her mother bought me new clothing. The ones I had been wearing for all those four months were now beyond foul. I was reminded to eat, bath, and attend to all my hygiene needs including washing that nasty wig.

My Mistress and her mother often commented about my growing beauty after a few weeks of decent feeding and proper bathing had offset the ravages of my hundred-day incarceration. Their remarks made me feel extremely uncomfortable though I couldn't understand why.

I shared a room with Mistress Julia and the king-sized bed. It was a small room with a large window on the first floor of the house. The boys and Daisy slept in larger rooms upstairs. My Mistress never asked for Special Services, thank the Gods, and I never offered them.

It is unclear if this is because I was unaware that I provided them. Despite my memories of trauma I had forgotten some services the collar assured and this was one of them or because she was just not interested. I had no concept of sexual drive or needs.

This adaptive function had not returned to my consciousness. I had no urges like nun, like the pun there? There was no one stimulating any carnal interests, so I had literally forgotten about sex. The old you don't use it you lose it came to be a true statement in my shattered brains during those many months under Mistress Julia's collar.

I spent my days helping Daisy around the house with cooking and housekeeping. She kept me busy in that big two-story house. I was pretty bad at it in the early days. I couldn't recall how to do anything. My Mistress's calm, patient mother re-taught me how to mop, sweep, scrub and make beds. I learned the basics in cooking – yeah sad, right as I used to be able to cook anything – and how to do laundry without turning whites, pink.

By the beginning of May I had gotten to be a stellar housekeeper and trusty cook. I did all my chores without complaint and minded my Mistress and her mother without causing any trouble. I missed my children terribly and spent hours scrubbing floors trying to remember my life before this epic failure. I still couldn't even recall the event that had led to my being put away. There were no memories for 1997, 1998, and 1999, at all no matter how hard I tried to focus to gain a few.

I spent my free time coloring books, playing with toys, and talking to Simon. My mind was now functioning at the level of a ten-year-old kid. I was still very childish and often didn't understand higher concepts. I could read simple baby books, but I was starting to pick up bigger words quickly. No one was helping me learn, I was teaching myself. My intellect was starting to return, slinking back slow but sure. If only I had some professional help, I would have improved much faster.

Simon had found his way to in Baltimore by the second day of my stay there. He hated the house, the town and everything about our situation. He and I were doing our best to get along but in truth, he was not even close to becoming a friend to me. He had known the shard Psycho but had never known me before I showed up when she died. Simon admitted that at first, he didn't like me very much. He said I was slowly growing on him, but he often said he wished Psycho had not gone away.

That hurt my feelings a lot. I never knew Psycho. Simon spoke of her as if the woman were a superhero, capable of walking on water. He said I was a pale, weak, useless shard that wasn't worthy of running the unit. He hated Mistress Julia a great deal as well. Simon cruelly said that a panty waist like me deserved a shit Mistress, so he wouldn't step in and even offer to mirror her.

I tried to remind myself that Simon was mean to me because he was grieving the loss of his best friend. I was trying not to take his hateful remarks personally. I also cut him slack because he had been so severely injured during the accident that killed her. I knew he was hurting. I could hear him wailing and crying constantly. It was heart wrenching to hear. I suppose I would be bitter and angry too if I were him with all that had happened.

Still, I wanted Simon to love me the way he had loved her so completely. I would have done anything to gain even a kind word from him. Psycho was gone forever. He was stuck with me now, even if he hated me to his core. Somehow we would have to make it work.

It was the first day of May and spring had finally arrived in the north. Not that I would know. I was never allowed outside the house.

I was washing one of the millions of windows in that place listening to Simon criticize my window washing techniques when my Mistress came into the room to talk to me.

"Alex, the neighbor Gus has a bunch of clothes he needs mom and you to wash for him. His washer broke and I offered that he could use ours. Come with me and mom and help us haul the bags. The idiot didn't bother to even go to a laundry mat until every fucking stitch of his clothing was filthy." She sneered appearing irritated by this task.

I stopped washing the window and looked at the floor. "But what if someone sees me? I would have to go outside?" I started to wring my hands feeling extremely nervous.

My Mistress rolled her eyes. "We are just hauling the laundry over. It will take like five minutes, dummy. No one will identify you in five minutes. Come on, move your ass. The faster this gets done the sooner you are safe back inside. Mom is waiting."

I followed her and Daisy out the door feeling my heart pounding like a heavy metal drummer on crack. We walked down the cul-de-sac road then turned down the small winding driveway that led to Gus's mansion.

My Mistress alleged that when she had approached the old childhood friend to see if he could get her work at the local prison, where he was employed as a guard, they had instantly connected on a lover level.

My Mistress talked non-stop about how wonderful this man was to her and told Daisy that as soon as her divorce from Earl was official, she and Gus would get married. I just rolled my eyes when my Mistress talked of her love for this guy. I didn't understand a lot of things, but I sure knew one thing. Mistress Julia only loved money. If she was courting Gus it was not because she adored the man. She desired his wallet and the glorious life he could afford to grant her.

Gus was wealthy with trust fund money from his deceased grandmother. The lady had left him a minor fortune when he was still just a teenager. Now at the age of thirty-five he was well accustomed to the finer things in life. He had built the largest house, bought the finest cars, and almost anything else a person can buy with that kind of cash.

Even though he had far more money than he knew what to do with he had been working loyally as a prison guard since his twenty-first birthday. My Mistress found it distasteful that her boyfriend felt the need to work such a dangerous job when there was no need for the paycheck. Gus had told her he did it to keep his life interesting and because he loved he challenge of keeping the bad guys where they belonged behind his bars.

The three of us walked up the steps to the humongous house. I looked up to see a porch light nearly as big as a chandelier to light this entry for giants. I briefly wondered how many people it would take to clean even the living room in this place.

A large man came to the door. The man I assumed was my Mistress's beau Gus was around six-foot-tall and built like a linebacker who had one too many keg parties. His paunchy gut made him appear shorter than he was. He had dark brown eyes and almost black hair with a heavy moustache and brows. Gus's skin was deeply tanned making him appear almost Hispanic or middle eastern in decent. He smiled happily at the three of us to expose perfectly straight and unnaturally bright white teeth.

"You are a mess Gus. You need a woman around to keep you on the straight and narrow. I have been saying it for years," said Daisy laughingly.

He nodded his head in agreement. "Daisy you are absolutely right. When are you going to marry me and make all my dreams come true, hot momma," he teased.

Daisy slapped his shoulder lightly. "Now you stop that you bad boy. You need to take this young lady of mine off my hands and make her an honest woman. Leave my old bones to rust like they should." She pointed to my Mistress.

Gus narrowed his eyes at Mistress Julia. "Oh, I think only the devil could make that lovely minx into an honest lady, Daisy." He flashed her a sinister smile.

My Mistress chuckled. "Well then, we are a match Gus, because if you are not the devil's boy you are at least his stepson."

The three of them laughed while I reached out and started to haul a big green duffle bag off the porch. I was in a hurry to get back inside before anyone saw me. My attempts to escape caught the eye of the dark eyed homeowner.

"And who is this vision Julia? A friend?" I stopped cold in terror realizing a stranger who may call the cops, hell was a cop, had spotted me.

My Mistress chuckled. "Oh that is Alexandria. Don't mind her Gus, she is just a retard you know."

Gus snorted. "Julia, that is rude. You don't call them retards. They have feeling too you know."

Mistress Julia laughed. "Since when did you grow a heart, you beast. Alexandria come here and say hello to Gus. Be nice and don't act shy. He isn't going to bite."

I dropped the laundry bag I was dragging and began to wring my hands keeping my eyes down "I am tired, can I go back inside now," I whined while walking up to stand next to my Mistress practically hiding behind her so the man could not get a good look at my face.

My Mistress ignored my statement. "You know what Gus? Alexandria here can color ten pages in a coloring book in just one hour and has several hot wheels cars. You should see her collection." She said sounding proud while putting her arm around my shoulders.

Gus sucked in his breath feigning shock. "Wow that is something. I am impressed. What is your favorite picture to color," he said sounding excited.

I continued to wring my hands while shrugging. I felt the two of them were patronizing me, but I could not be sure. I did enjoy coloring and I did have several hot wheels cars. I had traded my other toys with my Mistress's children to get more to add to Richard's red corvette.

Mistress Julia rubbed my shoulder smiling. "Yes she does, Gus. She loves the dogs and puppies the best. Don't you, Alexandria?"

I nodded now really feeling they were being assholes.

Gus shook his head. "Well, that is really nice. I love dogs and puppies too. They are a lot of fun. You have good taste Alexandria. Oh, my what am I to do with three pretty girls living right next door? It will keep me up tonight you can bet." He breathed out appearing frustrated.

My Mistress rolled her eyes. "You had better not be up tonight, lover boy. Keep that in your pants. Let's go mom, Alex, it is getting to deep here for me and I am wearing my good shoes if you know what I mean," she said while guiding me off the porch.

We grabbed the laundry bags and hauled them back to Daisy's house. It took me all day and half the night to wash and fold all those clothes. I didn't mind. It was something to do. I had not seen Simon since earlier when I had left. I wondered if he had finally given up on trying to learn to like me.

The next day the phone began to ring off the hook. Daisy would answer it and become angry then hang up. This happened several times. I kept doing my chores trying to mind my business. Then around dinner time when my Mistress came back from wherever she had been, likely out catting or drinking knowing her, Daisy told her that Earl had been calling all day.

My Mistress said she didn't care if he did call, she wasn't speaking to him. However, that night the phone rang nonstop. Mistress Julia could take no more by three in the morning. She answered the phone angrier than I had ever seen her.

"What the fuck do you want Earl? No, no, go fuck yourself. Stop calling this house asshole. Yeah, well good luck. See you in court." She slammed down the phone then went and unplugged all the phones from their outlets.

The rest of the night was quiet. The next day, a package arrived. Earl had sent my Mistress a VHS tape that said 'play me' on it.

At first, she was going to throw it away, but Daisy told her to watch it in case there was some threat he would make on it. If he threatened her, it could be used in divorce court against him. My Mistress told me and her mother to stay with her while she watched it. She worried seeing Earl would upset her. Daisy popped the tape into the video player.

A man was sitting at a kitchen table that I had seen in my dreams. I suddenly realized this was Earl and that place must be my Mistress's house. I had been at that very place in one of the chairs that surrounded him.

Earl told my Mistress he would not stop till he had his boys back. He said a lot of hateful things about her history as a hooker and called her a lazy whore. It was all the usual name calling and bitterness that comes from the mouths of a lover scorned. Truth was I had to agree with old Earl. My Mistress had been unfair and cruel to him by taking his children without provocation. He had been a fair, loving and kind husband to her. She didn't leave him for being abusive, a cheater or even indifferent. She left him because he had bored her.

The tape went on for about thirty minutes when suddenly Earl picked up a little pug dog. Apparently, the dog had been scratching and whining just under the table at despondent husband's legs. I had a picture that named his dog. His name was Jake.

Earl was petting the little dog and telling my Mistress this dog was all she had left him to remind him of the love they had shared. I watched the dog smiling wishing that I had met Jake in person when I had been in Cumberland. Jake just sat there on the tabletop enjoying the petting and attention Earl was showing him while he cursed my Mistress.

Then to my horror, Earl reached into his lap, you couldn't see it in the video under the tabletop and retrieved a large butcher's knife. In a single stroke he ran that blade into little Jakes unit causing the pup to scream out then collapse on the table. Earl was laughing maniacally while the dying Jake wailed shrilly trying to get up, laying in a widening pool of blood.

I covered my eyes shrieking in horror as the pup's sounds of agony grew weaker. I went to the floor rolling into a ball wailing at the sounds of Earl murdering Jake on the tape, while my Mistress and Daisy watched in silence.

I could hear Earl pull out the knife then stab the helpless fur baby once more. Jake went silent as the sound of the blade plowing into the wood of the table echoed in my heartbroken ears.

Earl said, "You are next bitch." Then the tape ended in the static.

Daisy got out of her seat and turned off the TV then stood over my weeping unit. "Earl is insane, Julia. You had better get that lawyer fast, honey."

My Mistress snorted. "Typical hill people. He kills a little dog and thinks that scares me? Fuck him. Alex get off the floor and stop acting stupid. Help mom finish lunch as I am starving."

I couldn't catch my breath. "He killed the puppy, Mistress. He killed Jake," I screamed out in agony over the lost little fur baby.

My Mistress scoffed. "Ah shit, I keep forgetting what a fucking retard you really are. Yeah, he killed Jake. He didn't kill me or the boys or any human. He is just a bully. Jake was old anyway. So, what? Now get up and do what I said before I kick your ass. Jesus, I will get a new dog. You act like that was the only one in the world. Go now, your sobbing is getting on my last nerve." She kicked at me.

I got off the floor still crying like a child but followed Daisy into the kitchen to cook. Daisy handed me a paper towel and told me to sit down till I could calm down. I was wiping my eyes, when I remembered eating paper towels and pancakes in Vegas. There was someone with me. A man with blue eyes that burned like ice.

His face was there but his name or association with me was not in my memory. A pug like dog, like Jake only black and white was barking at this man. The dog was mine. He was usually calm as a river in France. Seine, his name is Seine.

I saw Jake dying in my mind. Fresh pain began in my chest breaking me away from my new discovery of a black and white bulldog named Seine. How could Earl do that to that sweet little pup? Jake never hurt anyone. It wasn't his fault my Mistress left him. No, it was mine. I killed Jake. My Mistress had to leave because she broke me out of the mental hospital. I really started wailing when I realized that. If I had not let her do that, then Jake would not be dead.

I was so distraught that Daisy told me to go to my room. My Mistress came in after I had laid there weeping in guilt and misery for hours to call me names for being so retarded over a dog. I just took her verbal abuse about my simplistic mental health and lack of usefulness to her and Daisy. I knew I wasn't getting any better. My Mistress's children were more sophisticated than me and they were under ten years old. She only succeeded in reminding me that I was a retarded loser who was a burden to anyone who bothered to care for me.

My depression over seeing Jake murdered by Earl followed me into the next day. I moped around the house doing my chores sighing and crying. I didn't even bother to color or play with my cars. Simon wasn't speaking to me and I had caused an innocent to be stabbed to death. I had lost my kids, and the world seemed so dark and bleak.

I laid in bed that night wishing I could remember who I had once been. Simon told me Psycho was a superhero who could beat anything. I shuddered realizing whatever killed her had to be beyond horrible if she was truly what he said she was. Otherwise, how could she have died and left me to run the unit? What if that whatever it was, came back to finish us off? I felt the tiny paws of mice running down my spine while I fretted in the darkness about mysterious monsters waiting to stab me to death like that little helpless pug dog.

The next morning my Mistress came and removed my collar. She told me that later that afternoon she had a job interview set up for me. Mistress Julia told me that in Baltimore people were more cosmopolitan. They were aware of lifestylers and seeing me in a collar could lose the employment opportunity for me. Apparently the normals and vanillas didn't like my kind.

I was told to shower and wear my best clothes. I did as commanded, but I was trembling in fear the whole time. I was worried I would not get the job. I needed work so I could get my kids back.

I finished my job cleaning myself up, then went to the kitchen to be inspected by my Mistress to make sure I met her standards for well groomed. I knew she and Daisy were stuffing a large turkey Gus had sent to Daisy as a gift to the family. When I walked in Mistress Julia turned and smiled.

"Well you look very pretty, Alex. Good job. See the monster turkey for dinner. Can you believe how big it is?" She pointed at the bird.

I shook my head. "Make sure you don't leave it on the counter. My Master did once, and it went bad. Carla can't cook a turkey, huh?" I stood there confused feeling that statement came from somewhere else, but it mattered a lot somehow, but how?

My Mistress laughed. "My God, I can't decide if you are just plain crazy or plumb retarded. Either way before we go I need you to run next door and get my coat from Gus. I left it there last night like a moron. It is supposed to get cold tonight so I will need it. When you get back, we need to get moving for your interview. So, hurry up please."

I felt my blood turn to ice in my veins. I didn't like being alone and Gus's house was a bit of a walk. "Mistress couldn't we just drive over and get it before we leave?"

Mistress Julia's smile twisted to a frown of anger. "Do you see that I am busy helping mom? What the fuck do you think you are doing still standing here? Get your ass over there, knock on the door and get my God damned coat. Then get back here. Do your job, Alex, now." She pointed to the door.

I looked at the floor and wrung my hands now realizing she was very angry. "Yes Mistress." I took off for the front door took a deep breath then ran fast as I could to Gus's house.

I figured the sooner I got that coat back to her the better. I needed to get the job and being late would promise I wouldn't be hired. I wanted to see my kids so bad I was ready to dig ditches to earn the cash to buy that lawyer.

I knocked on the door, then stood back keeping my eyes downcast while wringing my hands. I heard Gus say he was coming. The door opened and he stood there looking at me appearing surprised.

"Yeah? What can I do for you, uhm, Alexandria, right," he said looking me up and down strangely.

I shrugged then began to tug at my wig hair nervously. "Mistress Julia said for me to get her coat. I came to get her coat please mister," I babbled a tad.

Gus smiled warmly. "Oh yeah that's right. She left it didn't she? Well, let me get it for you. Wait right here." He closed the door most of the way when he left.

I saw him returning through the beveled glass of his fancy entry area. He reached out across the threshold to hand me the jacket. I reached out to grab it while mumbling 'thank you.' As my hands closed on the coat, he pulled back on the coat hard. I was knocked off balance from the unexpected motion. I staggered forward slightly. In a flash Gus grabbed my arms and jerked me through his entry way. He had no difficulty tossing my tiny unit, compared to his bull sized one, face first to the floor just inside his house. I heard him close and lock the door behind me.

I scrambled to get off the floor in a wild panic, but Gus moved fast as lightning. He grabbed my ankles and flipped me to my back. I kicked in terror trying to get free as I screamed for help. Gus just laughed while he dragged me along a hallway just off from his receiving area.

When he stopped in front of a small door. Gus let my ankles go. But before I could get up to run, he reached down and pulled me to my feet by grabbing the front of my shirt. He then took me by my left upper arm and opened the door with his free hand. I struggled, spit, bit and tried to get lose, but the man was far too big and strong for me to even make him flinch.

He hauled me down a flight of stairs that stretched into darkness below us laughing at my pathetic attempts to break free of his iron claw grip and my childish pleas that he let me go. No matter what I did I couldn't get away from this monster. When we reached the bottom of that long wooden staircase he flipped on a light switch.

I stopped struggling. I felt the air rush from my lungs. I was paralyzed in complete horror of the sights in front of my eyes and laying there in the center of it all was my collar.

Okay, warning, the next chapter is very gruesome and graphic. Get ready because Master Gus has just arrived.

Chapter 92: Gus's Fantasy
Master Gus

Not a good day. When it comes to Master Gus a single scream is worth a thousand words, trust us. Nothing in our lives, not even our sicko mom, had prepared us for this the most dangerous of all twenty-eight Masters.

Our mind was still recovering from its epic fall. The only one who knew the kind of danger we were in had put us there. We were completely on our own. Live or die, with only the mind of a ten-year-old to figure a way out before it was too late.

Are you ready to find out what lurks in the darkness of a demon's heart? Well, too bad if you aren't. Mistress Julia didn't give us a choice. She sold us away. We belong to this Monster now. We are in big trouble. If we don't escape it will be one hole we won't be able to dig out of.

For this chapter you will need to grab that mallet and a butcher blade. You may need both. Be prepared to sacrifice everything to keep his fantasy from coming true. Try to remember Simon will forever love you if you can make it through this nightmare. We are about to prove that while Psycho may have been a superhero, Alexandria is the true Goddess of Survival.

20th Master (collar-no key)
Master Gus – the Pig Monster
Reign May 5th to May 6th, 2000

"Oh, hell yeah I remember Alexandria. Only I seem to remember Ginger called her Psycho. Man, she, and that red head were hot. Seriously though, you are offering me a shot at holding her collar. Fuck yeah, count me in. What do I need to do? Wait, if you are her Master why would you share?"

--**Master Rebecca to Master Boyd discussing Interim collaring of Alexandria, October 2000.**

CAUTION: *THIS STORY IS GRAPHIC, GRUESOME AND SICK BEYOND IMAGINATION. PLEASE BRACE YOURSELVES OR DON'T BOTHER TO READ ANY FURTHER – I AM NOT KIDDING.*

My unit began to tremble in terror. Gus tightened his grip while chuckling low under his breath. He was enjoying the horror he had elicited in me by this scene.

"Do you like it? I had to go through a lot of trouble to make it perfect, but you are worth it. I have waited so long for this moment. I wanted it to be better than my fantasy. Well? Answer me, what do you think Alexandria? Tell me," he said while jerking my unit hard.

My lips felt stiff and frozen. "I don't understand. Please you are hurting me mister. I want to go home." I felt the first tears roll down my face.

Gus scoffed. "Well, Julia said you are a retard, but surely even you can appreciate what I prepared for our fun. Never mind, I will enjoy it, that you can be sure of. You really have no choice. I bought you fair and square. One hundred thousand dollars for a pretty girl, that no one can trace or will ever miss. One that can't be tied to me in any way. Julia is a fucking genius. She brought me even better than I could have imagined. Young, dumb, and beautiful, and most of all small enough to keep under control. The collar business is a bonus." He reached out and rubbed the tears on my cheek.

I couldn't tear my eyes away from the scene in front of me. The basement was empty of the usual clutter of an underground storage area. The concrete floor was lined with white colored Vis queen. In the center of the room was a single wooden post that appeared to be holding up the ceiling.

A single chain coiled on the ground with a metal wrist manacle was bolted into the heart of it. A small rolling table was just off to the left of the restraining column.

On the table was a decapitated pig's head with its eyes open wide in terror and its tongue hanging out in agony. A variety of knives, a mallet, and a spoon lay next to the dismembered swine. The tools of a butcher to be exact.

On the ground next to the table lay an old Polaroid camera. It was there ready to memorialize any sight Gus desired to enjoy after his prize was just a memory.

To the right of the post on the floor was a large, covered basket. It was quivering with movement from within. I could hear the gentle cries of puppies within. It sounded as if there were an entire litter trapped in that woven prison.

In front of the post was my collar surrounded by thudding devices and rope I recalled from my darkest recovered memories.

This was without a doubt Gus's own personal torture chamber. Fear filled my head making the room start to spin slightly while I scanned the room. I instinctively knew I needed an escape route and fast.

I saw a small window that had been blacked out located on the farthest wall. There were empty shelves covered in dust and dank. Sewing mannequins were piled in a heap laying in a distant corner.

The dimly lit area was very small. I noticed another chain locked door. I realized this likely indicated this was only a part of a larger room. Then I noticed the posters that lined the place like gruesome wallpaper.

Naked woman of every color all in various sexually suggestive poses. Each female appeared to have been butchered and most seemed dead.

Some were bleeding with many cuts, some had their intestines hanging out of their mouths, vaginas, or holes in their tummies. Others were missing eyeballs, fingers, legs, breasts, or heads.

The pictures were incredibly old, dog eared, and some were in black and white. All were paintings or drawings but not real photographs. These ladies were Gus's Pin Up Girls. They had been hanging in that room a long time.

"Well, you are not much of a talker. I like that. A girl who knows her place will keep her tongue a lot longer. I have use for it anyway. Now get on your knees and let's get this collaring business over sweetie. I am ready to get started." He pushed me forward roughly knocking me to the floor on my hands and knees.

I tried to get up. Gus laughed while he dropped down pinning me with his weight to the Vis queen. He grabbed the manacle and locked it on my right wrist. Then got off me while reaching out to pick up my collar. He stood over me while I got back up to my knees trying to pull my restrained arm from the metal bracelet.

"You are going to be so much fun. I admit, this is much more thrilling than I ever imagined it would be. You know, I have beaten down grown men since I was a youngster. Those big guys can fight, you know. I love to hit them, watch them bleed, hear them beg and plead. That has kept me satisfied for years. But it is not the same. I can beat the shit out of them, but I can't kill one. I don't like fellows, so fucking them is out of the question. I get a hard on but nowhere to put it. It was always my real dream to have a girl all my very own to do as I pleased. I could beat her, fuck her, cut her, and then kill her when I am tired of her." He rolled the collar in his hands with a strange look in his eyes.

I could barely breath gasping in a crying jag. "Please mister, I just want to go home. I am scared. Mistress Julia is taking me for a job interview. I have to go please, sir," I whimpered not truly understanding what had happened thanks to my still deficit mentality.

Gus looked at me in shock. "You are retarded. Holy shit. I thought Julia was fucking with me. Okay, let me explain this in a way you can understand you stupid slut. I am the Master now. This is your collar. Your Mistress sold you to me. I am going to put it on you and then you do what I say or I will hurt you badly. This is your home now. Got that dummy" He walked over to my crying unit and roughly put the collar around my neck and locked it without any other words.

I wept in misery while that pig head stared at me, and the basket made little crying sounds next to me on that floor. Gus stood there as if thinking, then he smiled evilly. He gathered up his ropes and thudding devices. He took me by my upper arms and stood me up. I tried to struggle to get out of his grip. He kicked my left leg hard and told me to be still or he would beat the shit out of me.

I whimpered and sniffed while he bound my wrists together. He then threw the rope around a beam in the basement ceiling and pulled my limbs above my head when he pulled it tight. He tied off the end to the post holding me up so I couldn't run, put down my arms or move very far from my spot.

I was really wailing at this point. I could recall this sort of behavior from my broken memories. Gus was going to hit me with those floggers and cat o'nine tails. Gus was sweating and smiling as he walked in front of me to admire his work.

"This is more like it. Nice, keep crying honey. I like the sound. You can even scream if you want. Begging would be even better. Just remember how lucky you are. I am your Master now. When I am done you will be completely mine in every way. You see I am going to be your last Master. You will stay with me forever. I dug the hole in the backyard yesterday. I am going to have my fun with you, then you are going to make my darkest fantasy come true. See these girls on the wall? They are jealous of you, Alexandria. They are just posers. You are the real thing baby. All they could do is watch me get off. They couldn't get the pleasure of being involved, you know. But you little gal, you are going to please your Master in every way. Then to honor you I will come see you every day. I will never forget the gift you will give me." He came forward and forced his mouth to mine holding my head so I could not escape his foul mouth.

Master Gus then let my head go and walked to the pig head table. I turned my unit wild with terror to keep an eye on this insane man. I watched in disbelief while he petted the dead boar while chuckling. Then he picked up the large butcher blade and came back to my hanging unit. I began to scream and kick at him fearing he was going to cut me up like the woman in the posters.

Master Gus just laughed at my useless attempts to keep him at bay. He reached out and grabbed my clothes pulling them out, then ran the knife down the length of it. My Master continued using the knife with expert precision until all my clothing was cut into ribbons. He pulled the mangled rags off and threw them into a pile on the floor.

He returned thc blade to his table then turned to admire my naked unit. I stood there wearing only my boots terrified beyond, unable to understand why this man was doing this to me. I was willing to wash his big house or dirty clothes, but he was hurting me. I simply was unable to grasp anything other than he wanted to hit and then kill me for some reason.

"Very nice. Now this is quality pussy. I am going to enjoy this so much. Your skin is so fucking pretty. I am going to blow a load before I can finish skinning it all off. Shit, I guess I had better get it all out of my system first. I waited too long to lose my shit before I get everything ready. Oh well, no hurry. I have two days off. I will just have to fuck my fill so that when I am finally ready to get what I paid for I will keep my cool. No problem, I can do this," he said while rubbing his chin appearing deep in thought.

"Please Master, I can go cook your dinner now. Can I go? I am cold, please?," I cried out like a child.

Master Gus laughed hard. "You are cold? Well, let your Master warm you up. Then when you are nice and hot, we will cut off all that smooth skin and I will warm myself up while you bleed to death on my cock. Doesn't that sound like fun?" He picked up a flogger while still chuckling hard.

"No, please don't cut me. Don't hit me. I will be good, Master, please," I wailed out while he turned my unit away from him.

He struck me with the leather flogger across the shoulders sending me into screams of agony. I plead, begged, screamed, cried, struggled, and was even struck in the front trying to wiggle out of the rope that bound me like a piece of meat hanging from the ceiling.

When Master Gus tired of the leather flogger, he switched to the cat 'o nine, then to a leather strap.

His cruel thudding devices welted, cut, and bruised most of the back of my unit from neck to ankles, and some across my chest and front of my thighs due to my attempts to get away. I had fallen into a moaning, wailing mess before he finally tired of his game of tenderizing his prize.

He put down his implements and stood behind me admiring his handiwork. Master Gus reached out and ran his hands roughly along the cuts, welts and bruises causing fresh screams from the feeling of burning, shock and pain.

My Master laughed each time I yelled. He began to poke hard with his fingers into the deepest injuries appearing to be very thrilled by my animal like scrambling to try to avoid his continued torturing.

Master Gus soon tired of this game as well. He untied my arms allowing me to fall to the ground on my hands and knees. I was exhausted from the trauma. I couldn't find the strength to stand. My right arm was still chained to the post. I knew I wasn't going anywhere, unless I could rip that arm off.

My Master went upstairs leaving me weeping in a heap on the floor unable to get my shit together. I couldn't think a single coherent thought. All I knew is pain, fear and despair.

He returned with a wooden chair from a kitchen table. Master Gus sat it just within reach of my cowered unit. He took the seat and watched me for a few minutes appearing to relish my despondence.

"Beating your pretty pale skin was fun, but just not enough to get me hard. Don't get me wrong, you beg beautifully. It was like mother's milk to my ears, but still my dick is a picky guy. He demands real excitement before he can join our party. Ah, you know what? I have just the thing. I planned for everything you know." Master Gus got up and grabbed the whimpering basket and returned to his seat.

He told me to look at him or he would beat me some more. I pulled myself to a sitting position from my fetal one using all the strength I had left. I gasped for air as my bottom and back of my legs squealed out to my brain in torment.

My Master smiled diabolically while he opened the lid of the basket. Out popped five little furry heads. Golden lab puppies no more than six to eight weeks old. They all began to whine and try to struggle to get out. My eyes went wide, forgetting my pain for a moment.

"Puppies, oh Master, please can I hold one please? I want to hold one." I shuddered but came forward thinking that I maybe I was getting a puppy for being good while my Master hit me Yeah, I was that fucking stupid, sad really.

Master Gus laughed. "Julia told me you like puppies. Aren't they pretty? There are five of them. If you had to pick one for you, which would it be?"

I bounced in joy. "I can have one? Thank you Master. Oh, I love them all. I want that one." I pointed at the golden little brown eyes puppy closest to me staring at me with his little pink tongue rolling out while he yapped at me.

My Master nodded. "Good choice. Here you go Alexandria, you can hold your pick." He scooped the puppy up handing the bundle of fur to my trembling bruised hands.

I immediately hugged the excited puppy to my face while he licked and struggled to paw me. I giggled in delight forgetting all about the cruel situation I was in, and the monster sitting in the chair watching my thrill at the little dog with a look of pure evil on his face.

He allowed me to hug and cuddle the puppy for several minutes before he spoke. "You have a name for him?"

I shook my head. "Not yet Master. He will tell me what he likes to be called soon. He is just a baby you know." I smiled but it melted when something in my Masters eyes told me there was something wrong here. Something bad was happening, oh God.

He grabbed one of the other puppies from the basket and threw it hard into the floor. I screamed in horror while he grabbed all of them one by one throwing them to the floor injuring each little life. They all yelped in agony. I came forward to try to help them. He stood up fast and threw the basket at me and the puppy causing me to cower back for a moment.

It just seemed to keep on getting bigger and bigger until finally I was remembered that this was not a good thing. Sadly, Master Gus was an exceptionally large man, in girth, height and penis size.

My Master reached the point of readiness for penetration. He ended his cruel breath play blow job by grabbing my shoulders and pushing me to my back. I tried to keep the puppy tucked tightly to my breast, but Master Gus grabbed him by his neck and wretched him from my grasp. He flung him hard into the post. The puppy cried out and fell to the ground limp.

I let out a mournful shriek while Master Gus forced himself inside me, sending the sensation of tearing and pain through my traumatized mind like hot lightning.

He grabbed my breasts, rough housing them harshly, while he thrust his manhood brutally ripping my female parts. I could not understand the horrific situation as my damaged brain went haywire. I started guttural screaming out of my brain with anguish.

This angered or thrilled, unsure here, Master Gus. He thrust harder and leaned down biting me on my shoulders and neck. He slapped my face several times appearing to try to get me to shut up.

I was beyond reason. His rape was more horrific than I could have handled in my best of mental states. In my incapacitated intellect it was devastating.

Master Gus did not come to a quick orgasm. Instead he flipped my wailing unit to my stomach. He laughed while he sodomized me dry.

My howls of horrendous pain and screaming caused him to bite and hit me again. I could think of nothing but the dead puppies and agony that filled my nether region. I was blinded by it, unable to see, hear or move while he reached his orgasm deep within me.

My Master dismounted and pushed me face first to the ground panting and laughing at my guttural wailing. "Now that was a fuck. Damn, you may be retarded but guess it doesn't take intelligence to suck a dick. Now I am going to grab a bite to eat. You rest up. I am going to want to do some more of that in an hour or so." He slapped my welted bottom hard making me yell out while he got up and left the basement to get his dinner.

I could hardly move from the torturous pain my Master had subjected me to. I reached deep inside and found the strength to crawl towards the little pup he had tossed away when he raped me.

I saw his little brown eyes staring at me, pleading for help. As I slowly approached him is tail began to wag wildly. I swallow my terror. He was alive. I had to find a way to keep Master Gus from finding out. He would kill him like the others.

I picked the puppy up and realized his injuries were terminal. His back legs were hanging useless and his abdomen was split open, his little guts were hanging out. I opened my mouth to wail but only air came forth as my chest felt like it was imploding. The puppy licked my hands and wagged his tail while I picked him up off the floor carefully.

He snuggled close to my battered unit as I gently held him close. Even dying, slow and painful due to the cruel treatment of a human, he showed me nothing but unconditional love.

I felt that my brain would shatter into pieces as I watched the light going out of his eyes. I whispered begging anyone who could help me to not let the puppy die.

With a gasp and shudder his light went out forever there in that basement hell while I wept beyond misery, beyond terror, beyond despair.

It felt like my heart was going to stop beating while it broke inside my chest. Then suddenly, a strange feeling overcame me. It was another of those strange episodes where weird scenes would fill my head, memories of a life I used to know.

Images of a bleeding Karrie filled my mind's eye, and a man with dark brown hair. He was my true Master. This man's name was Boyd.

He lived in a place that was called Wheatly and he knew where to find my children. Julia was a liar. This man called Boyd had Simon's key and my collar.

I saw them in the hospital, the one she had kidnapped me from. This Gus person was a kidnapper too. No, he was worse. He planned to be a murderer.

I looked back down at the lifeless little dog. I petted him and sung him a song about horses I once had sung to my children when they were little. I knew the baby dog was tired and needed to sleep now. Like his brothers and sisters.

They were all sleeping. I had to stop crying or they would find no rest. I took him while I crawled to the other mangled little fur babies.

I grabbed the basket and gently put them all back inside. Side by side so they would not be lonely for each other. They were so pretty laying there. I marveled that more well-behaved pups no fur momma could boast.

I shuddered and gasped feeling the despair within try to come back. No, the puppies were not dead. They were just sleeping. No need to be crying about tired puppies.

Simon came through the wall while I rocked and sung to the napping babes. He heard my terrified cries.

"What is going on Alexandria? The unit is hurt. It is bleeding. Something is wrong," he said shaking all over in fear.

"We are kidnapped by a killer, Simon. If we don't find a way out, he is going to murder us and bury us in the back yard," I said smiling while I reached into the basket to pet one of the dead pups.

Simon gasped. "Oh no, Alexandria. We have to get out."

I nodded "I know that Simon. I will get away. I must find Boyd. He is the Master. Julia lied to us. She kidnapped

101

us from the hospital. She has sold us to this man for one hundred thousand dollars." I tranced slightly while looking at my Simon starting to lose my mind from the trauma, what little I had no doubt.

He shook his head. "How will you get away? What if Boyd is not the Master? I cannot remember him. Are you sure you are remembering right?"

I smiled. "No. I am not sure. Boyd could have been our Master a long time ago. He may be dead like Matt. I must try to find him. I remember he loved us once. He said if we were ever lost or scared to call him. It is a directive." I could see his blue eyes as he said this to me in the darkness of my mind.

Simon looked startled. "It is a directive. Yes, I remember those words that it is a directive. A black car, dancing with gypsies, drinking from a ditch."

I nodded. "Yes, this Boyd was important to you Simon. You picked him for Psycho. I will see if he wants an Alexandria but first keep your voice down. The puppies are sleeping. You will wake them." I closed the lid and rocked the basket gently.

Simon looked at my right wrist. "The manacle. You can't get out with that on. It can't be picked. What are you going to do? Oh God, we will die here," he wailed out in fresh terror.

I looked at the table with the pig's head on it. "See that table, Simon. See the knives? I will cut off my hand when

Gus goes to sleep tonight. I will cut it off and run away with the puppies. We will find the bus place and go back to Wheatly. We will find Boyd. I will do what I must to be free."

He opened his eyes in shock. "You would cut off our hand? Do you know how much that will hurt, Alexandria."

I smiled. "Yes, I am sure it will hurt bad. But I will cut it off. I won't let Gus kill the puppies or us."

Simon shook his head. "Julia or the police or someone will come help us. No, don't cut off your hand. Oh there has to be another way."

Master Gus opened the door above and started down the stairs. I put my finger to my lips cautioning Simon to be still. I would have to endure whatever this monster was planning for me.

I could only hope he would keep his promise of using both days to get around to killing me.

He laughed when he saw me cradling the basket of dead puppies. "Put them all to bed did you momma? Well thanks for cleaning up the mess. I must admit this has been more fun than I ever thought it could be. Maybe before I skin you, I will get some more puppies and skin them first. Would you like that?" He chuckled.

I looked at the floor keeping my mouth shut. I knew there was no response on Earth to that foul threat. I decided not to speak to this pig monster anymore. He was a murderer. Even if I could get away, he was killing puppies and pigs.

I wished I had magic powers and could grow into a giant. I would stomp him until his guts came out of his asshole. I would let prisoners from his job stick their dicks in his mouth and up his ass while he screamed dying. Dark I know but shit I was thinking it. So being honest.

Master Gus went to the table with the pig and wheeled it over to where I sat with the basket, "Well, now for a real treat. I am going to show you what I will do to you tomorrow. I have been doing this since I was just a young boy you know. All these years, I would skin pig heads, when I could get them. I used to skin dogs and cats, but their eye sockets are too small to fuck you know? I need a big eye hole to get all this man inside."

I listened in total disgust while Master Gus began skinning the pig head with precision and speed that was frightening. He told me that his fantasy since a young age had been to skin and removed the living eyes from a human girl while she screamed in agony. He said he would dream of fucking her while she lay dying. After she died, he would keep having fun for a bit longer by having sex with the corpse through its eye holes.

My intellect was still very stunted. However, Master Gus had just taught me what sex was in a most foul way. I sure as shit understood skinning, popping out eyes, and being dead. This time I finally got the horror of this situation loud and clear:

This sicko was going to skin me alive, pop out my eyes, and fuck me while I died slow.

Then he was going to violate my corpse by fucking my empty eye sockets.

Holy fucking shit snacks.

He already had dug my shallow grave in the backyard.

That is what he paid one hundred thousand dollars to do.

The kidnapper Julia sold me to a fucking serial killer wanna-be.

When Master Gus had finished working on the boar, head was nothing but muscle, not a stitch of skin remained. He smiled while he boasted to me that it only took him ten minutes to complete the job.

"I can likely get most of your belly and maybe your upper arms, thighs and cut off your breast, but then I will have to start fucking, I think. You won't last long with most of your skin gone even with my fast hands. Don't worry, I will finish the job once you are gone. Oh, but the best part is for last, watch this." He took the spoon that he had sharped the end of and dug into the pig's head till one of its lidless eyes popped out across the table.

It made a sound that made my stomach sour. Master Gus laughed maniacally while he dug out the other eye. Then he took one of his knives and carved on the empty right eye socket of the head. He made it big as possible. I realized in horror what he intended to do. I tried to swallow my spit, but my throat had closed in from fear.

"Ah that will have to do, my beauty. Now you get me all prepped with that soft little mouth of yours and let's start round two." He walked over to me undoing his pants.

He kicked the basket out of my lap and grabbed my neck while forcing his cock into my mouth. He warned me that biting him would result in him ripping out my teeth so I wouldn't do it again.

Once again, he forced his manhood down my throat roughly while holding my nose closed so I couldn't breathe. This time I vomited from the forced deep throating.

He just laughed then went back to his foul enforcing of oral sex. He obtained a full erection then pulled back from his cruel game. I braced assuming he was going to rape me right away but instead he went back to the pig head.

He demanded I watch or pay the price while he stuck his hard on into the hole of that pig head. He couldn't get it all in there of course but he held it still while he thrust into it moaning out how he couldn't wait to do this to me. I sat there in stunned terror as I watched this scene right out of madness.

Master Gus did not orgasm into the dead pig. After several minutes of foreplay he turned and look at me smiling. His cock dripped with tissue from his eye socket rape of the pig head. I began to retreat far as I could go while he came to rape my unit again.

I screamed in panic while he pushed me to my hands and knees mounting me from behind. Master Gus pinned me with his massive weight while he forced himself into me with a single horrid stroke. He began his violent carnal congress ignoring the foulness of the pork that he violated coating his manhood.

He continued his raping of my unit by holding off his orgasm for an extended time. He accomplished this by constantly dismounting, forcing me into a new position, then re-entering with brute fury causing my vaginal canal to rip, bruise and ache unlike anything one can imagine unless they have been violently raped with no lube. This was not a turn on for me, a dry vagina is not a nice day.

When Master Gus finally reached his climax, I was no longer fighting. I had given up and just laid there while he pounded his strength and seed into me as deep as he could go. His sweat was dripping onto my face while he finished his brutality balls deep with a loud yell.

I no longer felt any tears coming from my eyes. I hated this man above all people on Earth, except maybe for Julia. I decided I was more than ready to cut off my hand. I was leaving. I would not allow this creature to kill me. No, I was going to live.

Master Gus looked down into my hate filled eyes. "That was even better than the first time. You are getting good at this Alexandria. Too bad you won't be able to enjoy the next one as much. For now, I am beat. Torture and rape will take it out of a guy. I hope you don't mind if we finish this in the morning. I need a couple hours to rest up. This has been so much fun. I think I will have to do it again. Maybe Julia can get me another girl soon. The only bad thing about being a picky man like me is that the best ladies are hard to come by. I had thought about keeping you around for fun and games a bit longer but shit, I can't wait. This is too fucking exciting. I am like a kid in a candy store. I will miss you a lot. You never forget your first you know? That is why I made sure to have my camera ready. You should be so proud of yourself. You will die tomorrow knowing you made your Master a very satisfied man. How many people can say they truly brought someone else total happiness? You come here so I can get you ready for bedtime. Get some rest beauty. Tomorrow is your big day." He uncoupled, then grabbed my arms dragging me back to the post.

He forced me to sit down while he tied my wrists behind me to the pole. When he felt sure he had me secured he stretched and yawned.

"Good night beautiful. Sweet dreams. See you in the morning." He leaned down grabbed my head and began forcing a kiss when suddenly my wig came off into his hands.

He jumped back as it fell to the floor. I sat there glaring at him with anger. Somehow, luck or not who knows, that wig had held up during all his raping and beating of my unit until that moment.

"Holy shit, you're bald." He looked at the wig as if it were going to bite him.

Master Gus picked it up and examined it. "Well, this is not okay. I guess it will make skinning easier, but I paid for a whole girl not one missing part already. I just assumed you shaved to keep your kitty clean. You are actually bald everywhere. This is bullshit. I have been ripped off. Fucking Julia." He threw the wig onto his steps then came back to stare at me.

"You are still a pretty little thing but those scars on that head. Is that how you got retarded? Someone hit you in the head. Yeah, someone already busted your torture cherry. You have been beaten up and raped before, haven't you? This is not your first time. You are not fresh at all. Well, I am going to get what I paid for anyway, but that God damned Julia is giving me a discount. Fucking lying cunt. She said you were not a virgin,, but innocent as a kid, not with marks like that you aren't. You know what? You don't even deserve to wear my fucking collar, you whore." He reached into his pocket and took out the collar key.

Gus removed it from my unit mumbling how he had been robbed. He threw the collar on the steps with my wig then stood above me appearing angrier by the minute. He walked to his pig table and grabbed a small pocketknife then returned.

He crouched down in front of my bonded unit. "You are not fresh meat. You are nothing but an old used up fucking whore. You probably faked the whole thing. How many floggers, dicks, and ropes have you had? Can you even count that high, you retard? Probably just one of Julia's old trash road whores. Yeah that is what you are, Alexandria. How old were you when you first started sucking dick for nickels?

Where you ten? Thirteen? When whore?" He opened the pocketknife growling appearing furious.

I just glared at him. He could say what he wanted, use me as he pleased, even kill me, but I would be damned if I would speak to this pig monster.

Gus grabbed my knees spreading my legs wide then pushed the small knife into my vaginal opening. "Move and you will die. You answer me whore."

I screamed in fresh agony as I felt him wiggle the knife within me threatening to cut worse than he likely already had. The burning was almost unbearable. Fear filled to a breaking point. I thought he was going to start skinning me right that second if I didn't do something fast.

"Please, Mister. I just wanted a puppy. I don't understand. I am scared. Please, I want to go home," I cried out in a child-like voice.

Gus's eyes went wide. "Fuck, I can't believe this shit. Julia really did sell me a used up retarded whore. I thought it was cute at first. I thought you were born that way. The innocence was sexy but those scars. You have been knocked stupid not born that way. Useless, you are fucking useless. I should just skin you right now, fuck you and get this over with. The fun will be less knowing you are dumpster trash." He sat there appearing to think on that a moment while

I held my breath fearing to move an inch with his knife inside me. I was silently crying. I just assumed this was it. I was about to die like the puppies.

Instead he pulled the weapon out of me, blood began to seep onto the Vis queen between my legs, slow but sure. He had cut me deep inside with that knife. Gus looked at the small pool and began to laugh.

"Well I suppose I was wrong. Looks like you had a cherry after all. See you tomorrow slut. Be ready to suffer. I am going to make God damned sure you hurt." He stormed off taking the knife, my wig and the collar up the stairs with him.

I sobbed for a few minutes as the burn from the cut began to ache between my legs. I knew I had to get that stopped up fast. I focused all I had while I started working the poorly knotted rope that bond me to the pole. Within only about fifteen to twenty minutes I had freed my wrists. Even slow, I could still get out of poor knot bondage after so many years of it.

The blood was pooling where I had been sitting. I had already been bleeding a bit from his violent rapes and his large member, but this was a scary amount of blood.

A woman can die from such an injury as this. Somehow, I knew that. I crawled to the ripped-up clothing still piled in the floor. I took a long strip of my cotton shirt. I rolled it up and packed it inside my bloody cavity.

Then I took more of the cut shirt making sure to over stuff the area to attempt to provide pressure to stop the internal bleeding. It was the best I could do without emergency aid. If the cut were not too deep, I would survive it with this make-shift bandage, but if it were then nothing would save me from slowly bleeding to death.

Next, I crawled to the table with the skinned eyeless pig head. I took a deep breath and grabbed the big butcher knife. I looked at my hand realizing I could just cut off my thumb. Then my hand could slide free of the metal cuff. If I could not get my hand out, I was prepared to end my life to keep Gus from doing it the way he intended to.

It was then that the mallet caught my attention. Cutting off my hand or thumb could result in heavy blood loss. I may pass out or bleed to death before I could get away. Worse, I would have trouble hiding a bloody stump at the bus stop. If I broke my hand, then no blood and I hoped the hand would come out.

I took up the mallet and put my right hand, I am right-handed just so you know, on the floor flattening my fingers. I knew I only had to break my thumb but if I missed too bad for me.

I reared back the mallet high above my head taking several deep breaths. I did my best to brace myself as I knew I would have to be silent. If I screamed or the hammer made a sound, Gus could come back. This was going to test my ability to do what it takes to live.

Simon stood there in silent awe as I brought down that mallet with all the strength I could muster. I kept my sights on the target, my right thumb.

The connection was a perfect aim. The mallet crashed down breaking my thumb right at the palm knuckle. White hot agony raced up my arm to the top of my head. I groaned but bit my tongue and held my breath refusing to scream out from the incredible pain.

Simon let out a gasp. "You did it Alexandria. You broke the thumb. Hurry, hurry, run God damn it. Go to Julia's break in, steal some cloths and money. Get to that bus and go find Boyd. You have to go now or die."

I nodded as I moaned out pulling the manacle up my wrist toward my now mangled thumb harshly. The broken digit folded up to make my hand unnaturally small. The agony was not describable using words, just know I nearly bite off my tongue to keep from screaming. No matter the pain, it had paid off. I was now free to run away.

I looked longingly at the basket with the sleeping puppies., "The puppies Simon, we need to bury them."

He shook his head,. "If you fool around, they will be, right next to us in the back fucking yard. You can't help them anymore. Run, now."

I sniffed back my tears as I went to the small blacked out window. I quietly took the wooden chair to aid me to climb up to it as it was more than six foot up the wall. I unlocked the hinge that held it closed. It opened much to my elation.

I was worried I would have to break it. It took a bit of a struggle to pull up and get my unit through but I managed to squeeze out to the world outside that basement hell hole. I was injured with a broken right hand to boot.

It was very dark. I could tell by the way the air felt it was likely early morning, possibly after midnight. Without a second hesitation I ran naked, bloody with part of a shirt packed in-between my legs across Gus's huge yard right to Daisy's house.

I fell several times in the dark, but I did have my boots on still. He never removed them thank the Gods. I went around to the window that belonged to the room Julia and I shared.

I had recalled when I washed the windows, I had forgotten to relock the ones in this room. Julia had interrupted me to help her and Daisy haul Gus's laundry. I had meant to return to lock them but never recalled it. I hoped no one had discovered my mistake. One I was glad I had made for a change.

I used my left hand to push the window up. It didn't offer any resistance. Another lucky break for a change. I could see Julia sleeping in the bed through the murky darkness.

I was beyond angry and considered strangling her right there. Instead I clumsily fell through the window deciding I would kill her and Daisy if they woke up. I would have to do it or they would send me back to Gus so he could finish me off. I am not a killer, not like those two wastes of space are.

I very quietly opened the drawer and took out a hoodie and jeans. I put on the clothing. I covered my bald head with the hood and pulled the string tight around my chin.

I searched in the dark room on my hands and knees until I found Julia's purse laying in the floor. I took out her wallet and found it flush with cash, likely from her selling of my collar, the bitch.,

I took all her ill gotten money. I quickly waded it up and stuffed it into my jeans. Then I grabbed all her tampons, five of them, and stuffed them into the hoodie pockets.

Just before I left that place, I grabbed my little black bag full of my hot wheel's cars and colors. I crawled out the window not even bothering to close it as I took off running fast as my beaten, fatigued, mangled unit could go.

I was beyond scared. I didn't know where the bus stop was or how to buy a ticket. I feared Gus was coming or Julia.

Every sound made my heart stop in my chest. I ran up that long street and took a right. I seemed to remember that was the way we had come. I prayed I was headed back towards the city.

I started jogging then slowed to a rapid walk when I could go no more. Not far down the road I ran into a street schizophrenic.

She was wearing every item of clothing she owned in the world. I counted five shirts, two sweaters and one coat with a hat over a stalking cap.

She had two large trash bags full of items she had collected from dumpsters. I noticed her glasses were broken and she had no teeth. The lady was likely only forty but looked seventy.

I looked at the ground wringing my hands while I approached her slowly. "Excuse me. I am lost. Do you know where the bus station is? I can trade."

The woman growled and mumbled. "Yeah maybe, what do you got, chickee."

I reached into my black bag. "I got crayons, a bag of skittles, and a pack of cigarettes." I showed her the items.

She nodded. 'Yeah I will take them. You go there and turn to the other side. Keep walking and the bus will run you over." She pointed ahead.

I nodded then left her items of trade on the sidewalk and ran off in the direction her bony finger pointed me. I know she picked them up where I left them.

I know how to speak her language. She told me to go to the stop sign and the turn right and the bus stop was right there around that corner, close enough to be hit by a bus in fact.

The homeless schizophrenic wasn't joshing me. I found the Greyhound station right where she said it was. I almost died right there from relief as I walked across the parking lot towards the big glass encased building.

Homeless people were everywhere laying around trying to stay warm in the darkness. I just ignored them and went inside, unsure what to do next.

I stood in the lobby wringing my hands, pacing scared and confused. A man behind a window asked me if I needed help while he shot a look at the security guard standing next to him. I walked to that window and kept my eyes down ready to run if the cop made any moves toward me.

"Yes, I need help. I am trying to get to Wheatly, Oklahoma. Do you have a bus going there," I barely whispered.

The man smiled. "Yeah I sure do. You got money? It is pretty expensive to go that far you know."

I nodded. "I have money. How much?" I pulled out my cash to show the man.

He looked at the officer and nodded that he had no need to worry. I was not a homeless person looking for trouble. I was a customer looking for a ticket.

The man helped me get my ticket and explained to me there were many stops along the way. He said it would take four days to get home because the bus made so many, and I would be stuck in Nashville for a few hours to change buses.

I wrote down all he told me in a coloring book with a red crayon. He chuckled at my doing that, but I didn't care. I was just so happy to be going home. My bus was leaving in fifteen minutes.

To my relief he told me I could go get on my bus right away to get a seat. It was bus number 56 headed to Nashville. I smiled as I thanked him and rushed outside to find my ride out of that horrible nightmare called Baltimore, Maryland.

I was lucky to get there just in time to catch the one leaving at six in the morning eastern standard time. It only took me moments to find my bus number. I walked up the steps and down the aisle of big, cushioned seats on each side. I chose the back seat which could only be shared by two people and was closest to the bathroom.

I sat down and closed my eyes praying that fifteen minutes would hurry. I knew Gus and Julia, who was an early riser, would be awake by now. Maybe there were already looking for me. I was so fucking scared.

Each person who got on the bus sent lightning terror down my spine. I watched the passengers loading praying the next would not be there to drag me back to be skinned, raped, and murdered.

Surprisingly, few people got on the bus before the driver entered and closed the doors. I looked around to see the bus was only three fourths full, lots of empty seats were available.

The big lumbering vehicle lurched forward and the driver announced we were heading for West Virginia. I watched the city go by as we raced west headed towards home at last.

I sat back as the last of that wicked city's lights faded into the distance behind me. I took my first real breath since I had broken my hand a few hours before.

I got up and went to use the bathroom. I need to remove the packed cotton shirt. To my dismay I found my cut was still bleeding. It had slowed only a bit.

I inserted a tampon hoping that I could gage the seriousness of the injury. I then discarded the gory shirt shreds into the tiny garbage can.

I looked at my thumb. It was swollen, purple, black and ached so badly I thought I would die. In fact, everything ached even my teeth. My throat was sore from screams and friction of a forced blow job, my skin was on fire from the beatings.

I looked in the mirror while the pathetic image of a small trembling hooded schizophrenic stared back. My left eye was black, and my lip busted. A small purple bruise was on my cheek and a dark purple handprint was around my throat. I smiled at the girl in the glass.

Simon was standing behind me. "You did it Alexandria, you escaped. Oh my God. You saved the unit all by yourself. You hand, the break in, you are amazing. I love you so much." He began to tear up showing pride in his face.

"It was for us Simon. For our children. We will find Boyd. The police will take us back to the hospital. They will want to fry our brains. Julia stole us from them. The hospital will want to hurt us some more. I think we were there for doing something bad. No matter what. I love you too. You are my best friend Simon. You are the only one I can trust in the whole world."

He smiled. "I am honored to call you my best friend Alexandria. We will rebuild and start over. You are not weak at all. You are a Goddess on Earth."

I shyly looked down smiling as he attempted to flatter me. "Thank you Simon. The bleeding won't stop. I think we are going to get sick from it. We need help from a doctor. He must sew us up. Could we sew us up you think?"

Simon shook his head. "We don't have any needle and thread. You will have to tell the police before they put us back in the mental hospital. They will get us to help."

I sighed. "Okay, if we don't die in four days."

I went back to my seat and Simon sat next to me smiling proudly. I had finally earned his love the way Psycho had. She never got away from anyone without help like I just did.

My shard was not the impulsive fighter she had been. Mine was the patient winner. Simon was in rapture that I had escaped the hands of a would be serial killer by being willing to sacrifice my hand or be willing to kill myself if that didn't work to keep Gus from getting his kicks, to save his unit. Psycho was a badass, but Alexandria is a survivor.

Despite my horrible pain, extreme fear that Julia and Gus were coming to find me, and severe aching, the movement of the bus lulled my exhausted person to sleep.

I began to dream of a lonely two lanes road. It had trees on each side. I was driving in a panic, trying to outrun someone in black.

Oddly, I was driving backward and fell into a ditch. The man in black pulled me from the car. I was scared and crying. He took out a pen and wrote his phone number on my left arm under his letter B. B for Boyd.

I woke with a start. "Master Boyd, he wrote his number on our arm," I said out loud to Simon.

I pulled up my sleeve best I could groan from the screaming broken right thumb. I could see the B scar but no phone number.

"Maybe if you go to a phone and look at it hard the numbers will come back to you," said Simon as he gazed at my skin deep in thought.

The bus stopped in West Virginia. The driver announced we had thirty minutes to stretch our legs, smoke and get food.

I followed the other passengers out watching with extreme caution for any signs of Julia or Gus. I didn't see anyone who even resembled the evil pair. I knew by now they both were hunting me.

Gus could not allow me to escape now that he had raped and left all his evidence behind. Julia would want to collect me to keep the money she had gained by selling my collar to him.

I was daft but not that fucking gone. I was in danger, I needed help. I walked into the bus station and went to the pay phone to see if I could get some.

I dialed several numbers believing I had remembered the number from my dream correctly. Each time I was disappointed when I asked for Boyd.

Most hung up calling me a nutjob. I was near tears about to give up when I tried one more series of numbers.

The phone rang three times then a man answered, "Hello?"

I took a deep breath. "I am looking for someone named Boyd. I think I know him. My name is Alexandria. I think he was my Master, but I can't remember."

The man let out a gasp. "Alexandria? Is this a joke? Wait, it sounds like you. You are alive. Where are you? Oh my God." The man let out a wail and began crying.

I didn't understand. "Please sir, do you know Boyd? I need to find him. He said it was a directive. I am in trouble. I can't stop the bleeding. I am so scared. Julia and Gus are coming. If they find me Gus will bury me in the back yard. I have to go soon, please help me," I babbled out now crying almost as hard as the man on the phone.

The man took a deep breath. "Don't hang up, Alexandria. This is Boyd. I am your Master Boyd. Where are you, baby? Tell me where you are right now. That is a directive," he yelled into the phone.

I was startled to hear those words. "I am in West Virginia, Master. I am on a bus coming to Wheatly. They say it will be four days. I am scared Gus and Julia will get me or I won't have any blood left."

Master Boyd took a deep breath trying to contain his excitement, fear and surprise. "Okay baby, what is your bus number? I will come pick you up during your first layover. You know what that is?"

I shook my head now crying harder. "No, I don't understand Master. What is a layover?"

He spoke softly. "Honey that is a place the bus stops to change to a new bus. Did they tell you where that would be? Think hard now, try to remember. Where will the bus change and what day?"

I thought hard and remembered. "It will change in Nashville at noon tomorrow Master. They told me that bus 56 will be bus 78 at noon tomorrow." I smiled through my tears happy to recall something for a damned change.

Master Boyd chuckled. "Okay, go back to your bus. Get in your seat and don't get back off that bus until you get to Nashville tomorrow. I will be there to take you home. Do you understand?"

I nodded. "Yes but how will I know it is you, Master?"

He sucked in his breath. "I will be holding red roses for my One and Only that God has brought back to me alive. I love you Alexandria. I am so happy you never forgot that."

"Okay Master, red roses. I will look for you in Nashville. I am scared of Julia and Gus, Master. Can you bring a gun? If Gus finds me he will kill me." I started sobbing again.

He sniffed loudly. "I will not let those monsters get you sweetie. Alexandria listen carefully, do not get back off bus 56 until tomorrow in Nashville. That is a directive. Hang up and get back on the bus now."

I hung up the phone as he ordered. Simon and I rushed back onto the bus immediately. I sat in that seat for the next twenty-four hours terrified, in agony, and watching for any sign of doom each time that bus stopped to pick up and let off passengers.

It felt like forever before the bus driver announced we were about to stop in Nashville. He thanked all of us for riding with Greyhound as he parked the bus and opened the doors. I stood up feeling faint.

The world spun for a moment while I hung on to the seats for support. I had used all of Julia's tampons and I still was bleeding. The wound was not completely closing, I needed stitches.

The line of people moved slowly, exiting the bus. I looked out the window for signs of Gus, Julia or the man called Boyd. I saw a man holding red roses.

He was tall and slender with dark brown hair and a handsomely sharp face. The man was dressed in black he was watching the people getting off the bus. Even from that far I could see his eyes, blue like ice.

I remembered his face from my dreams and scattered memory. This was the one who had Simon's Key. My real Master.

I started down the steps, but Master Boyd ran up them. Without a word he grabbed my arm and pulled me after him rushing across the bus parking lot. His head was watching all around us as if worried we were being followed for attack.

I was wanting to beg him to slow down. His grip was tight and hurting my already battered unit. I didn't dare say a word. Something told me he had reason to act this way. I knew he was there to make sure I was safe. I assumed he had seen evidence that we were in danger.

Then I saw the problem. Julia and Gus came out of the office door watching Master Boyd and I as he practically ran with me across the Greyhound property.

I almost fell in sheer terror at the sight of them standing not more than twenty or so feet away. They both were glaring at me trying to decide what to do now that my Real Master had me in his possession.

Master Boyd stopped in front of a black car, also from my dreams but slightly different. He opened the passenger door and gently pushed me inside slamming it closed behind me.

My Master ran around the car jumped into the car, started it and sped off away from the evil pair who never took their eyes off us.

I trembled while watching them shrinking in my review mirror realizing had I not found my Master they would have caught me in Nashville. I leaned back letting out my breath in relief, agony and because I had been holding it all that time.

Master Boyd let out his breath too. "I am sorry baby for scaring you. I saw Julia. I am not at home. I was not sure the cops would do a thing about them and to be honest, I didn't know if you would be on that bus. I only hoped you were. We need to get you to the police station or an emergency room and file a report. I want those kidnappers arrested. Honey you look horrible. What did those assholes do to you. Are you hurt? You said you are bleeding?" He stole glances at my battered face.

I looked at the floor as I began to cry again. "Gus he used a knife to cut me. He hurt me bad Master. He killed the puppies and was going to kill me too. He was going to bury me in a hole in his back yard. I had to break my thumb to get away. Julia sold me to him Master. I am sorry. I was so scared."

Master Boyd winced as he heard my words and looked at my disfigured right hand.

He teared up as he reached out and took my left hand into his. "It is okay baby. We are going to the doctor now. I want you to tell them what Gus and Julia did okay? Don't be scared. I won't let them get you. You are safe now. When you are all fixed up, we will go home. I will spend the rest of my life making up for failing you so badly. I am getting a second chance to do this right. I won't lose you a second time."

I glanced at my Master feeling sad. "You are taking me to the mental hospital again. I know you are. Julia stole me from there. It is okay you don't have to lie to me. I just want to see my children and Seine first before you let them take me back."

Master Boyd appeared startled. "Baby, you were released from the hospital. Julia kidnapped you while you were waiting for me to pick you up. You are never going back to Harbor View ever. You are coming home with me. Your children and Seine are waiting to see you. We have been looking for you for more than five months. Don't you remember?"

I closed my eyes hardly able to believe my ears. "I am really going home now? You are not lying to me, Master? I just want to go home please." I waited to hear the answer as my heartbeat faster in my chest.

My Master kissed my knuckles. "I would never lie to you, Alexandria. Once we see the ER doctors and file a report, we are going home. You are never leaving again. That is a directive."

Master Boyd followed the road signs until at last we arrived at the Nashville city ER. He opened my door and helped me out shaking his head in anger while looking at my busted hand and beaten face.

I heard him mumbled, 'animals,' 'crooks,' and 'scumbags' under his breath as he took my left hand and guided me through the electronic doors into the waiting area.

He signed me in then took a seat next to me while we awaited our turn. My Maser had requested a female police officer be called in to witness my exam due to suspected rape and/or assault.

I had not told Master Boyd that Gus had raped me. He already just assumed that was why Julia had kidnapped me and Gus had purchased me in the first place. This was not his first trip with me due to a crime against me of this nature.

Master Boyd had been down this despicable road with me several times before.

I have had enough for this chapter. I am sure you can understand. The only time I have ever discussed the above information was the day in Nashville when I had to make the report to the authorities about it. So, tough thing to re-live, tough thing to read I am sure. I cannot edit it. I can't bear to read it again so please forgive errors. I warned you was gruesome. I actually did my best to protect you from the worst descriptions. I could have gone further into detail, but I don't think anyone should have to add that to their memories. I already have a hard enough time with it myself. And you know me, I am tough as old shoe leather, right? Sure.

Chapter 93: The One and Only Alexandria Recovery of the D/s Power Couple Master Boyd & The Fall of Mistress Julia and Master Gus

You know just how fucked up my life is when the title above brings us, maybe you too, relief. Our longtime friend, that had betrayed us by rape, then forced his collar at gun point had become our savior. Who would have believed him to be the actual good guy after he caught us alone in Darlin with the key and collar?

You shouldn't be too surprised by this unexpected twist. In the world behind the shattered looking glass, nothing is ever what it appears to be. Master Boyd would continue to astound, surprise, and protect us for several more years to come. He will be the third longest serving, and second greatest Master to ever hold Simon's Key. This complex man is also one of only three people that we will ever completely love. The three are submissive Matthew, Master Boyd, and Master Jon.

Most important of all the schizophrenic cop Master Boyd was destined to be Alexandria's Mirror of Origin. Without his core delusion and undying affection, we may have never recovered our shattered mind. He rebuilt the baby shard with his own hands. It would take him full four years to define our borders, cement our identity, and become the person who drafts this story tonight.

The attacks by the killer team of Julia and Gus bonded the psychotic pair more tightly to each other. An epic battle of schizophrenic versus psychopathic power couples would rage hotter than the fires of Hades itself. The prize everyone was fighting for: The One and Only Alexandria herself.

Ready to find out the rest of the story? Of course, you are. Okay, just try to remember that only in the land of madness does everything go exactly the way you want it to. In the world of the Real, nothing is ever fair. If you are still believing that it is, it is time to wake up because you are obviously dreaming.

Now lay back, let the doctor look, don't fear that officer. You can talk to her, she is here to help you. Let your Master hold your left hand and accept his band of gold. You can't handle the circle of silver, not after what you just went through. No worries, Master Boyd understands. It is time to take a breather. You need a rest and time to rebuild. Take your time, just focus on getting well. We will be waiting for you when you are ready.

"You have to believe me Alexandria. I had no idea what kind of a monster Julia was. She fooled me too you know. How can you dare to blame me for any of the troubles you have had? You are still schizophrenic, right? You would not have even been in Harbor View had you not been Psycho. How the fuck is that my fault?"
--Sheryl denying playing any part in the abduction of Alexandria by Julia, June 2000.

130

The nurse called my name. Master Boyd got up and took my left hand guiding me through the doors to the exam room. A woman police officer was there in the hallway. I started to panic thinking my Master had lied to me about going back to the hospital. Why not Julia, Gus, hell everyone lies to me.

"Whoa baby. The officer is here to help us put Gus and Julia in jail. I want you to calm down and tell this nice lady what happened when you were with Gus. That is a directive," said Master Boyd holding my hand tight so I could not escape as he dragged me into the little room.

I whimpered with fear but recalled this man with ice blue eyes was mean. I dared not test him. He might beat me. I was tired, weak and my unit ached everywhere. I couldn't take anymore swats, slaps, or whippings.

Master Boyd helped me to sit on the high table while he told the woman cop that I had just escaped a kidnapping, probable rape, and attempted murder. The policewoman looked at me with pity while he told her I was intellectually disabled. He told her that getting information from me may be difficult thanks to my well documented brain injury. She nodded that she understood the situation.

She smiled appearing friendly as I sat there trembling in terror. "Hi Alexandria, I am Officer Meeks. Would you mind if I talk with you for a little while about a man named, she looked at the paper she was writing on while talking to my Master, Gus?"

I twirled my hoody strings looking at the floor. "He killed all the puppies. Gus was going to kill me and bury me in the back yard. He cut me and hurt me too. Can you please make him go to jail? I am scared of him," I whined out like a child.

Officer Meeks nodded. "Well I will need to know more about Gus to do that sweetie. Can you tell me where he cut and hurt you?" She was writing stuff down in her note pad.

I sighed. "He cut me here (I pointed at my vagina) and he hit me with whips. Then he put his boy parts in my mouth, and other places," I whispered that. I saw Master Boyd wince and sit down appearing upset for some reason.

Officer Meeks looked up seeming serious. "Can you take off your clothes for me and put on that gown over there? I want to see what Gus did. I will go outside for a minute so you can have privacy okay?" I nodded that I could do that for her then watched nervously as she left me alone with my Master.

I tried to get my hoodie off but with my broken thumb I was having difficulty. I got it hung up over my head. Master Boyd stood up and came over to aid me in removing my clothing. He started to reach for me and I flipped out hitting him hard screaming no.

My Master put up his hands in surrender and back off toward the door giving me space. He had for a moment, forgotten that a male anywhere near me after a brutal rape was not a welcomed sight.

I stood there glaring at him. "You don't touch me. No one better touch me. I will bite them, kick them, and hurt them." I stomped my foot in anger like a pissy kid.

My Master looked at the floor wringing his hands. "I wasn't thinking Alexandria. I am sorry baby. Just put on the gown. If you want help, ask me. I promise I won't touch you."

I kept a baleful eye on him while I finished disrobing. He gasped in horror when I was finally sky clad and reaching for the gown.

"Christ, what did they do to my Alexandria, the fucking animals," he yelled out while rubbing his hands through his hair eyes wide and agitated.

My unit was bruised, welted, cut and bloody from head to toe, front and back. My tampon was now leaking down my legs in a slow stream. It was overburdened by the flow from the knife gash in my vaginal canal.

His yelling frightened me. "You stay over there. Don't come closer. I will hit you," I threatened.

He just nodded then took his seat and covered his eyes, sniffing as if crying.

I continued to watch my Master with a suspicious look. I seemed to remember he liked to do what Gus was doing to my unit. I had memories of him hurting me just like him with his own male part in my girl places, mouth, and bottom.

I wanted nothing to do with that bullshit. No more of that sex stuff. I had decided nothing in the world could be more awful than having a man pushing himself inside me every few hours. Puppies get killed, blood comes out and its painful.

Once I had the gown on, I returned to the table and sat back down. Master Boyd was breathing hard, and sweating, no doubt incredibly stressed out. He opened the door telling Officer Meeks I was ready for her.

Obviously, she got one look at my battered skin suit and immediately called for a rape kit, and full examination to be done with results to go right to the crime lab. She and Master Boyd sat in the room while the doctor, they called in a woman physician (smart move), came to repair the damage.

My Master got more upset with each detail I or the doctor gave to Officer Meeks. The lady cop was careful to ask her questions in ways I could understand. I told her about the pig head, the puppies, the plastic on the floor, the hole he said he dug for me, even the posters.

I went on to tell her about Julia taking me to a room with a chain and a cot. I told her I was there a long time, but she fed me and gave me a bucket to potty in, and coloring books.

I was unable to tell them details such as last names, dates, locations (other than Baltimore Maryland) or addresses. I was able to give detailed descriptions of my poor treatment by Julia, Daisy and Gus.

I told her Daisy was nice because she only hit me when I dropped something or burned the dinner. Not like the other two who hurt me a lot.

Officer Meeks often had to take breaks from the room and would come back with red eyes. Master Boyd left the room while I told the story of Gus putting his cock into the pig head and then into me. He couldn't bear to hear any more details. It was killing him. My Master had failed to protect and defend his collar. He was having to face the consequences and so was I.

The woman doctor seemed to get upset like the cop and my Master when she examined me. The doctor's face became pinched and angry looking while she looked my unit over. That scared me a lot. Then she ordered a bunch of shots to help kill the pain so she could sew up my unit, including inside my private parts.

I threw a fit of terror when the nurse arrived to start giving the anesthetic and run an IV. I was afraid of needles due to the bad experiences at Harbor View. Several nurses had to be called in to restrain me and the doctor ordered I be sedated for my own safety. I was injuring myself in the struggle. The nurse gave me a shot in my hip, and I felt sleepy and my fear went away. I just laid there watching everyone feeling relaxed and confused.

The doctor finished her job at patching me up then told my Master and the lady cop that there was no doubt I had been raped and repeatedly beaten by the use of fists and implements. She added there was evidence that the perpetrator had used a small blade in at least one of his sexual assaults. I told them that.

The doctor shook her head in disgust as she said the cut inside my girl part and in other places on my unit were infected. The hospital staff immediately began treating me with antibiotic medicine, IV fluids for dehydration, a blood transfusion, lots of stitches and my thumb was rebroken and set as it had started to heal wrong.

The diagnosis given to Officer Meeks and my Master was *'victim of violent multiple sexual assaults, and batteries that without treatment would have resulted in death (attempted homicide). Injuries included: mild concussion, anemia from blood loss, mild/moderate dehydration, numerous contusions/abrasions/cuts, broken right thumb, several cracked ribs, severe Post Traumatic Stress reaction, and moderate bacterial infections in the vaginal canal and open wounds on back/buttocks.'*

Officer Meeks informed my Master that her hands were tied in arresting Julia or Gus even if she could find them. The alleged crimes happened in my home state (Julia's kidnapping) and in Maryland (Gus's sexual assault and attempted murder). She stated that since both offenders resided in Baltimore, she would send the report to that city's police for further investigation.

Master Boyd was furious. He told the cop he had seen the offenders only a few hours before at the Greyhound station in Nashville. There was no doubt they had traveled to

Tennessee with the plan to kidnap me and then commit murder to keep me quiet.

Officer Meeks told him they likely had split running for home to destroy evidence before being questioned. After all, they knew he was a police officer himself. Master Boyd was surely going to the authorities with his battered and raped fiancé. She assured him she would send the information to the cops in Baltimore herself.

My Master had no choice but to trust the lady cop. He was not in his own jurisdiction and he was aware of how the law works. Julia and Gus would have to be investigated by the cops in their home state. All he could do is hope that the rape kit would yield enough biological evidence to point to Gus as the rapist, and Julia would then be prosecuted as an accomplice, maybe Daisy too.

The hospital decided to admit me overnight for observation and to make sure I was responding well to the antibiotics. They allowed my Master to stay in my room due to the sensitive nature of my being there in the first place. They asked him if a rape crisis counselor would be helpful, and thankfully he declined. Master Boyd assured them he would get me to all the proper services the second we got home.

It was his belief I had been through enough and needed rest more than anything else. He was correct. Had they sent one more person to ask about Gus and Julia, I likely would have come unglued. I wanted to forget those two monsters and that horrible basement like I did everything else but no one at that fucking hospital would let me.

They kept me mildly sedated during my twenty-four hours stay. Master Boyd never left my side except to call home to spread the good news. His Alexandria was alive. He slept in the chair next to my bed that night. Later he would tell me, despite the chair being uncomfortable as hell, it was the best night sleep he had in over five months.

I don't doubt him. I know I slept like a baby myself for the first time in a long time. The nightmare that had begun one year before, almost to the day, was finally over. I was going home at long last.

The next day I was released into my Master's care. The nurse wheeled me to his awaiting black car. I could clearly see the Chevelle in my memories. Slowly, 1997, 1998 and even 1999 was starting to leak back into my consciousness. I still had an exceptionally long way to go before I would recall even half of my life before Doctor Baker's little experiment stole my mind.

Master Boyd gently aided me into the seat, and we took off for Wheatly without any further fanfare. We sat in silence for quite a while before he cleared his throat appearing eager to speak to me but unsure how to approach his desired subject.

"Uhm, baby, do you remember me other than I am your Master? I mean, do you remember that I am your, uhm, husband," he said pensively.

I shook my head. "No, I didn't know we were married. That can't be Master. Simon says I can't marry a Master. You are not my Master anymore?" I raised my eyebrow at that wondering if he was not the reigning Master than who was?

He chuckled. "Oh no I am still your real Master. See I have Simon's Key." He pulled the item out of his shirt to show me it still hung on the chain I could see in my mind's eye.

I was very confused by this. "Master, Simon says it is a Key rule I can't marry a Master. How can you be my husband? I don't understand."

Master Boyd stole a sheepish glance at me. "Simon made an exception for me, Alexandria. He also said there a man couldn't be a Master, but I am your Master and I am a man. I want you to put my ring back on your finger. I brought it with me. You are my One and Only Alexandria. I want to go back to being yours too like it was before this nightmare. We love each other. Please try to remember." He reached into his breast pocket and produced a gold ring with a red stone.

He held it out for me to see with his right hand. I took the ring and examined it. I closed my eyes and saw the back of a squad car. He was sitting in the front, it was dark. My Master got out and came into the back seat. He, oh God, he hurt me.

I opened my eyes glaring at him with hate. "You did what Gus did. You made me give you my collar and stole

Simon's Key. You are a rapist. How can I love you," I yelled as I threw the ring back at him angrily.

Master Boyd's blue eyes filled with rain. He wept silently while I snuggled near to my door watching the scenes of a world that was completely new to me rush by. He didn't try to speak to me again the entire way six hundred and ninety miles home, an almost nine-hour ride.

My Master spent most of it despairing in the knowledge that the only thing I could recall about him was his cruelty towards me. To be fair, he had raped me, forced the collar at gun point and spent almost a year violently sexually assaulting me after all that. His expecting I would recollect the slow onset of love and trust that had built after such a vicious start, was a bit much to expect. Especially after the trauma I had just barely survived.

The doctor had warned him that my hand would take eight to twelve weeks to heal. I could not engage in sexual contact for at least six weeks, and even then, she asked him to take it very slow and be conscientious of the horrors I had just endured. I am sure for my sex addicted Master, who had already waited almost a year to enjoy carnal congress with me, it was a bitter pill to swallow.

My Master was in his residual cycle. Harbor View and heavy antipsychotics had helped him clear his head of significant psychotic process. When not prodromal or acute, he was a romantic, loving, kind, generous, honorable, and clever man. Had he never developed Schizophrenia he would have been the kind of lover or husband any girl would be beyond lucky to call her own.

I suppose the Gods decided to take pity on me one more time. They had already helped me by aiming my mallet true, allowing those windows to open that night, and putting that beautiful schizophrenic street woman in my path. They had been with me when that bus took off only fifteen minutes after my arrival, and they came to me in a dream to remind me of a phone number that would save me from my pursuers. How could I have dared to expect them to reach out and grant me any more mercy after all that?

Well, the Gods graced me with their blessings one more time. My Master was not in a psychotic cycle. He accepted my rejection of his love with quiet dignity and respect for the fact that he had caused that by forcing my collar during his nasty acute. He felt guilty that his violent hands had helped, along with Sheryl and DCFS, to lead to my deep life altering break from reality.

He had kicked himself thousands of times that he had not just commanded I quit the job and leave Sheryl to rot. He had allowed me too much freedom of choice and as usual I chose the path to destruction. My Master was aware that is why I wear a collar. I cannot be trusted to do what is right for me. His weakness at fearing my hate if he had directed I leave DCFS had been a key factor in my eventual blowing of my final gaskets.

Master Boyd had committed me to Harbor View. He had tried to sign me out when he realized the danger but then lost control as my guardian when Doctor Baker had the hospital court order my treatment. He had also been late the day Julia took advantage of a lackadaisical discharge process by the mental hospital.

My Master had suspected the foul Julia of my kidnapping but in an impulsive move, got himself stuck inpatient leaving the monster Mistress free to drag me off to my doom. Master Boyd knew he had missed every opportunity to stop the horror that sat next to him in his car. As my Master he had sworn to protect and defend his collar. He had done such a terrible job he had even had his submissive poached by a bona fide human trafficker. All the above were not things he was ever going to forgive himself for.

Master Boyd was and is schizophrenic. He was no doubt a rapist, of me at least. He had made many mistakes and failed as badly as any Master could. Yet, he was also intelligent. My Master believed God had granted him a second chance to prove he was worthy to be my Dominant. He decided on that long, sad ride home to dig his boots into the ground and hold on to his One and Only's collar with his hands, heart, and soul.

He was determined to do whatever it took, no matter how long it took, to help me get back to the best functioning possible. My Master believed, in time, he would find a way to get me to love him again.

He told me later that on that ride home he swore to his God he would never allow me to be hurt like this again.

Master Boyd was tired of sitting in waiting rooms while physicians stitched up the latest wounds, rapes, and damaged caused by monsters. So was I.).

Master Boyd took me straight to my Maiden Mary's home to see my children and Seine for the first time in a year. I didn't recall seeing them in the hospital and didn't know them while there either.

When we pulled into the driveway my heart began to beat rapidly. I could remember this place, and the beautiful woman who lived here. She was my friend Mary. I began to tear up in joy as I got out of the car and the lady in my memory stepped out squealing in extreme happiness at the sight of my unit.

My children and Seine rushed out of the door past her running for their mother, dancing, laughing, and shouting in pure jubilance. I imagine this is what it feels like to be a rock star, just on a much smaller scale.

I crouched down as the three of them approached. All of them dog piled me almost immediately. I yelled out their names, while crying in pure elation ignoring my injuries while I basked in the re-bonding and pure love only a family can ever genuinely enjoy. I fell to my back laughing hard as their weight pulled me down. Even Seine couldn't get close enough to his returned momma as he playfully fought for his spot in my arms for hugs and adoration.

Everyone, including Mary, had believed me long dead. I can only imagine what it was like for Mary to see me returned alive after so much grief at my loss. I can, however, tell you for me it was pure joy. I really thought I would never hold my kids, Seine or my Maiden ever again. The homecoming was, well there are no words strong enough to describe the feelings of reunion after all that terror and time.

Master Boyd and Maiden Mary watched the celebration with smiles of satisfaction on their faces. It was without a doubt one of the finest days of my life. Good thing too, after so much pain, I was in desperate need of a few fine moments in my miserable life.

We went inside where Mary had made a big meal, cake and the kids had decorated the house in welcome home mom paraphernalia. I sat in the living room floor playing with my children. My daughter was about to be ten years old, my son only eight. My beloved Seine was almost five. On that floor we all shared about the same mental age. For the first time in my life, I was the perfect mom. I could finally relate to my children on their level.

I showed them my hot wheels collection and coloring books. My son and I played cars, while my daughter colored in my books. I could hear the discussion between Mary and Master Boyd as they watched us interacting on the floor.

He told her about the discovery he made in Nashville and what had happened to me during the five months I was missing. My Master informed Mary that Julia and Gus would likely try to abduct me again unless they were arrested for their crimes.

My Maiden frowned. "Oh my goodness. Boyd, surely they will put those fiends under the fucking jail for what they did to Mother. Look at her. She is a mess." She clicked her tongue in disgust.

Master Boyd sat down watching me with his icy gaze. "No Mary, they will let the bastards get away. They are too far away for me to put serious pressure on the authorities. Alexandria is a poor witness, and the doctor told me thanks to her quick actions that likely saved her from bleeding to death she ruined the DNA evidence. The doc didn't think they got a valid sample despite all the evidence of assault. Worse still, the sonsofabitches have time to clear up all the collaborating evidence. It will take days for the Baltimore cops to get out there to question those assholes. By then there won't be shit around to prove my girl is telling the truth. Julia and Gus saw me haul her away. They know where we were heading. You can bet your bottom dollar they ran home to pick up their toys. They will deny what they did and say with Alexandria being so simple it could have been anyone. Without more evidence tying them to this crime, nothing will ever come of it. I have been in law enforcement too long to lie to myself. Those two will get away with it unless I go take care of business on my own."

Mary's eyes went wide. "Boyd, you can't go beating the shit out of people."

My Master turned and set his sight on her and said coldly, "I am not going to beat anyone. I am going to bury them in the hole Gus dug for Alexandria. All three of those fuckers."

My Maiden shook her head while sitting down next to him. "Boyd, you need to think of Alexandria, if you kill them, they will put you away. Then what will she do? The state will ship her off to some retardation place, and the kids will go to Timmy's family. Shit, they were already trying to make a play for them. They may still if they find out how mentally fucked up she really is. You need to focus on helping her get well. If you really love her, that is what you will do. Let the law handle those monsters, you take care of your own."

Master Boyd growled. "They need to pay Mary. How can you expect me to just sit here on my thumbs? The sonofabitch raped her with a knife, God damn it. Who does that? He was going to skin her and fuck her empty eye sockets. Where you not listening? I can't let that kind of abomination just walk away free. What if he gets another girl? What if Julia helps him? What if there were other girls already, Mary?"

Mary took a deep breath. "I know what you are saying Boyd but look at Alex. Look at her. You do it, you will get caught. The world is full of shit like those two. You must let it go and try to start over. I don't want to hear any more about this. You compromise me just by making the threat. What if you did it and they asked me if you told me? I don't want to lose my freedom and home. Haven't they done enough to this family? Think man, think."

My Master sat there glaring at her angrily for a moment then got up and tore out the door to pace on the porch. He knew she spoke wisdom; he just didn't want to hear it. I listened to them talking and agreed with my Maiden. My Master needed to help me find my way back to where I had been. If he went around killing Julia and Gus, not that I would not have liked to myself, then he would surely go to prison.

I was daft, but I understood he was my guardian. I also knew he was the only thing keeping me from another mental hospital. I may have hated him for being a bastard himself, but I had to tolerate him or pay the price. I watched him walking back and forth appearing to work himself into a frenzy. My Maiden sighed and shot me a look of worry. I nodded in an unsaid agreement that he needed to be spoken to by the victim herself like it or not.

I got up and went outside to see if I could calm him down. When I stepped onto the porch, he stopped pacing and stood off to give me my space as I had demanded. I told you he was and is clever.

"Master, I don't want you to kill Gus and Julia or beat them up. I want you to stay here with me and the children. Seine wants you to stay too. Don't go to Baltimore, please," I said while staring at the wood below my feet feeling anger toward this hideous man who had hurt me so many times, according to my Looper anyway.

Master Boyd let out his breath. "Alexandria, those people may have hurt other girls and may come back to hurt you some more. No one is going to do anything to stop them. Do you understand that?"

I nodded. "Yes Master, I do. Gus told me I was his first girl. He was mad that I didn't have hair. He wanted the girl he would kill to have hair. He didn't kill me though. I got away. I am never going back either. Julia and Gus were liars. That collar was fake. You helped me get home to my children and you have Simon's Key, you are my real Master. You need to take care of me like you promised when you took the Key, right before you raped me. I remember what you did to me in the back seat of the police car, Master. You should be in jail like Gus," I yelled out in rage.

My Master gasped. "You submitted and gave me Simon's key, Alexandria. You accepted my collar. It is not right to accuse me of what Gus did. His collaring was fake. Mine was real. Special services are the rights of the Master. I took what was mine by the rules. That is not rape. Simon says so."

I looked up startled. "You are a liar. Simon never said anything about that to me." I was terrified by the look of honesty in my Master's face. What if he was telling the truth?

Oh shit, if that were true then he could do what Gus did all he liked. I really needed to talk to Simon and fast.

Master Boyd looked at me hard. "I am not lying Having sex with your Master is part of the service provided for services given to you. Ask Simon."

I started to wring my hands with anxiety as the memory leaked into my consciousness that 'special services' are sex and are guaranteed to a Master. "You stole Simon's key, not fair," I whined realizing I was in big trouble. I didn't want to ever have sex again.

Master Boyd scoffed. "I didn't steal his key Alexandria. You gave it to me willingly. You questioned the first time, so I offered to give it back. You gave it to me a second time too. You must believe me. We worked this all out a long time ago. I admit we did start off wrong. I did things I am not proud of today. Then you punished me for it. We were equal. We started over, and you loved me like I love you. Please try to remember."

I looked at my left arm. "You love me? You burned me. You raped me. You hit me. That is not love, Master," I yelled back now feeling very frightened because somehow I knew he was being honest. I did love him for some fucking reason despite all I remembered he did. How could that be?

My Master shook his head. "Yeah, I did all that Alexandria. I won't lie to you ever again. I was sick when all that happened. I have schizophrenia too, like you do."

I gasped as all my breath left my lungs. "What? You have schizophrenia, like me?"

He nodded while looking at the ground appearing ashamed. "I do. I should have told you a long time ago. I got sick and came after your collar the wrong way. When I got better, I made it up to you. Equal service for equal service, Alexandria. I can't ask your forgiveness. There is no way to have that. Instead, I did my best to be a good Master and a loving husband to you. I wish you could remember that. I won't live without you. You are my everything. I will do whatever it takes to win your heart back, to prove I am a worthy Master and husband if you will let me."

My chest ached with the realization I wanted nothing more than to be with this man. I could clearly see his attacks, cruel behavior, and violence toward my unit, but still I felt a need to be near him. It didn't make any sense, but it was true. There was no doubt I was deeply in love with him.

"You don't touch me. You keep away. I will be good and make your dinner or clean your house, but no special services. I won't do that, not ever." I stomped my foot like a child but meant every word I said to him.

Master Boyd nodded. "Okay, fair enough. You come home with me, and I will keep my hands to myself. Unless you ask me to be with you, I won't touch you." He looked at the ground wringing his hands appearing to trance slightly.

I looked back inside at my children and Seine. "I want to stay with my children and my dog. I don't want to go home with you."

He shook his head. "Alexandria, you are very ill. Mary doesn't have the skill or money it will take to help you get well again. You can't manage your kids or even Seine like you are now. Come home with me and I will get you the right help. When you are back to yourself, you can do whatever you want. I must demand you come with me to our home for now, that must be a directive sweetheart. You don't know what is best for you. I won't screw this up again by giving into unreasonable demands. You can come willingly or I will do what I must to drag you home. I don't want to be an ass, but this time I will be if you make me." He appeared genuinely apologetic about his directive to return to his home while leaving my children for Mary to continue her care of them in my place.

I felt I may cry at his words, but I knew he was right. "How long till I can be with them again?" I sniffed back my disappointment.

Master Boyd shook his head. "Honey, I can't tell you that. I know if we work together, we can make you better, maybe even better than before. You must learn to trust me. You will have to work hard with the therapists. Do what they tell you to do. I believe in you. I know you baby, you are the toughest person I have ever met. If anyone can come back from this it will be you. It is time to go home. Go say goodnight to the kids and to Seine. I promise we will come see them every day until you are well again."

I of course argued to stay longer, but in the end Master Boyd got his way. I had to kiss my sad children and distressed Seine goodbye. Master Boyd herded me to his Chevelle then made sure I got in. We took off for the white A-frame house I had seen in my dreams that he called our home.

We pulled into his driveway. I stared at the giant's belly just behind my Master's house. I recalled Simon told me the giant was so big he was under the ground, only his stomach protruded. I was in awe of the beauty of this place. I had never seen anything so green, wild, and vast. My world had been the dark cell of Harbor View, the dusty shed with Julia, the drafty interior of Daisy's house or the dark horror filled basement, for so long I forgot what fresh, free air even smelled like.

I got out of Master Boyd's car hypnotized by the amazing natural scene all around me. It was funny Psycho had noticed the landscape, but not like Alexandria was. Suddenly, the colors were more brilliant, the sounds of the world crisper, and the smells of the real more enticing than ever known before. Something new was stirring within. I could see the way everything was connected from the ground beneath my feet to the sky above my head. I wanted to replicate it somehow.

I followed my Master inside while craning my head to try to capture everything with my camera eyes. It all just made sense. I wondered how I could have missed it before. The lines, the curves they were invading my mind driving me near to madness. Master Boyd noticed my odd grin in my attempt to drink in the sights all around us.

"Alexandria baby, you doing okay? What is on your mind? Glad to be home maybe?" He stood at the door watching me with curiosity.

"Do you see it? Can you hear it? Master it is calling to me. I need to, I don't know, but I have to answer it." I said still confused as to this odd new sensation bursting inside my mind.

He shook his head. "You have been off medication for a while now. Don't worry, that is our first step, then back to rehabilitation too. I have the Occupational and Physical

Therapists all lined up. You are no longer on probation, they finally ended it. If you stay out of trouble, the court will only pull you in for medication checks if you call their attention to yourself." He motioned me to follow him.

I walk inside and looked at the place from my memory. I was most unhappy to be back in this house of pain. The cold icy hands of fear flowed down my spine like electricity. I could only remember the first several months of Master Boyd's reign. Gothic Barbie's punishment of my Master was also forgotten. It felt as if I were back in a similar situation to that of Julia, uncertain of what he may do to me. I only recalled he could be abusive and definitely rapey.

Master Boyd smiled at me with a look of extreme happiness. "Welcome home baby. I thought I would never see you again, but here you are. My prayers were answered. You can never know how wonderful it is to have my One and Only back where she belongs." He sat down on the couch still looking at me with adoration.

I looked at the floor wringing my hands unsure what to do. "Do you want me to make your dinner or clean the house Master?" I thought maybe if I were busy, I could work off some of my growing anxiety.

My Master sat forward. "I would like to just hold you if that would be okay? I won't do anything more. I just want to feel you in my arms. I have ached so bad to just have you in my embrace." He was looking me up and down with a look of desire that made me feel even more afraid.

I twirled my hoodie strings. "I don't like to be touched, Master. Can I just color? I want to be with my children and Seine now. I am scared," I babbled out now feeling incredibly stressed.

He frowned. "No, I said I won't do more than just hold you. Come here and let me snuggle with you Alexandria. I have been tolerant, and I understand your fear, but you are my wife. Sooner or later we will be a couple again. Maybe you just need a reminder of what we were to each other before this all began. Now sit down next to me, it is a directive." He pointed to the couch seat appearing mildly irritated.

I began to shake my head tearing up. "Please Master, I don't want to sit. I need to color. I can give you one of my hot wheels to not have to be over there." I was twirling my hoodie cords hard with panic.

Master Boyd stood up almost in a rage. "Trade me a hot wheel to avoid letting mw hug you. Are you kidding me? This is bullshit. I can't take this. My fucking wife hates me that much." I winced as he yelled out the words.

He stood there glaring and breathing hard appearing unsure what to do. I was openly crying at this point assuming he was going to punish me for refusing to let him touch me. To my surprise he stormed off to his kitchen. I heard the back door slam as he left the house.

I didn't know what to do or if I should even move. I waited for what seemed like a long time. I thought he went outside to get a whip, strap, or flogger, but he didn't come back. My legs were tiring of holding me up and I was starting to calm down. I finally sat down in the floor and took out my crayons and began to color, slowly forgetting what had just occurred.

My Master had gone outside to take out his frustration and anger on his shed. He understood I had been severely traumatized by Gus's attack. Master Boyd was sensitive to my limited mental abilities as well. He knew getting upset in front of me or worse, forcing anything would not bode well for his bid to re-gain my affections.

The scene of my refusal to let him anywhere near me under any circumstances followed by his furious departure out to his shed would replay dozens of times over the next six weeks. I would always forget the entire fight within about twenty minutes. He would take over an hour each time to get his anger demon under control.

At night I would refuse to sleep next to him in his bed. He allowed me to take the couch without quarrel. I awoke many times at night to see him sitting in his recliner watching me but never speaking a word. I believed it was all a dream.

Thanks to his severe acute cycle in February, Dennis had removed him from work until July. My Master had nothing to do in the first several weeks of my return home each day. He spent his every waking moment trying to find ways to bring me back from the brink of intellectual weakness and chronic forgetfulness.

Master Boyd brought the best occupational and physical therapists, females only, he could find into the home to work with me five days a week. I restarted on my antipsychotics and Master Boyd lobbied the courts to appoint a new psychiatrist. Doctor Baker was officially removed and replaced by Doctor Williams.

Every day my Master would call the Baltimore police trying to put the pressure on the lazy cops to investigate my allegations. Almost two weeks after I had escaped, they finally followed up on my claims. By that time, Julia had coaxed Daisy and her children into claiming they had never met an Alexandria. Gus had cleaned up his crime scene leaving nothing, not even a tack in the wall from his nasty posters, to be found.

The Nashville doctor had been right. My attempts to save myself from bleeding to death had corrupted the semen samples. The police were left with only the word of a mental midget against a well-respected prison guard.

As my Master had predicted, Gus and Julia were going to get away with all of it. Neither were implicated in so much as a speeding ticket when rushing home from Nashville to hide the evidence of their dirty deeds.

I was left without justice and those monsters were left to roam free. Master Boyd feared they would either try again with another girl or even come back after his own. As the days passed, he became more paranoid that their attack was imminent.

My Master's hypervigilance at a second attempt to kidnap me resulted in knee jerk overprotection. He kept me isolated from everyone other than immediate family or professional nurses. I couldn't even go to the bathroom or out in the yard to play without him standing there guarding me. He was always present, never taking his cold blue eyes off every move I made.

He continued to take me to spend time with my kids and Seine daily and stayed out of our interactions, but he denied anyone else access to visit with me, including the Coven, Linda and Dennis. My Master had become a micro-managing overly vigilant guardian.

The lack of social stimulation had the unintended side-effect of less than stellar recovery from my brain injury. My Master was not pleased with my snail-paced progress. My memory was not improving, and my behavior was still exceedingly immature. You would have never suspected I was a 4.0 graduate with a bachelor's degree in anything.

My mental age was still testing out somewhere in the ten to thirteen-year-old level by the beginning of June. I was prone to baby talk, magical thinking, tantrum throwing, fits of crying for no reason, and still preferred playing with toys, pets, or coloring books to speaking to another human being. It was starting to appear that I would not recover just as Doctor Baker had told Master Boyd.

Then in the second week of June I had a massive Grand Mal seizure. Master Boyd was watching as I played with my hot wheels in the living room floor when I looked at him appearing agitated to tell him I could see a light around his head. I fell to my back almost immediately after going into an epileptic fit. My Master rushed me to the hospital and I was held overnight for observation.

When I awoke it would soon be discovered that my mind had just taken another unexpected turn. Only this time it was for the better. It would take several weeks for everyone to discover just how much that seizure had improved my situation, but I was aware immediately, something was different.

I could hear my Master talking to the nurses about my condition. I suddenly understood complex words such as neurological, fatigue, aura, and seizure activity. I laid there listening to her tell Master Boyd that my phenobarbital was not adequately controlling my brain hiccups.

When he returned to my room, I almost sent him to the floor by stating, "Tell the nurse that if the phenobarbital is not working adjusting a dose of Depakote would be the next step in controlling the rolling epileptic process. I realize this would not be the drug of choice with my liver malfunctions, but the benefits may exceed the drawbacks." I looked at him to see if he would relay my message.

He stood there his eyes wide and jaw on the floor for several moments. "Uhm okay, yeah Depakote. Alexandria, are you feeling okay?"

I smiled. "I feel fine Master. I am having a nice day."

Master Boyd looked at the floor appearing unsure what to say to that., "Uhm when we get home, I have a present for you."

I nodded. "Okay Master, but I don't remember doing anything to earn a present."

He chuckled. "You are here. That is enough."

Later that afternoon I was discharged into Master Boyd's care. For the second time in only four weeks I was wheeled out of a hospital to the awaiting black Chevelle. I was getting really tired of doctors, therapists, and psychologists. I suppose that didn't have to be said but there it is.

When we got home Master Boyd presented me with several artist's canvasses, oil paints (base colors), a classic brush set and a painter's easel. I was not only surprised by the gift but unsure how he had managed to sneak it past me since the man was never out of my sight anymore.

He explained to me he had kept it stored in the extra room he had built while I was away at Harbor View. Master Boyd told me he bought these items when I was about to be released but never got to give them to me thanks to Julia's poaching job. He had thought I would enjoy painting since I seemed to enjoy using the crayons so much and thought painting was a step up in creativity.

I had been a bit curious about the locked door just off from the kitchen. I had never been allowed to see inside that room. It was padlocked and for whatever reason my Master never bothered to explain to me why. In my lowered mental capacity it had not occurred to me to ask about it.

After he gave me the paint set, it become a goal of mine to find out what other cool items he had stored in there. Oddly, whenever I would ask about seeing what was behind the door, he would change the subject or ignore me.

His evasive behavior about this hidden place only helped to fuel my eagerness to know what was in there. I began to watch him constantly hoping to catch him going inside. I decided if he ever did, I would take the chance of getting caught and punished just to get a peek.

I enjoyed the paint set a great deal. It was evident very quickly that my new vision of the world of the real translated to an uncanny ability to replicate what I could see with my naked eyes. I had a knack for mixing the paints, knowing the lines, and just understanding the proper brush required for each stroke. I had run through all five canvases with full paintings in only three days.

Master Boyd was not only impressed by my strange new skill, but he was also in awe of it. He began to formulate a long-term plan of action to keep me too busy to ever consider returning to the employment rat race or even desiring to.

He had always wanted his One and Only to stay home and care for him, his house, and her children. In my sudden aptitude in self-contained creativity he believed he had found his answer at last. He went out of his way to encourage the beastly growth of my inner artist. My Master heaped canvases, paints of every type (from watercolor to acrylic), artist pads, and brush sets of embarrassing numbers.

I would thank him for his gifts and used them to my best ability. He seemed satisfied with this at first but as the third week of June began, I noticed his sudden attempts to try to find excuse to touch me anywhere he could.

After my seizure, I had noticed he was becoming bolder in his behaviors. He would reach out to take his plate or fork but accidentally rub my hand, or he would brush up against my unit while walking through the house.

By this time, he was so brash I would come out of the shower to find him standing there holding my towel wanting to assist in drying me off. I would decline every time but he kept trying and always stood there to watch me dress.

I could see the desire was rising in him to painful levels. It scared the hell out of me. I wondered how long it would be before like Gus he would just hold me down and do whatever he liked no matter how much I protested.

Then at the end of the third week in June, six weeks had passed since my escape from Baltimore in case you are wondering, my Master left me with my Maiden and children. He had not left me alone anywhere since I had gotten back. I enjoyed his absence immensely.

It was wonderful to be able to just be myself with my kids and Mary without Mister Eagle eyes right on top of every move I made. I didn't even consider why he had left or where he may have gone. If it was not around me, I was happy to say good riddance. I was dismayed when he returned after only an hour of freedom from his microscope. Oh well, it sucked to be me.

Master Boyd was ready to take me back home almost the second he returned. He angrily told me to get in the car and stop offering argument. I kissed the kids, Seine and hugged Mary then did as I was told. He sped off appearing to be in an extreme hurry. His agitated behavior frightened me a bit.

When we got to the house, he demanded I go inside first, again a weird behavior for him. I just raised my eyebrow but did as commanded. He flipped on the living room light and there in the floor was the most beautiful female Boston Terrier puppy in the world looking at me.

I fell to my knees as she ran toward me yipping in a baby voice wagging her stubby tail. She jumped at me demanding I adore her, and you know me, I never could say no to a beautiful girl.

"Do you like her Alexandria," I heard my Master say from behind me as the pup began to bathe me with her wide bulldog tongue.

I giggled. "I love her Master. Where did she come from?" I looked around to make sure her mother was not hanging out somewhere looking for her pup.

He chuckled. "I got her for Seine. He needs a One and Only, a wife. Do you think he will like this lady?" He looked at the floor sheepishly.

I smiled warmly at him. "I think he will love her the way I do. This was very nice of you to do for Seine, Master. I know he gets lonely." I picked up the wiggly black and white baby.

Master Boyd walked over and took a seat on the couch. "Yeah, I know how he feels. Do you think he would be sad if his wife here didn't love him back?"

I frowned at that. "Why wouldn't she love him back, Master? Seine will make a great husband. He will protect her and take wonderful care of her. She is very lucky. He will love her with all his heart."

My Master nodded. "Yeah, but that doesn't mean she will appreciate him for it. She is very small and he is big. At first, he will be too rough with her. She may not forgive him for that when she is bigger. Then Seine would be lonely, wouldn't he?"

I looked into her buggy brown eyes., "Yeah, you are right that could happen Master. I suppose I had better keep them apart till she is bigger so she doesn't hate him." I realized my Master was wiser than I had given him credit for as Seine likely would be rough on a little pup at first.

Master Boyd looked at me appearing very stern. "Alexandria, I am not going to try to play anymore games. You understand service for service, I want a service for Seine's One and Only. You may keep her, but you have to give me something in return." He kept his gaze fixed on my face while I looked back in surprise.

"I don't understand Master. If this is for Seine, why are you asking me for a service trade?" I was confused by his statement.

He shook his head. "Seine can't take care of a puppy. You and I will have to raise her for him. That is asking me to do his job for him. He gives you love in return for your gift to him. He will not love me in return, never has no matter what I have tried. You will have to either provide a service for him or I will not provide my home. She will have to go live with Mary and Seine. He will be mean to her and she will hate him for it, like you do me." He looked at the floor.

I looked at the puppy desiring nothing more than to have that little beauty in my presence. I wanted so bad to raise her big enough to give my fur buddy a companion. Helping me raise a puppy was an expensive service in time and energy. What he was offering, his request would be just as onerous, no doubt.

"What is the service you request in return for the puppy, Master." I looked at the floor feeling a bit anxious.

Master Boyd sighed. "I want to be able to touch you, that is all. Just touch you whenever I like and wherever I like."

I winced. "I will not touch you back. Master, I don't want to have sex with you. Will you kill this puppy now like Gus did," I growled back now gripping the baby dog tight, ready to run to save her life with nightmare memories of dying little ones filling my mind.

My Master gasped. "I am not going to hurt that puppy. Not even if you say no. Get that shit out of you head right now. I am not a monster. I just want to touch you. You don't have to touch me back and I won't try to force sex on you." He glared at the floor angrily.

I was still ready to haul ass but was now willing to listen to the offer if it didn't include intercourse. "You just want to touch? Nothing else? And I can keep the puppy for Seine and you won't make me have sex, that is all? Are you trying to trick me Master?"

He nodded. "I get to hold and touch you without making you have sex. No tricks. That is the service I want. Do we have a deal?" He appeared to be holding his breath.

I looked back at the puppy. "Does she have a name, Master?"

Master Boyd smiled. "I call her Ma Chère. It means 'my darling.' Seine is named after the river in Paris. It was only right his One and Only be French. Do we have a deal? A service for a service?" He looked at me lovingly.

I took a deep breath then nodded. "It is a fair trade, Master. I thank you for giving Seine such a gift."

Master Boyd let his breath out appearing beyond grateful. "Okay, then we need to get Ma Chère all set up. I have everything she needs, follow me Alexandria." He stood up taking me and the pup to the locked room in the kitchen.

I was shocked. A puppy and finally seeing what inside the secret room all in one day. I felt like I had hit the jackpot of lucky. I watched in hushed anticipation as he unlocked the padlock. He swung open the door and flipped on the light switch.

The room had no windows and the walls were unfinished plywood. The floor was naked cement. It was small, not much bigger than the average home's bedroom. In the center of the room was a baby's playpen. Laying on the floor next to it was a water and feed bowl along with various chew toys designed for a teething fur baby.

I was a bit disappointed. I had expected magical creatures, possibly a dragon or at least boxes of hidden treasures inside. If nothing special was ever there, why the padlock? Why didn't he build in any windows? It seemed weird to me, but then again Master Boyd was hard to understand. He often confused me. This was just the latest in his impressive list of odd behaviors.

He and I played with Ma Chère laughing and enjoying her energetic antics for quite some time. My Master appeared to be in an uncommonly good humor. He allowed the pup to wrestle his pant leg and laugh till he nearly split a side when she fell head over heels trying to attack one of the larger puppy toys.

Despite the thrill of the new pup I kept a baleful eye on my Master. I didn't trust that he was not planning to hurt me or Ma Chère the second I had let my guard down. Gus taught me to never trust a monster. They can seem so sincere and even give you the impression everything is going to be okay. The second you stop being afraid, they will swoop in and make the terror hurt twice as bad. Master Boyd wasn't fooling me. I just knew he was waiting to make his foul move.

To my surprise when the pup fell to sleep, he gently picked her up and put her into her playpen without throwing her to the ground. In fact, he appeared to be as careful with her little unit as he would a piece of glass. Ma Chère never even stirred from her slumber thanks to my Master's easy touch.

He put his finger up to his lips in a motion for silence. We tip toed from the room to allow the fur baby her much deserved rest. Master Boyd left the door slightly ajar in case the little one awoke and needed to call out for aid later. I stood there in the kitchen looking at the floor both apprehensive and relieved at the same time.

My Master had not killed the puppy, yet, but now that she was asleep, I assumed that he would want to be granted his desired service. Master Boyd did not leave me to wait for my call to pay back his generosity for very long.

"Alexandria, I have kept my end of our bargain. It is your turn to serve me back in return. I want you to come with me. I want you to remove all your clothing and lay in the bed next to me. That is a directive." He reached out and grabbed my wrist but didn't squeeze it as he pulled me along to his bedroom gently.

I felt as if the air was not getting into my lungs as we got closer to his desired location of his request of service. He stopped at the door and turned around appearing to have heard my shallow, rapid, panicked breathing.

"Baby, calm down. I am not going to hurt you I promise. If you get scared, I will stop. We are going to take this slow. I want you to feel safe. There is no reason to fear me. Please trust me." He reached out and gently stroked my cheek.

I closed my eyes feeling tears forming behind them. "I am already scared, Master. Please I can't go in there."

Master Boyd nodded. "Okay, we won't go into the room. If you feel safer here, then here is where we stay." He reached out and began to unbutton my blouse.

I kept my eyes closed while he very gently removed my garments. He had been with me naked many times since I had come home but this was the first time he had been allowed to handle me in any way.

I felt the tears rolling down my cheeks while he wrapped his arms around my waist to pull me close to his fully clothed unit. He snuggled my face into his chest while stroking my back in a tight hug.

My Master laid his head on my own and breathed deeply of my skin while mumbling that he loved me with all his soul. I could hear his heart beating faster and feel his erection pushing into my stomach through his pants. My fear was peeking. I was sure that at any moment he was going to attack and take me against my will.

Instead he leaned down and kissed deeply while holding me in his embrace. His oral adoration was passionate and well executed. I could feel his interest was coming to a fevered maturity. If he were going to rape me, it would have been at that moment.

He let out a groan of frustration as he suddenly broke his mouth from mine. My Master pulled back running his eyes across my unit longingly. Then he left the room rushing out the back door for his shed without saying a word.

I stood there panting in fear, confusion, and relief. He had kept his promise to me though there was no doubt restraining his urges were almost more than he could bare.

I waited several moments. When he didn't return, I put my clothing back on and dried my tears. I checked on the new pup then went to my tasks of making my Master his dinner and attendance to his house chores. When he returned from working out his aggression he sat at the table and ate his meal without requests for any further service.

That night I still refused to go to his bed and he didn't ask either amazingly. I decided to forgot the couch preferring to sleep in the spare room next to Ma Chère. In the early morning hours, I heard a stirring at the door. I opened my eyes but didn't move.

My Master was at the door watching me sleeping on the floor. He didn't appear to have any affect on his face. I didn't allow him to know I was aware of his presence. Master Boyd was still as death, appearing deep in thought. I felt a chill rock my unit. I wondered if he was considering hurting me or the baby dog.

To my surprise he entered the room then laid down next to me on the concrete floor. I felt his arm reach out in the darkness then drop very gently draping my shoulders. I gasped in fear as he pulled in the slack of his limb dragging me across the floor. I was enveloped into his chest as he wrapped himself around me. I didn't move a muscle out of pure terror. I heard his breathing become slow and rhythmic. Master Boyd had fallen into a deep sleep in only moments while spooning my unit.

The next morning, I awoke still cuddled in my Master's arms. He had been awake for a while, so he told me, but had been enjoying the feeling of holding his One and Only while she slept. He told me knowing I trusted him enough to sleep was a step in the right direction to rebuild our life as husband and wife.

I didn't understand what he was talking about, but I didn't argue. Ma Chère was waking. She needed to piddle. We stretched, both got up stretching, working out the kinks in our muscles from hours of laying on the hard floor. I took the whining Ma Chère to the back door so she and I both could attend to our calls from mother nature.

"Don't wander far, either of you," my Master said while yawning and following us outside heading for the trees to pee as well when the phone began to ring.

"Who the fuck calls this early," he said while he eagerly looked at his chosen spot to empty his bladder, then to his squatting female wards.

He continued grumbling but gave in to the signaling phone before attending his own needs. Ma Chère and I finished our natural tasks and returned into the kitchen to find Master Boyd angrily yelling into the receiver.

"Try me. You come on anytime, you stupid bitch. Where are you right now? Shit, you need not come to me. I will happy to meet you anywhere. Come on, Julia, what's wrong? Chickenshit when you deal with someone who isn't helpless? Hey, bring your boyfriend Gus with you. I have something for him too. I am warning you, if you come near my girl again, you better get ready to retire early if you catch my drift. I don't give a good God damn if I do go to prison for it." He slammed down the phone red faced and still breathing hard in intense fury.

I hugged my little fur baby tightly feeling my unit trembling in terror. I realized Julia and Gus had finally decided to make their move. Master Boyd saw me standing there shaking in fear.

He shook his head then held out his arms. "Don't be afraid, Alexandria. This time, I won't let them get you. No matter what I must do, you are going to be safe from now on. Come here and let me hold my girls. It is going to be okay, I promise."

This time I didn't hesitate. I ran to his embrace burying my face into his chest willingly. I heard him let out a cry of joy as I snuggled in close. Master Boyd was thrilled that he was getting through to me. He understood that this simple

171

display of trust meant he was close to reclaiming all that belonged to him.

Master Boyd told me he loved me while he wrapped his arms around Ma Chère and I tightly. I tolerated his reemerging excitement over my being within his grasp while I prayed he had plenty of bullets in his gun.

If Julia and Gus were coming he was going to need them.

Chapter 94: Seine and Ma Chère
Recovery of the D/s Power Couple
Master Boyd & The Fall of Mistress Julia
and Master Gus

Here we are back again to deal with the evil power couple of psychopaths, namely Julia and Gus. Master Boyd has been doing his best to help his collar find her way back from Hell, but will it be in time for this most epic final showdown? Well of course it was, or I would not be here writing today. Despite your knowledge of who is going to win this fight, the journey to the victory is as weird as it ever will get. Nothing before this can even come close in comparison, and nothing after will be quite the same.

Ready to take a walk on the borderline between right and wrong? Ah, wait, you have been here with me before. Just never went this far. Oh well, desperate times, yadda yadda, and some shit. For this chapter bring your Master Boyd, a will to survive, matches, a lack of moral values, and a shovel. Have you ever seen his cool handcuff trick? Then, you simply have never lived. We shall see what is below. Don't worry, Julia and Gus are already there, hee-hee.

"Boyd, I have fucking had it with the two of you. I have tried to stay out of it, but your life is a mess ever since you started a relationship with Alexandria. Son, I am giving you two choices. You send her out of your house or I will do what I must to end this crazy love affair. Some people were never meant to be. Deal with it. Do you want to find

out what I will do if you ignore me on this one more time?"
-- **Dennis threatening Master Boyd, September 2000.**

My Master held me tightly basking in the glory of my coming to him of my own freewill. He had not held me like this since before Julia's cruel poaching trick in December a full six months earlier. Master Boyd was in no hurry to let me or Ma Chère out of his embrace.

I stood there feeling the warm furry unit of Seine's perfect female partner. She was like her betrothed, calm, easy going, and patient. She yawned while never taking her deep brown bug eyes off her human parents.

"I could do this all day my love, but Ma Chère needs breakfast. Your Master does too. Can we do this again later? Would you be okay with that?" He held me out looking into my eyes to make sure I was not just trying to humor him.

I nodded. "A deal is a deal. You can touch me as you like, no sex. I don't remember setting a limit but I should have."

Master Boyd raised an eyebrow. "You know Alexandria, sometimes you say things, I mean it is like you are better? I don't know, I guess it is wishful thinking on my part."

I took a deep breath. "Uhm, no it is not wishful thinking, Master. I have been improving daily for a while now. I just didn't say anything. I can understand you and everyone else most of the time. I woke up remembering I hold a bachelor's degree in Biology and Psychology. I still can't remember a

174

lot of things I guess, but I am not intellectually disabled. I wish everyone would quit saying that. I am a lot of things but retarded is not one of them." I looked at the ground realizing my Master would likely be pissed off finding out I had said nothing of my improvement to anyone.

He gasped. "Wait, you didn't sound like a kid there like when you asked about the Depakote in the hospital. How long have you been better?" He was looking at me in astonishment and confusion.

I pulled away. "About two weeks I believe. When I woke up from the seizure. It did something. I think it has fixed my problem with comprehension somehow. Not sure how. I just know that since then I have been not retarded."

Master Boyd looked at the ceiling appearing thrilled or possibly thanking God. "That is wonderful, baby. Wait, why didn't you say anything?" He really looked confused at that point.

I chuckled bitterly. "Because I know if you thought I was better you would want to do what Gus did. I don't want to have sex anymore. Not with you, not with anyone. You are a rapist plain and simple. You may not kill puppies and fuck pig heads, but you are like all the others, just a foul man who thinks with his dick. I assumed the only reason you were keeping your hands to yourself was because you thought me simple. And your guilt, which you should feel, you put me in Harbor View and you let Julia get me after Doctor Baker finished frying my fucking eggs. There it is, so go ahead and punish me if you want. You leave the pup alone and forget it if you think touching me will lead to more. Not gonna happen Master." I walked off into the spare room to feed our baby dog while my Master stood there with his mouth open in shock.

I sat Ma Chère on the floor to grab her puppy food. She was like her companion greedy. I laughed when I poured the food and she stuck her head into the stream knocking food all over the place. Master Boyd had finally recovered from my bomb shell revelation. He stood at the doorway.

"She is going to be a clever dog. Good pick for Seine no doubt," he said sounding a bit irritated.

I nodded. "Yeah I agree. I do appreciate her Master. It was exceedingly kind of you. I hope you know I mean that." I didn't take my eyes off the munching puppy.

He let out his breath loudly. "Well, after what happened I thought it would make you feel better. Look Alexandria, I would never, I mean I know I did in the beginning, but we worked that out. I wish you could remember that honey. I don't expect you to just jump in my lap and be okay with special services overnight. I would be lying if I said I didn't wish that, but I won't force you. Never again. We agreed on that a long time ago. You are right, I fucked up with Harbor View and with Julia too. I won't deny either of them. I hope one day you will forgive me for it. Until then, if you don't want me to touch you, I guess I can learn to live with it. I just want you safe, happy and if that is what it takes, it sucks to be me, doesn't it?"

That made me laugh hard. "Okay Master as you say. My turn to be honest I don't believe a word of it. I will not deny you the service you requested for the puppy. So, you can relax. I will never come to you willingly and I know you. You will not keep your promise. When that happens, I will endure your bullshit like I always do with all you shithead Masters. It really kills me you know. You arrogant pricks think I should adore you. For what? Doing what any fucking decent human would do. Service for service. What a joke.. You know some folks out there have people who care for them and don't make them pay for the pleasure. Not my stupid ass though. I get to wear a collar, put up with assholes like you, and scrap on my knees while you play God, then expect me to love you for it. I am sure you put me in Harbor View because you didn't like me not kneeling fast enough. You wanted me out because your dick won't suck itself. Now you stand there acting like I have a fucking choice. When you want to take me, you will. It sucks to be me, Master. Get over yourself." I turned and glared at him full of hatred.

Master Boyd stood there stunned into silence for a moment. He shifted his feet while I held my defiant gaze on him like the accusatory finger of victim toward an offender.

He nodded "Yeah, I can see why you feel that way Alexandria. The Key and collar have not brought you anything but pain. I offered you a band of gold and my heart. You said you didn't want it. Psycho said that. You are not her. So, I offer it again. Be my partner, my equal. Get off your knees and stand beside me as my wife, not my submissive. I love you with all my heart. Whatever I must

177

do to prove that I will do it. I want your love back, not your service. If service was the only way to know the joy of being with you, well I did it. If I could have it the proper way, I would choose it every time. You have to believe me when I say that. I am offering to give you freedom from the collar. Just be my wife." He looked at me his eyes pleading for mercy.

I snickered. "Are you now? Well isn't that mighty white of you Master? I do believe releasing me from the collar is not in your power. Only Simon can do that."

Master Boyd scoffed. "I am his representative am I not? If I say you can drop the delusion of the Key and Collar I speak for Simon."

I stood up smiling widely at him. "You Masters are something else. Simon allows you to carry out his will. If he willed you stop, he would tell me. I have had enough of this bullshit. You would allow me to drop the Key and collar only if I stay your wife. If I said no I want a divorce – I didn't recall we were not married yet in case you are wondering – you would say oh wait, you keep that collar and I will hold Simon's key so do as I say Alexandria. I am not a fool, not anymore Master. Do what you think you are entitled to do and I will continue to hate you for it. But don't insult me again by calling it love when it is clearly controlled exploitation on both ends."

I pushed past him headed to the kitchen to start his breakfast. Master Boyd stood there a few minutes appearing deep in thought. He watched me start his eggs and bacon silently. I knew what I said hurt his feelings. I didn't care. It was the truth or it was at least the way I saw it.

Psycho had never truly questioned the delusion that kept her submissive to those who demanded payment for the gift. As Alexandria, I was not so quick to agree to this solution to my lack of a crucial support system. The Key had failed over twenty times in only thirteen years. By this time, I had an impressive resume of rapes, beatings, assaults of every kind, and scars that reminded me of what a loser Psycho had truly been. Harbor View, Julia and Gus were just the latest nightmares to add to my dark memories.

This time I had almost not survived, the exploitation of my mind or unit that was directly tied to my following that damned Key. I believed it was time to reassess my choices, my goals and decide where the fuck I was going in life.

After all, I was twenty-eight years old. Did Simon think we would be able to keep taking this kind of abuse forever? I was not young and resilient any longer. With thirty looming, it was time to get serious. I had gotten super lucky this time. Maybe next time, Gus or another would get what he paid for. Marriage to a rapist, sometimes abusive, sex addicted, schizophrenic, paranoid, police officer was just another symptom of the weakness of Simon's persistent delusional process. Where Psycho was an impulsive doer, Alexandria was and is a cautious thinker.

Master Boyd went out the back door likely to finally relieve his momentarily forgotten bladder. I finished up his breakfast, then set his plate on the table. He came back inside with his head lowered.

"Okay, you are right. I want you for my wife, my submissive and I don't have the power to release you from following Simon's key. That said, since you are refusing my offer to be a partner then I demand you wear my ring and I will bond Simon's Key to your collar. I did fail to defend and protect Psycho. Since my original collaring ceremony was with her and not you, I will have to re-submit you to my will. We will just have to start over. This time I will not break my promises no matter what I have to do to keep them." He threw the collar onto the kitchen table.

I stared at the silver ring with my eyes wide feeling fear filling my unit. "I don't want to re-collar. I don't want to wear your ring either. I have the choice to refuse to submit. You are right, I am not Psycho. I am someone else completely. Whatever agreement you had with that idiot shard is null and void. I don't know you. What little I do remember about you, I don't like. Psycho may have thought you great, but I think you are a weak keyholder at best and a damned opportunist at worst. You can't get a lover because you are a twisted fuck. Your answer is to hold me hostage, force your will and your fucking ring upon me. Sick is what you are Master Boyd. You need to get a therapist and I need a God damned divorce attorney." I glared at him filling with anger at this thinly veiled attempt to consummate his collar therefor bypassing my refusal to provide special services of the collar.

He winced at my words. "I expected you to say that. You are most definitely not Psycho, but you are hardheaded like her. I am going to forgive you for it because you are confused baby. You obviously forgotten why you wore that fucking collar in the first place. You can judge me as harshly as you want. Like you, I don't care either. What you are saying is partly the truth. No one else would ever have me, that there is no doubt. You are my One and Only Alexandria, like it or not. I can't get another. God only makes one for each of us. The marriage was consummated a long time ago. There is no turning back now. I won't stand to be without you anymore. I can wait till you are ready for my collar, but you will wear my ring as my wife from this moment on. I don't want to be cruel but I told you I will do whatever it takes to protect and defend you Alexandria, even from yourself." He held out the gold ring with the red stone glaring back without wavering from our stare down in a battle of wills.

I didn't even glance at his ring. "I would prefer punishment Master," I growled.

Master Boyd grimaced while he reached into his shirt and pulled out Simon's Key for me to see, "I am going to give you a moment to take that back. You had better use that big brain. I am the keyholder like it or not. You will do what I say and be grateful for my continued grace of allowing your chastity from my sexual desires. I wouldn't test me if I were you. I have been patient, generous and even will tolerate continuing to not receiving special services until you are ready, but I won't bend on the ring. I will warn you I will only give you so much time to be ready for my recollaring and bed as well. Understand that if you fight me on this and I must force this ring on your finger it will be easier to take the next step and force the rest that I want too. You belong to me, that is final. We are not vanilla, Alexandria. You know God damned well I don't have to be nice. It is because I love you that I have been so far fare to you. If you are going to hate me anyway then I am only tempted to give you plenty of reasons." He smiled a checkmate smile.

I sneered. "Okay, fine, I will wear the ring. I will not submit to your collar. I will find a new Master. You failed anyway. Psycho is gone. I have the right to choose my own holder of Simon's Key. Give it back now." I took his ring and put it on my left finger then holding it palm up I smiled back my own gotcha smile.

Master Boyd's smile melted into a look of surprise "You can't do that. I will not give it back." He quickly hid the key back in the safety of his shirt collar then snatched up the collar too holding it tightly.

I laughed. "Well then keep them both. You will not talk me back into wearing that damned thing anyway. I will cook your dinner, clean your house, and keep my service agreement over the puppy but that is it. Sooner or later you'll be ready to hand me off to someone else just like all the rest of you did. I am not the least bit worried about it. You had better eat your breakfast before it gets cold."

My Master looked down at the plate of food and growled. He then violently flung it like a frisbee into the kitchen wall.

"I am not hungry," he yelled out as he stormed back out the back door taking his collar with him.

Simon walked into the kitchen while I chuckled over my Master's nasty temper tantrum. "What is happening, Alexandria? I seem to notice irritation in my Keyholder. What have you done?" He sat down in a chair holding his head as if it ached.

I shook my head. "Nothing that shouldn't have been done some time ago. I told Master Boyd he sucks, and I won't if you catch my drift." I went to the sink to get a rag to clean up the mess.

Simon looked at me in utter horror. "What the fuck do you think you are doing? You don't piss off the Master, stupid. Christ, how fried are your brains?"

I turned around to shoot a look of disgust at my friend. "Master Boyd failed. Do you see Psycho? No, he her get killed. The he nearly let me get killed, hell all of us. I must think of that each time I move my fucking thumb. He is just a sicko rapist punk. I am going to steal your key back and blow this pop stand. I am sick of him breathing down my fucking neck. Too late now, isn't it? I have to spend the rest of my shitty life worrying about Gus or Julia jumping out at me."

My Simon put his finger to his lips to motion I be quiet/ "Alexandria look, I confess I have no idea why Boyd holds that key after what he did but I do know he saved us in Nashville. I do know he loves us too. You discount that. You shouldn't. Our memory says no one else ever did."

183

I chuckled angrily. "Yeah, Wild Side did. You told me not to go with him. So much for love, Simon. Instead you gave me a fucking key to follow. It works great. I mean look at our Master out there pacing in the back yard. Oh wait, you can't see or hear him anymore, can you? You are blind and deaf. Shit, you know what? You always were a fool. Thanks to that Keyholder our connection is weak. If I lose you, well nothing will matter anymore anyway now will it? So, now you want me to let this loser try again? How many times do you think we can take ECT or another sexual assault, or another beating before you disappear completely? Look at him. He is fucking nuts. What is he even doing?" I pointed out the window to my Master pacing in the backyard while talking to him appearing agitated.

Suddenly I noticed my Master had a halo. I remembered what that weird visual hallucination meant. I barely was able to call out for Master Boyd as my eyes rolled back into my head and my unit fell to the floor in another epileptic Grand Mal.

My Master had heard my call. He came running inside to find me in a full-blown seizure. His training in handling my brain hiccups paid off. My Master was able to keep me from breaking any bones or biting off my tongue as the fit raged for a full two minutes.

He was able to rouse me within fifteen. I was groggy but conscious. Master Boyd wanted to rush me to the ER, but I assured him I was fine. He helped me to my feet while we went to his room to run a shower and change my clothing. I always lose bladder control during one of these nasty things.

This time I didn't argue while he aided me to bathe, dress and return to the couch for rest. I was angered that it was a chore he likely got a cheap thrill from, but I was too weak to protest. This seizure had been rough. I was grateful to find my intelligence was not hurt by it, but a bit shocked at memories of a woman named Sheryl. I also now could recall the foul trick, in detail, that Julia had played on me while I waited on Joppers and Master Boyd.

Master Boyd demanded I lay on the couch with my head on his lap for the next few hours while he watched me for further epileptic activity. He just stroked my head appearing deep in thought, but he didn't bother to speak. I laid there with my eyes closed resting.

Once we were sure the seizure had passed, we loaded up Ma Chère and took off to visit the kids and Seine. I was still feeling weak, but I was fairly sure I was up for the epic meeting of my best fur buddy with his life companion.

The meeting and beginning of a lifelong love affair between Seine and Ma Chère was a sight to behold. My long-time buddy was excited, as usual, when he saw the black car. He came flying off Mary's porch full speed attempting to beat the kids to get adoration from me. That day, he stopped short having caught a whiff of something different about his fur momma, but what?

Seine approached with much caution sniffing the air seeming unsure what to make of the strange air and small whining noises coming from inside my shirt. I walked into the house with a throng of kids and my furry friend close on my heels all desiring to see what I was hiding from their view.

Once inside I sat into the floor and produced the ecstatic Ma Chère. In typical bulldog fashion she stood her ground while all the kids clustered together squealing in delight. She was small, fat and beautifully marked with a white blaze on her chest and forehead like her much larger One and Only Seine. Ma Chère looked around at all the excited faces opened her near flip top jaw and yipped as if letting them all know she was ready for her inspection.

The children, mine and Mary's were immediately wrapped around her paw. Seine stood there his head cocking back and forth. He would shoot a look at me, then Master Boyd as if asking, is she for me?

He eventually got his chance to check out this most interesting of bundles. He prodded her in her tiny bottom with his big nose. She turned around quick as a cobra and bit his nose. Seine jumped back a mile in pure terror. Everyone laughed as Ma Chère then took off in chase after her much larger companion. Seine was terrified. He jumped onto the couch running right to Master Boyd's lap begging for protection from the scary, yipping baby Boston on the floor glaring at him.

My Master stroked the trembling Seine in his lap with a look of pure shock on his face. Seine had never liked Master Boyd but that day Ma Chère had been more a threat to my fur buddy than my Master apparently. I picked her up and attempted to put her with Seine and he tried to crawl behind Master Boyd in horror.

Seine stared at Master Boyd while his bugging eyes seemed to say, "damn can you help a fellow out man? I mean I know we usually hate each other but today, well you are the biggest here so save me please."

Ma Chère sure made for strange bedfellows of those two old enemies that lazy afternoon. The entire room erupted in wild howling laughter while the male sides of the One and Only huddled together on the sofa praying their female counterparts couldn't reach them to do whatever evil they had planned.

Eventually, all the children and fur buddies calmed down. Seine and Ma Chère quickly worked out their differences and became fast friends. Mary started a late lunch while my Master followed her in the kitchen to talk. I stayed on the floor with my kids and the pups but kept my ears focused on this seemingly private discussion going on between my nefarious Master and nosey Maiden.

"Mary, you are a damned saint. I don't think I tell you enough," said my Master.

Mary snickered. "You pay me enough Boyd. Hell, thanks to you my kids are going to get to go to college. Besides, Mother's kids are a dream, always have been. Now what is this all about," she said sounding suspicious.

Mary was no fool, my Master wanted something no doubt. I was curious to that myself. I got up and sat on the couch to get a clearer listen to the discussion without having to be obvious about it.

"You got me Mary. Well, I was wondering if it would be too much to ask you to keep Ma Chère for a couple days? I must go back to work in a week, and I wanted to use the last days to take Alexandria on a little vacation, you know just the two of us. I am sure you are aware that since the accident, our relationship has been strained." He threw a glance my direction and I quickly looked at the kids and dogs in the floor pretending not to have heard his bullshit about taking a vacation.

I saw Mary look worried. "Oh that is terrible Boyd. I know Mother loves you. She has just been through a lot is all. If you give her time…."

My Master interrupted her. "I am going to give her all the time she needs. I just think maybe getting out, maybe camping, will help to strengthen our bonds. A change of scenery, you know?" He smiled at her appearing sincere.

She nodded. "Of course Boyd. The pup is a cutie. Seine will be a bit pissy about having to share the kid's attention, but you fellas get over that don't you?" She chuckled at that.

My Master laughed and agreed with her. I sat there angrier than a wet hen at his conniving with my Maiden to get me without even my new puppy. Master Boyd knew I would never stir shit in front of my kids with him. I was stuck, stewing in my juices while he and Mary continued to talk about the weather and other superficial topics.

I didn't know for sure what my Master was up to, but I assumed whatever it was it was surely geared toward him getting his collar around my neck and his hands down my pants, grrrr. Why the hell would we need to take a vacation anywhere? We had not worked in months.

It smelled like a rat to me. I decided the second we were on our way home I would give him a piece of my mind about it. I would then have him return for Ma Chère the next day, no one being the wiser about our tiff.

Master Boyd and I didn't linger too much longer after dinner. He pointed out my need for rest after the morning seizure as the culprit behind our skipping out so rapidly after eating. I didn't argue for more time with my kids like I usually did. I was in a hurry to tromp his ass for daring to send our puppy to a babysitter when we had only just brought her to our home.

My brother the sun had just set and my father darkness pulled his blanket across the land as we sped off for home. My Master barely pulled out of the driveway before I lit into him with a full verbal assault. Initially, he was yelling back, but then suddenly became quiet. I hurled more foul insults calling him names such as liar, rapist, and abuser. He still didn't retort. I was working toward my next series of finger pointing when I noticed his silence was not the only odd thing about his behavior.

He was watching his review mirror and speeding up ever so slightly, to a dangerous level for the dirt road he was navigating.

"What is going on Master," I said trying to sound angry but feeling a bit of panic starting in my chest.

He shook his head/ "Maybe nothing. I think that car is following us but I am not sure yet. Do you recognize it? Is that Julia's car? It is not the Acura. Did she get a new one?"

I looked into my mirror and saw a yellowish vehicle only twenty feet behind the Chevelle. "No that is not the one she had while I was there, nor Daisy's car. Gus had a jeep. What makes you think they are following us?" I narrowed my eyes wondering if my Master was just attempting to deflect a fight. If so he was doing it in a way that was not cool.

Master Boyd sighed when the car pulled off onto another side road. "Well, I guess I was being, uhm, they weren't following us. Just nerves. I swore they have been behind us since we left Mary's. I really thought they may have been tailing us." he shot an embarrassed look at me.

I crossed my arms. "The only person who chases after people around here is you. Guilty conscious if you ask me or paranoid."

My Master's face started to twist into anger, but he took a few deep breathes appearing to calm down. "I am not going to argue with you, Alexandria. You can say whatever you want. We are going camping and that is final. I think maybe if you got out of the house, you would start to feel better."

I glared at him openly demonstrating hate. "I fucking feel fine. It is you who is not feeling good these days. Why would I want to go out into the weeds and get eaten up by insects? I am perfectly happy in the house. I have no interest in camping, especially with you."

Master Boyd scoffed. "Okay, glad you got that out of your system. If you are done now, then let me just say we are going camping. That is final. You will have fun you'll see. That is a directive in fact."

I rolled my eyes. "Another infamous directive that you don't have the power to command. God this sucks. I hate this." I pouted but there was nothing I could do about it.

He was right, like it or not he was my Master, and my guardian too. If he said we were going camping, tough shit for my unemployed, schizophrenic ass.

We pulled into the driveway in an uncomfortable silence. Master Boyd got out and directed me to follow him. When we got into the house, he told me to sit down in the recliner. He had another present for me. I sighed while he went into his bedroom. I listened while he dug around, likely in his closet, the came out with a box. He laid it on my lap and took a seat on the couch.

"Open it Alexandria," he said while looking at the floor appearing still upset over our fight in the car.

I took off the lid to find an exact duplicate of the wig Gus had stolen from me contained within. I smiled realizing that I would finally be able to wear something besides hoodies. I hated being bald so much. Master Boyd could be a real shit in many areas, but the man was amazing at choosing just the right gift to melt even my cold heart.

"Do you like it," He asked without inflection.

"You know I do, Master. It is just like my real hair was." I pulled off the hood of my shirt and carefully put the wig on my head while heading for his bathroom mirror to make sure I got it straight.

Master Boyd came in to find me working on the adhesive tapes to make sure the wig would hold to my bare skin. He smiled appearing very captivated by what he saw.

"There is my Alexandria at long last. You look beautiful with or without the wig. You have always taken my breath away. I never have seen a more perfect," he trailed off looking at the floor appearing sad as he remembered I hated him.

I shook my head and ran my hands through my new locks. "It is a gorgeous wig. Thank you Master. I do appreciate it. Wait, do I have to trade a fucking service for this too, like the puppy?" I narrowed my eyes in suspicion ready to rip the hair off and throw it back at him if he even dared to ask for more than my verbal gratitude.

He looked at me appearing startled. "Oh God no. I would never ask for a service over a wig. That is like making you serve to wear clothes. That is not proper. I wouldn't dare."

I snorted. "When has that ever bothered you? Being not proper that is. I seem to recall I did have to earn my clothes from you."

Master Boyd looked at the floor. "I guess that is possible, and if you say you remember that I have to believe you. Alexandria, it is not an excuse, but I get psychotic too. I did a lot of rotten things while I was psychotic. I hurt you, I know that. I accepted your anger over it and though you don't remember, your punishment too. You must try to learn to trust me again. I am not letting you go. Even if you make every moment of our lives miserable. I am asking you nicely to try to let the past go and let me do right by you. Otherwise, well, to be honest this is getting old. Before you got sick, we would fight, makeup, fight some more and then back to the makeup. We were meant for each other, but you just won't accept that. What must I do to get this to stop for good this time?"

I scoffed. "I am going to clean that mess up in the other room then do some painting. I am done talking to you for the night. You don't listen worth a shit, Master. I have been telling you for years what to do to end this constant battling but you are apparently deaf." I pushed past him headed to his kitchen to attend to the mess from his breakfast throwing fit that morning before my seizure.

I was scrubbing the wall when he walked into to join me. He sat in one of the chairs watching for a bit while I washed his dishes. Silently he got up and approached me from behind. He wrapped his arms around my waist pulling me toward him.

193

"I just want you to love me again, Alexandria. I would do anything. I am your slave. Wait, what the fuck? Did you see that?" He let me go and leaned into the window behind the sink straining his eyes to look through the darkness.

I was startled by his sudden strange behavior. "What? Huh? I don't see anything Master. Did you take you medication today?" I looked but only saw the outline of his shed.

He looked back at me still appearing concerned. "No, I forgot it. Did you take yours?"

I rolled my eyes. "No, we are both having a fucking psychotic episode, Master. I thought for a moment you were my Master and supposed to remind me, and you are seeing shit out the window that isn't there."

Master Boyd shook his head. "We can both take it now and then let's go to bed, both of us in the same bed. No more cement floors. I am too old for that shit."

I snorted. "But you want to camp. Like the ground is softer. Christ Master, take you medication before you get any crazier." I went back to drying the plates.

My Master stood there considering what I said for a moment and appeared to want to say something more but thought better of it. He stormed out the back door headed for his shed instead. I just shook my head as the glass in the window shuddered as he slammed it closed behind him.

"Nasty temper, always such a nasty temper Master," I mumbled to myself while I put the plate up into the cabinet.

194

I went into the living room to set up my easel for painting. I had been replicating the south end of Darlin cemetery from my broken memories of the garden of stones. I heard Master Boyd come back into the kitchen opening his refrigerator door.

I smiled as I recalled the two of us running across his yard in the dark to throw out all his poisoned food. It was then I recalled the back seat outside of Vegas, wait, in the woods down the road while we ran from 'they.'

Master Boyd was telling the truth. I had been his willing sex partner and he was a generous lover. How could that be? Sex is horrible. I liked him doing that to me. That was insane. I was trying to understand these strange memories when Master Boyd walked up behind me. He cast a shadow across my canvas.

I was trying to decide if I dared to ask him about my weird recollection when he said, "Wow, I never knew you could paint. I thought you were too retarded for that." Only it wasn't Master Boyd's voice, it was the voice I recalled from the basement in Baltimore, Gus.

I turned around terrified out of my mind sure I had to be hallucinating. Gus stood there tall as a giant smiling diabolically. I let out a yelp and instinctively began to retreat rapidly. I was struck dumb unable to get my shocked mind to acknowledge that somehow Gus was standing in Master Boyd's living room. He easily knocked me to the floor and handcuffed my hands behind me before I could even comprehend what was happening.

"Damn, you are prettier than I even remembered. Don't be scared. It is okay sweetie pie, I've got your handsome lover boy out in the car waiting patiently. You wouldn't want to leave him lonely, now would you? You know I thought Julia was fucking with me when she said you two made a beautiful couple. That gal tends to be a lying cunt. This time she was on the level. Two blue eyed pretty schizos. Ah, this is going to make all the trouble you caused me worth it. I got a two for one special. Now, time to fly little loony bird. Let's go." Gus roughly grabbed my upper right arm hauling me right out the front door.

I looked around wildly for Master Boyd. He was nowhere to be seen. I briefly assumed Gus had murdered him in the backyard before he came inside and nabbed me. I struggled but just as before the big prison guard was too strong for me to even budge. He was even bigger than my Master.

I was caught tight. The fact that Gus was going to finish what he had started finally began to sink in. I felt my tears flowing fast and free as we approached the yellowish car sitting in the driveway behind the black Chevelle. Its motor was running. Someone was behind the wheel.

The vehicle driver's door opened, and Julia stepped out smiling. "You got her baby. Good job. Boyd is out cold still. He hasn't stirred an inch since you put him in the back seat. Damn if you killed him, well guess there goes our fun. I was hoping to get some extra cash. You really shouldn't have used that shovel. I told you your fist would do the trick. Shit babe. He's bleeding all over the back seat." Julia shoot a look into her back seat appearing disgusted.

Gus chuckled. "That is what the fucking Vis queen was for Julia. You know what? I like this Chevelle. I think since we are here, I am going to help myself. Hell, he isn't going to need it anymore now is he? I will come move him to his back seat. Let him bleed on his own upholstery. Will that make you happy, babe? You will need to hold on to this little whore while I move the big bastard."

Julia glared hatefully at me. "My pleasure honey. Bring that stupid bitch over here and you move Boyd. Take that fucking shovel out of my trunk too. I can't stand having all this evidence around. We can just sink his car in a lake or something when we are done with them. I told you Boyd is a fucking cop. Even if he is just a small town one you can't be too careful if you are going to off one. If it were just this dumb broad, yeah, we could wing this, but if you want Boyd too, we need to be super careful. You can follow me but remember no speeding. No sense in coming all this way just to get caught over something so stupid." Gus handed me off to Julia.

She gripped my upper arm tight while I attempted to kick her. She backhanded me but I kept coming at her till she punched me in the gut. My air left me helpless while she let me drop to my knees struggling to breath in complete blind terror. Julia stood over me with a victorious grin on her face.

"You almost cost me one hundred thousand dollars. As it stands you owe me for the five grand you stole from me.

Don't even try to deny it you bitch. You had the cops come and embarrass me in front of my mom and boys. I should kill you right now just for all that," Julia growled as she watched Gus pull the Vis queen and a very unconscious Master Boyd from the backseat onto the ground next to me.

I stared in disbelief at the blood pouring from a soaked patch of his dark hair. He was handcuffed like me, but my Master wasn't going anywhere. I assumed Master Boyd had run into Gus around the shed. It appeared likely Gus had stood there waiting in the dark for my Master to come outside, then bashed him from behind based on the location of the wound on the back of his head. I felt my chest start to ache as I realized, Master Boyd could be dead or dying. Being hit in the head with a shovel can kill even the biggest and toughest person. The amount of blood pouring out didn't look promising for his survival, not for long.

Julia saw this gory scene as well. "God damn it, Gus. He is leaking like a sieve. Take a minute and patch up that wound or he won't make it to the fucking first scene. Shit, I thought you wanted him alive? He isn't going to be for long like that."

Gus was out of breath from dragging my lifeless Master across the yard like a travois. "Fuck Julia, if I busted his skull he is a goner anyway. Hand me something. I will bandage the loon's head. Shit, just shit." Julia kicked me in the sternum again sending me back into my battle for air while she went to her trunk and got the first aid kit she had stored there.

Gus caught the box and quickly did a bit of field repair of his wounded prize. He used all the gauze in the kit and then wrapped My Master's head tightly with the rolled crepe bandage. I watched in utter despair as Master Boyd didn't move or resist Gus's rough treatment of him.

Once he had plugged the leak I watched the prison guard root through my Master's pockets. Gus smiled wickedly as he found the keys to the Chevelle in the unconscious cop's jeans. I could see that my Master's breathing had become slow and deep. I really began crying as thought to myself there was no way he was going to wake up from that blow to his noggin.

Despite my own desperate situation, I felt extreme guilt and sadness at how cruel I had been to Master Boyd since his rescue of me in Nashville. I watched unable to move as Gus picked up my injured Master and tossed him into the Chevelle backseat like a sack of potatoes.

I wondered miserably if I had not been such an asshole, would these two demons have been able to sneak up on my ever-vigilant Master so easily? I wanted to just die right there – also before Gus could do what he said he would, yikes – over my stupidity towards a Master who had done nothing but try to help me get well. I closed my tear-filled eyes and made a promise to the Gods if they let us live, I would never take Master Boyd for granted again.

Gus closed the door behind his human cargo and returned for the shovel. Julia nodded at the sweating pig

Monster then reached down grabbed my arm and demanded I stand up. I struggled only to receive a fresh kick to my gut.

The old prostitute then started dragging me with some effort toward the black car. Gus walked up holding the shovel while chuckling at her slow efforts to finish her kidnapping job. He opened the trunk of the Chevelle tossed in the shovel then slammed it closed. Quick as a flash he reached down and grabbed my upper arm and dragged me the rest of the way to my Master's car.

Gus lifted me like he had Master Boyd and dumped my restrained unit right next to him on the back seat. I tried to kick the door before he could close it. He caught my ankles and yelled for Julia to bring him the rest of the bandages.

In less than ten minutes Gus had bound my legs, blindfolded, and gagged me with items from Julia's kit. I could do nothing but sit helpless on the seat next to my Master while Gus started the black car and took off following behind Julia.

I laid there on my side weeping. I couldn't believe we had been kidnapped from our home in the middle of the night by a would-be murderer and human trafficker. This had to be delusion or hallucination. Nobody is that unlucky, right?

Yet, I could smell my Master's blood musky and heavy in the air. Gus's voice was singing along, badly, with a tune on the radio (he had turned it on right after taking off). I scooted a bit closer to my Master's mangled head trying to touch him with my unit, hoping he would know I was there next to him.

I know it was silly, but I believed with all my heart that if he were able to feel me he would fight harder to come back. We needed each other more than we ever had. If we had any chance at surviving whatever these two had up their sleeve it would take both of us, working together as a well-disciplined D/s couple.

I had no idea where the demonic duo was taking us or what they planned to do when we got there. The only thing I could clearly be assured of that night is that wherever we were headed, at the end of it, my Master and I would not be having a nice day.

We drove for what seemed like an hour or perhaps a bit longer before I felt the car pull off a main road and slow down. The sound of rocks pelting the undercarriage told me we were on a dirt road. I tried to listen hard and figure out which direction we were going. I just assumed they were going to take us back to Gus's basement in Baltimore.

A cold chill ran down my spine. It had just occurred to me that the two were not going to travel all the way back or wait that long to get what they had come for. The slowing of our speed verified my terrified suspicions. We were close to reaching our destination.

I leaned down close to Master Boyd's ear and whispered, "Please wake up Master. We are in a lot of trouble. Please don't be dead. I am sorry for being so awful. I love you Boyd. Please get up."

I listened to his breathing but heard no change. He was still either lost in a near comatose unconsciousness or dying.

Either way, I was apparently on my own. I doubted a mallet and an unlocked window would work to save me this time. I felt the car stop. Gus killed the motor.

My ears perked up as they followed his movements. He got out and was standing next to the window on Master Boyd's side. He and Julia were talking but I couldn't make out what they were saying. They both laughed several times. I felt fresh tears of hopelessness start to fall down my cheeks when my Master began to moan as if in much pain.

"Oh God, my head. Alexandria, help me, my head is killing me. Where am I," he groaned out sounding as if he were in a lot of agony.

I tried to speak but the gag only allowed for my own moaning back.

I felt him trying to lift himself up next to me. "God help me. My head, what is going on," he yelled out desperately.

I leaned closer to him hoping this would help to calm him down before Gus heard him. I feared they might hit him again if he didn't stop calling out like that. He felt me snuggle into him.

"Alexandria, where are we? Why am I in cuffs? My head, what is wrong? Please help. Anyone help," he bellowed out while attempting to weakly struggle against his metal bracelets.

I heard the door fly open on my Master's side. "Ah look what we have here babe. Told you I didn't kill him. He is alive. Looks like we will have a party after all," Gus said sounding very satisfied that his victim had survived his first violent attacks.

"Who the fuck are you? Where am I? What is wrong with my head? You sonofabitch. Did you steal my car," my Master said wildly sounding very confused and upset as he should have been.

Gus chuckled. "Ah, a feisty fucker. I like him already, Julia. Alright, enough of the questions and answers fella. Come with me. Julia grab the other loon. Get her out of the car and I will come back for her in a second. Let me get pretty Boyd settled and I will be back for his little cocksucker."

I heard my Master growl under his breath. "Julia? You are Gus, aren't you? Where is my Alexandria? If you have hurt her I will kill you, God damn it." He began to struggle hard against his cuffs.

"Whoa, now slow down there pretty Boyd. No one has hurt your retarded whore, not yet anyway. Don't worry, you'll get your chance, partner. You won't be doing anything other than what you are told to do. Shut your mouth or I will shut it up for you pal." I felt my Master being pulled away still fighting his cuffs with all his might.

Julia was laughing while she opened my own door and pulled me to the ground. I couldn't threaten of plead or even fight her. I tried to roll but she used her foot to hold me still till Gus returned to aid her.

In only a few moments I felt Gus's arms close around my waist as he picked me up like a wife being carried over the threshold. I groaned against my gag and wiggled but Gus just laughed at my futile efforts. I was trapped tight. He was in full control. There was nothing I could do.

I felt the cooling night air on my tear streaked face while I felt I was floating through the air in Gus's foul arms. I felt him take a step, and the sound of a wooden floor. The smell of this place was familiar. It was the shed. The one Julia had tricked me into after she kidnapped me from Harbor View. I could never forget the smell of that hell hole.

"Alexandria? What have you done to her you motherfucker. Put her down. So help me God, I am going to gut you Gus," I heard my Master yell out suddenly along with the rattle of a chain.

I suddenly realized Gus had chained my Master to the wall the way Julia had me for all those months. I swallow my terror trying to focus on working out a way of escape. Gus dropped me on the floor while laughing.

"You know I really am starting to like you pretty Boyd. You got spunk. That is good, I love a fighter. Now, you be a good boy and you will have your dumpster rat all to yourself in just a few minutes. If you make one move this direction, I will break her frail little neck. We understand each other?" I could sense that Gus and my Master were staring each other down.

"I asked you a question pretty Boyd. Are you willing to play nice or do I end your fun right now? Be sad to have to make you watch me break your toy before you even get to play with her," Gus chirped out sounding happy.

"Yeah, I heard you. I understand." I heard Master Boyd snarl out sounding angrier than I had ever heard him in my life.

"I knew you and me would be friends the minute I got a good look at you. What is in the water around here, Julia? They sure make some good-looking loons. Hell, you don't see this kind of quality among the Baltimore psychos," said Gus while I felt him wrapping a chain around my neck.

"Gus baby, these are home grown, top quality whackos is all. They keep this kind in the family attic away from all the crime and drugs that age out the common street loon. You just don't know about these southern people. They are all clannish and never throw away a family member just because they are retarded or think they are Napoleon. Hell, in the south they give them a badge, or make them investigators. I bet even the governor is half God damned cracked knowing this dumb ass State," Julia said sounding resentfully.

Gus took off my blindfold and removed my gag at last. "Hi there, beautiful. Bet you remember me. I certainly do remember you." He leaned down trying to hold my head and force me to kiss him.

I let out a wail as I struggled to break away from his incoming foul lips. "No, get away from me," I yelled feeling my stomach lurch threatening to spill its contents to the floor.

Master Boyd, who had been sitting cuffed and chained to the wall came off the floor. He slammed into Gus with all the force he could muster. Gus was knocked sideways right to the flood with a thudding sound.

My Master stood his ground in front of my unit defiantly. "Keep your fucking hands off my wife." He glared at Gus daring him to get up and fight.

Gus got up to his knees and glared back at Master Boyd. "Okay pretty Boyd, you can have your little whore all to yourself for now. I would knock your block off but that can wait. It won't look as good if I mar up your handsome face right this minute. I will deal with you in good time. Both of you settle in. Hope you don't mind, we decided to give you love birds the Dungeon Suite. Only the best for the talent, isn't that right sweetheart." He looked back at the smiling Julia.

"Yep, that sounds just about right. So, what do you think? Will this work? I told you Boyd was a looker. I mean I couldn't believe my eyes when he came looking for that psychotic idiot right there. I couldn't figure out why a guy like him would be so hot and bothered about finding his ward. Then I did some digging around and found out he is crazier than she is, and suicidal to boot. When I saw them running across that Greyhound Station, I realized they are hot enough to look like real professionals. No one would ever guess they are just schizophrenic trash. I thought shit. We could make some videos, then snuff them out on camera when we are tired of playing with them," said Julia while looking my Master up and down with a lustful smile.

Gus nodded as he stood up. "Well, sex films don't do much on the market like they used to in the 1970's and 1980's babe. Not since the internet came along. There is still some money for something special like what we have here. You can really push the boundaries with these two, the stuff the legit actors won't do. A snuff film to end the series, it could do well. If nothing else, it will be a lot of fun slowly ripping these two apart after what they did. I owe them both for calling the cops on me, and that little slut for ruining my fantasy." He glared at us both appearing indignant that I had dared to run from his raping and attempted murder.

Julia sat down on the overturned yellow potty bucket, it had been cleaned just in case you are wondering, appearing deep in thought. "I know people who could get enough to pay back double the trouble it cost us to get these idiots. The best part is all we have to do is keep them off their medication and they won't even know what is going on half the time. They give us any trouble just give them a few LSD tabs. I have dealt with enough of their kind over the years. They'll do all the shit no one else in their right mind would, but they never last long. They don't eat or take care of themselves. So, we won't have long to get this all done. Then dispose of their remains. We can't have any part of them found. It could be tied back to us you know."

Gus tore his eyes away from the angry glare of my Master "Yeah, so we could start filming up at my cousin's cabin just north of here. Lots of privacy and he won't ask any questions. That said I want to finish these two off at my place, back home. I want to take my time. Do it up right. I am going to skin that little cunt and make pretty Boyd watch me fuck her to death. Then I am going to skin him too. Afterwards I will toss them both in the same hole. Doesn't that sound romantic, you love birds? You'll be together forever and best part is you'll be stars. You know once it is on film it is forever. Your sacrifice will bring joy to a least a few hundred people. Makes me hard just thinking about it. How about you pretty Boyd this getting you hot too? Come on you can admit it to me, just guy talk you know." He chuckled hard at that.

Master Boyd just shook his head. "You are sick fucks, both of you. Tell you what. I'm glad you brought that shovel you hit me with as it will save me from having to go back home to get my own when I bury the two of you." He kept his stance in front of my sitting unit while I shivered in terror at what those two monsters just said they were going to do to the two of us.

Julia began to laugh wildly while Gus looked at her grinning with humor. "The more he talks the more I like him. He is definitely going to be a real pleasure to break in half. You did good baby. Let's go deal with that lawyer of yours and get this bullshit with your soon to be ex dealt with. I want to be on the road to my cousin's place by tomorrow late. We can leave the Chevelle here, right? No one comes around here. I mean I will be around, but I don't want to be hanging out waiting on you and have any nosy neighbors coming around to check on screaming or anything?"

She had trouble calming her laughter at my Master's furious response. "No one is coming here, trust me. Until this divorce is settled Earl can't do shit with this place. We won't be here but a day or two. Just make yourself at home in the house and keep an eye on our movie stars and I will make my business quick, then we can get to the pleasure. Just one thing, I want to watch this show. Promise you won't start without me?"

Gus laughed. "I will do my best to hold out. I am turned on just seeing that hot little mouth of hers again. I would like to fuck her right now while the boyfriend freaks out. Damn, it makes me about nutting just thinking about it. But tell you what baby, you get back here by tomorrow afternoon and I will keep it to myself till you can come watch the fun and games."

Julia looked at Master Boyd and me. "Nighty night psychos. See you tomorrow. Don't do anything we aren't planning to do."

She and Gus shot each other looks of triumph then he took her gently by the arm. The psychopathic duo left my Master and I alone in the shed while they slammed, then padlocked the door behind them.

My Master turned around to look at me appearing upset. "Baby, are you okay? Did he hurt you? Touch you I mean in any way?" He was looking me over as if trying to discover marks or wounds.

I shook my head. "Not yet Master, but he will be back. Now they are going to hurt you too. What are we going to do?"

Master Boyd just shook his head while he broke out of his handcuffs. "Well, first we see if we can pick these fucking locks. If not, then we will have to come up with another plan." He pulled his now free hands from behind him rubbing his wrists while he began to pull on the chain in the wall.

I broke out of my handcuffs while watching him jerking the metal links without any luck. "You can forget that Master. I tried that already, for months in fact. The locks around our necks are impossible too." I rubbed my now free wrists while standing up to try my own restraints.

He grunted, groaned, and used his feet to prop himself against the wall pulling with all his strength but neither the long chain nor the hook holding it moved an inch. Sweat had broken out on his brow and his color was paler than usual. I watched him do his best to get free while wondering if the blow to his skull needed medical treatment.

"Master see if you can pick the lock around my neck and I will try yours. We will never get out that way." I smiled at him thinking how wonderful he had been at stopping Gus from putting his mouth on me.

Master Boyd nodded and came over to look at my lock. He was breathing fast and shallow. I could tell he was anxious. I knew he needed to calm down to think clearly. I had been through enough of these hostage situations to realize wasting energy on getting upset only wore you out so you couldn't fight as well when the real trouble came through the door.

I reached out and stroked his cheek while his eyes examined the padlock closely.

He stopped and looked into my eyes startled by my loving gesture. "Alexandria?"

I grabbed his face with my hands and pulled him to me. I closed my eyes then began kissing him passionately with my tongue. I felt his tense muscles relaxing in response to my honest interest in him. My Master kissed back with intense eagerness. He bathed me with his tears of despair, gratitude, and honest love until I could taste them on his lips.

I felt him lose himself, forgetting the perilous situation for a moment. Master Boyd reached out and grabbed my shirt pawing my unit wantonly. I resisted his attempt to push me to my back to ready me for his coupling. He moaned out in frustration, then suddenly appeared to recall this was not the time or place for our re-bonding through our intimacy. My Master pulled himself off me and took several deep breaths with his eyes closed trying to cool his blood.

"Alexandria, you think we are going to die. That is what this is all about? You told me you never wanted to be with me again. Why did you change your mind or am I reading you wrong as usual?" He kept his eyes closed still doing his best to get his inner lust beast under control.

I chuckled. "Well yeah, I do think we are going to die, but that is not what this is all about. Just before Gus grabbed me at the house, I suddenly remembered you. I mean I recalled us. I remembered our D/s marriage. I remembered our love, the wedding dress, the Vegas trip, you stood up to 'they' ready to die to protect me. You did it again tonight. You are not a God, Master. Doctor Baker fried my brain and Sheryl set me on the path to Harbor View and Julia too. You warned me. You begged that I stop. I did this to myself. You are right. I wear the collar to protect me from my worst enemy on Earth, me. If we survive this I will proudly accept your collar and kneel at your feet like Psycho did. I will no longer deny you all rights. It was wrong of me to do that. You are right, we are not vanilla. Can you ever forgive me?" I looked at his feet feeling honestly terrible to be saying this to him now that we were going to die prematurely, painful, and foul deaths at the hands of Gus and Julia.

Master Boyd opened his eyes and looked at me with love in his eyes. "I can never blame you for anything. You are my submissive. I am the Dominant. When shit goes wrong, it is ultimately my fault. It no longer matters who made the mistakes. We are in a lot of trouble. No one is even going to notice we are gone for a week. Even Dennis thinks we are camping. It is very likely bad shit is about to go down for both of us. We must trust each other more than ever before. It may sound strange for me to say this, but despite this mess hearing you say you remember us and what we had makes me feel like I can deal no matter what. God told me if I have your love, nothing can go wrong. Do I have your love? Really have it the way you did before Harbor View?"

I smiled as my own bittersweet tears began to roll. "Yeah, you do Master. I love you with all my heart and soul. I love you the way you love me."

Master Boyd's smile was gorgeous as he heard those words he had missed for over a year. "Well, then my One and Only Alexandria, we had better put our shattered heads together and come up with a plan. I don't know about you, but I am not dying to break into film." He chuckled at his dark humor.

I smiled wickedly back at him. "Gus couldn't keep his pork greased fingers around the throat of one wiry schizophrenic. Now the arrogant pig is trying to take on two of us. Can you dig it?"

My Master laughed manically. "Oh yes my love, I sure plan to dig it. At least six feet deep. Oh, and when it comes to schizophrenics, there is really no such a thing as just two, even when there is only one you have a crowd." He winked with playfulness at his joke about our many shards.

I chuckled,. "Then let's have a meeting of the nations of Boyd and Alexandria. I hope you have a locksmith somewhere in your audience or at the very least swallowed one of your keys in the last two days."

Master Boyd shook his head. "I have tried to stop swallowing the keys all the time. Guess it was a bad time to kick the habit. I do have a plan, but it will only save us if Gus decides to wait until he gets to his cousin's cabin. The good news is we will survive it if he doesn't and we play it cool. Can you handle whatever comes?" He looked at the ground waiting to hear my honest answer.

I scoffed. "You know I can and I will endure, Master. I am an expert at suffering this kind of bullshit. Do you think you can handle it? No matter what comes through that door, no matter what he does, You have to get through it and then live with it."

My Master nodded. "Yeah, I did six years in prison, three stints in the Snake Pit, and now even a visit to the horrid Harbor View. Then there is what I see when I don't take my meds. I think I can handle whatever he pulls on me, but if you cry out. I will lose my shit. I am not as strong as you are, baby."

I smiled at him. "You know what? I feel the same way. If he hurt you I would lose mine too. I realized that tonight in the car when I thought he killed you. Ain't love grand? You know I was pretty tough before I fell for you, Master."

Master Boyd pulled me into a tight hug. "Baby, we are going to do this together. Somehow, we will get away and I will take you dancing in our secret spot. I will even build us a fire like the Boswells had. It will be like old times."

I laughed hard. "You romantic fool, Master. Tell you what, You get us out of this in one piece then I will make love to you in ways that are illegal in most States and unnatural on most planets."

My Master let me out of his embrace appearing suddenly profoundly serious. "Well shit. If you mean that, hell, I am going to chew through this chain. Stand back, baby. You don't want shrapnel in your eyes." I laughed till my sides split as my insane Master put the chain into his mouth and tried to gnaw his way out.

The sad truth is that we both were painfully aware we couldn't get out of that shed until Gus and Julia let us out. We were helpless to stop them from carrying out whatever foul desire they had planned for us. To alleviate our rising terror at our dangerous situation we joked, teased and cuddled through the long anxious night while awaiting our fate.

Chapter 95: Snuffed
The D/s Power Couple
Master Boyd and Submissive Alexandria

The chapter title does sound a bit creepy. Oh, now no worries. You should all be used to this nightmare we call our life by now. We are going to find out just how much Master Boyd trusts us and how much we trust him in return.

Hopelessly trapped and chained to a wall, no one could hear the D/s couple scream. The demonic duo of Gus and Julia had planned their horrible vengeance to the last detail. They had a bone to pick with the Dominant's collar, but to get their pay back, they had to dispose of the Alpha male too. They knew he would never stop hunting the hunters who want to steal his prize.

The schizophrenic pair await their fate hoping that the disease that has limited choices for them will offer a shield against the dirty realities about to come through the door. Turns out this time, being able to break from reality is the key to survival.

Take a deep breath. This is going to hurt just a tad. Okay we are lying, it will hurt a lot. You got this. We are here with you to guide you through the nightmare of total exploitation. No need to be afraid. When this is over, you will never doubt your inner strength again. So, grab you leading man, smile for the camera, and don't forget to make it look real. That is what acting is all about.

Three, two, one…action. Ah, looks like we forgot to practice our lines. That is okay, Master Boyd and I are pros at the art of the ad lib. Wow, working under a spotlight is tiring. Our Master thinks after all that hard work we deserve a vacation. We agree.

"Hey Linda, did I ever tell you about the time I was in a movie pilot? It never even made it to see the light of day. You see the driving force behind the film ended up on the cutting room floor. Then the rest of it got buried under a mountain of red tape and bullshit. It is a good thing I never put my heart into the role. I might have been crushed by the stress of it all. Don't get me wrong, making an overnight smash hit would have been nice. But getting the private pleasure of helping the director finish what he started, hell, that alone made it worth the experience." **--Master Boyd's dark humored confabulation, psychotic storytelling, to Linda during dinner with Alexandria in late July 2000.**

Master Boyd and I aided each other reapplying our cuffs. We knew the fact that neither Julia nor Gus had any idea we could get out of them was one of our only real advantages. He and I needed all the help we could get given the seriousness of our situation. Taking a chance of being double restrained was a risk we had to take. Besides, if they knew about our cuff trick they may use another way to subdue us. One that Master Boyd and I couldn't easily escape.

My Master leaned against the wall and slid down to his backside while I did the same next to him. I maneuvered my unit until I was in his lap with my head on his chest. Master Boyd did his best to aid me in my bid to find comfort and shelter by snuggling into his much larger frame. He laid his chin on my head sighing with resignation and frustration.

We had been working for hours to try to free ourselves from the chains. Nothing we had done even managed to loosen them from around our necks. Fatigue from stress, fear and lack of sleep was starting to settle into our bones. Panic can certainly wear a person to a frazzle.

"How long do you think we have been in here? Do you think it is morning yet," said Master Boyd sounding anxious.

I nodded. "Yeah, I think it is at least early morning Master. You were out cold for at least two hours. Then it seems to me many hours have passed since those assholes left us here. I can't be sure. I never was any good at understanding time." I listened to his heart speeding up as I pushed the side of my face closer to his chest.

"Then Gus will be back soon. There is no way he is going to wait for Julia. I could see that look in his eyes. Baby, he is going to hurt you and make me watch it." His heart was pounding like a heavy metal drummer under my head.

I nodded. "Sounds like it, Master. I will do my best not to cry, beg or scream. You could close your eyes and not watch it. Then you and I could break free when they haul us to his cousin's house. I doubt that guy has a shed. They don't know we can escape handcuffs. When they take off the chains we break out and run." I sniffed feeling terrible that that was the best I could come up with.

Even if we could get out of our chains, the door was padlocked from the outside. The shed had no windows and a solid wall and floor. We couldn't even bust through the roof. Until the demon's moved us, we were helpless and we both knew it.

My Master sniffed too. "I can't just sit back and let Gus, I can't. You know I will lose my shit."

"Then Gus will hit you in the head or beat you up so bad we will never get out. You are stronger than me. You must avoid getting beaten or knocked out no matter what he does. Do whatever you have to do to ignore it. Look, he will not kill me, not yet I think. Try to remember, only death is permanent. Everything else will heal up. Rape is just sex, a cut can be sewn up, ugly words don't matter. I can handle this if you can. If we trust each other, wait for the moment, do what they say. Then we can get away." I took a deep breath trying to steel my nerves for the nightmare that was sure to come through that door any time now.

Master Boyd nodded. "I hear you baby. I just want you to know, no matter what, I love you and always will. Gus and Julia can't take that away no matter what they do to either of us. I want you to, oh shit, I don't know if I can say this, uhm, do what you are told and don't fight back either. You do what you are told and maybe he won't hurt you as much. I am going to puke just saying it." I heard my Master swallow hard with nausea at his wise but hard to acknowledge words.

I kissed his chest. "Calm down Master. I won't take any chances either. We are getting out of this together. Stay focused on escape, and forget whatever you see, hear, or feel. Turn yourself off inside. We can deal with the pain later as long as we will have a later. Then we will have each other the way it used to be before this horrible shit happened."

We sat there making numerous promises of love and affection no matter the events that would surely come as that day progressed. He and I closed our eyes and did our best to rest. We knew there was nothing left to do but wait. We needed our strength if there was going to be a chance at survival of the human trafficker Julia and murderous prison guard Gus.

The sandman took us within his adoring embrace for at least a few hours. The sound of the door opening brought Master Boyd and I immediately out of our slumber to quick alert. Danger had just arrived to test our resolve and metal.

Gus walked in looking at us with a humored smile. "Well, are you two just cute as bugs in a rug. I never realized how pretty insects could be till now. I must say it warms my heart to see that even with your big starring roles coming up you both can relax and enjoy each other so much. Good. You will have lots of chances to show the world just how much you turn each other on very soon."

My Master's unit tensed under my own. I could tell his anger demon was rising. I snuggled my head close hiding my face in his chest. His breathing was shallow and rapid. The time we feared had arrived. Julia was not with Gus. He was doing what Master Boyd predicted, ignoring her request to wait for her attendance to abuse us.

Gus closed the door then turned to look us over. "Either of you hungry?"

We just glared at him silently. Neither was willing to respond. Master Boyd and I had agreed to refuse any food offered. Julia had already slipped me sedatives in the mash potatoes months before. We were not falling for such a trick.

He walked closer. "Ah, a pair of the coldest looking blue eyes I have ever seen just hating me. This is exciting. Like poking a snake in glass. I always did enjoy a bit of danger. Julia says you are a cop pretty Boyd. Humm, how did a loon like you get a badge and a gun? I guess out here in the sticks they are not too picky. I see you are though. That is one nice piece of ass you have in your lap. I did enjoy poking that little whore of yours and she can sure suck a cock too. Does she suck yours as good as she did mine?" He chuckled as he attempted to bait my Master's anger.

I felt my Master take deep breaths doing his best to just ignore the cruel comments. He was thinking before acting. I held my air hoping Master Boyd would keep his anger demon under wraps until the moment we needed it arrived.

Gus's eyes went wide in feigned surprise. "Ah, nothing to say about that pretty Boyd? Don't believe me, right? Yeah, she sucked my cock and loved it too. She may be dumb as a post, but God damn can she make a man feel good. Doesn't take brains though does it. That is why you like her isn't it? You can do whatever you want and then just give her a piece of candy or a puppy and she forgets about your dick in her ass. Got to love that. I am sure gonna miss it when she is gone."

Master Boyd looked at the floor now taking very deep breaths trying to keep his focus. I did my best to prepare. I knew where this was going. I had already dealt with Gus. He always liked to goad before he attacked. I prayed my Master was going to be able to handle the pain. It was coming no doubt.

Gus stood there in silence watching us, waiting for my Master to retort. When after several minutes neither of us had taken his verbal bait, he walked closer still.

"Well now pretty Boyd, you are surprising me my man. I thought you were feistier. Turns out I judged you too fast. You're not the tough guy I took you for. Hell, you are just a pussy. Oh, wait, I know. Your little whore lied to you. Told you she didn't enjoy me fucking her. Ah, that is it isn't it. You know, I know that is what she did. Women are dishonest all the time about their secret desires. You probably don't believe that while you fuck her, she is dreaming of me. Well tell you what partner let's have a demonstration shall we? You watch and then see if you believe her the next time, she says she didn't enjoy sucking my dick." He came forward rapidly and grabbed my upper arm pulling me out of my Master's lap.

I accidentally let out a yelp of surprise as Gus pulled me away from Master Boyd. My Master looked up with his eyes blazing full of hell fire. He jumped to his feet and bashed into Gus as he had the night before. Gus dropped my struggling unit to the floor as he staggered back from the force of their unit collision. I immediately got to my feet retreating to the wall while my Master rushed past me to guard my place of distance from the offender.

Gus recovered his footing chuckling evilly. "Now there is the pretty Boyd I expected. Nice. That is what I hoped you would do officer." The prison guard tackled my Master plowing him into the wall next to my trembling unit.

Master Boyd hit with enough force to shake the shed all around us. He let out a loud groan then without hesitation head butted Gus. The sounds of the big men's skulls colliding can only be likened to the sound of billiards smacking each other during a pool shark's first harsh strike with his stick.

Gus's knees wobbled as blood began to pour from a small cut caused by the hit. He grunted then punched my Master in the stomach. My Master had anticipated that. He had quickly braced for the blow. His abdominal strength held his breath inside his lungs despite the sucker punch.

Master Boyd had been without his special services for over a year. His frustration at that sad fact was paying off. His punching bag and shed had been overused in my place. My Master's muscles were in tip top shape. Gus would have to work hard to break this seasoned prisoner. Gus was quickly finding out Master Boyd was not one of the soft sedentary inmates he had become accustomed to. This one could fight back even cuffed and chained to a wall. He was making Gus sorry he had fooled with me.

My Master swept Gus's feet out from under him with his own. The Pig Monster hit the floor with a loud thud. Master Boyd went down using all his weight as he drove his elbow into Gus's sternum. Gus's air rushed from his lungs while my Master got up quickly and began to kick him with all his strength. I watched in terror, afraid Gus would hurt Master Boyd if he let up.

The overweight, outmatched security guard rolled just out of range of my Master's chain reach. Master Boyd hit the end of it like an angry pit bull. His face turned red as he choked himself trying to get closer. He was wildly trying to make connections on the unit of the now panting Gus.

"God damn, pretty Boyd, you are a tiger aren't you," Gus croaked out while getting up onto his hands and knees sucking in his breaths while grunting as if in pain.

"Come back here and fight a man, you chickenshit. You pick on helpless little girls and tiny puppies, but you can't handle it when you are equally matched. Fucking coward." Master Boyd spit saliva into Gus's face.

Gus began to laugh while coughing and wiping off the fluid. "I absolutely love you pretty Boyd. Now you are going to be a challenge. You are even more vicious than me. Tell you what, I am going to get the video recorder. You wait here. I have an idea. You are just going to love it." The Pig Monster got up and left the shed slamming the door behind him while rubbing his chest wincing in pain.

I ran toward my still fuming Master. "Master this is bad. You made him angry. He is going to kill us right now. Fuck," I said feeling, fear rolling down my spine in waves.

Master Boyd turned around still breathing hard from his excursion. "Baby, I was not going to stand there and let him rape my One and Only. I can't do it. I thought I could, but God damn it, I would rather die than watch that asshole hurt you," he yelled more passionately than I had ever heard anyone say anything before.

I felt the tears forming as I realized that Master Boyd truly did love me. I was not just a delusion, or his only choice. This was real love. I leaned my forehead into his chest as I was still cuffed.

"I love you Master. I always will. If you are to die, I am coming with you. When Gus comes back, I will follow your lead." I sucked in my terror and steeled my nerves ready to fight or die.

He looked down at me love filling his eyes as the storm clouds of his anger evaporated. "Those are the most beautiful words I have ever heard. When he comes back, if he tries to force himself on you, I will back up. Do what he says and keep him distracted. I will handle it from there. I trust you, please trust me." He leaned down and kissed me.

I nodded while closing my eyes feeling his adoration reaching into my soul. "I do trust you, Master. Whatever happens, we do it together."

Gus returned to find us embracing like this. "Ha! You two tried to start without me. Pretty Boyd, I see a little aggression turns you on too. A man after my own heart in every way. I guess that is why we are both cops, lots in common. We even enjoy fucking the same little slut."

Master Boyd growled. "I am nothing like you. Alexandria is my One and Only. She is not a slut and she will never be yours. Go fuck yourself, Gus," he said loudly while still nuzzling my face with his own ignoring our audience of one.

Gus laughed while he looked through his video camera at us standing there. "Ah, I won't be fucking myself pretty Boyd. I am going to fuck your One and Only. But first you will warm her up for me. Now here is your choice partner. You can do as you are told to her or I will get the shovel from the trunk and knock you into tomorrow again. Once you are out cold, well I will rip your little whore apart with my cock, got that?"

Master Boyd looked up from me. "Not about to happen. How about we do this? You come over here and let us go. Then maybe we will let you and your whore go. Keep fucking with us, then Alexandria and I will show you the proper way to use that shovel Gus."

Gus laughed. "You likely would pretty Boyd, but you know what? I expected you to ignore me. You are a tough guy. I am used to fellows who think they are bad asses. I could go get that shovel, it would be more fun. I hope you'd fall for the bluff. Trouble is I think another smack on that handsome head of yours may just end this home movie before it gets started. So, tell you what. I will just shoot you in the leg. Nah, you know what. I will shoot your little sweetie in the leg, bet that will get your attention." Gus pulled a small handgun from a hidden holster under his shirt and pointed it at me.

My Master's eyes went wide. "Alexandria, get behind me baby. Now, do it." I saw my Master begin to tremble. I knew from his nervous behavior the gun was real.

I shook my head. "No Master please, he will shoot you." I defiantly stood in front of Master Boyd refusing to follow his command to expose him to the bullet that was sure to go off any moment.

Gus chuckled. "Aw, now that is fucking adorable. Did she just call you Master pretty Boyd? So, that's what this was all about. You collared the little dumpster trash. Good for you. I did that too. Was a load of fun. I must admit I could get into owning her again. I was too hasty taking off my collar. I liked her calling me Master. Just like you do. Want to keep hearing her call you that? Well Master pretty Boyd, will you do what I tell you to do? Or do I shoot your bitch?" He cocked the gun.

Master Boyd's breathing began to grow shallow with anxiety. "Okay, put down the gun. What do you want me to do? I don't understand, be more specific."

The Pig Monster smiled widely. "Now that is better. Okay, this is what I want. I want you to fuck that little submissive of yours. That's all. Give it to her real good and like I tell you to do it. I know you won't mind taking my orders, but I doubt little retard there is going to enjoy it very much. I am going to have you hurt that slut. Then when you are done, my turn. We will start this movie out nice and slow. We are going to start with a brutal rape, you know nothing fancy. Then tonight when we get to my cousin's cabin, we can start bringing in the big guns. Torture, knives, the works. After I get tired of playing with you then we can end this masterpiece with a skinning. What do you say Master pretty Boyd, sound like fun or what?" He turned on his grey bulky video recorder pointing it at my Master to film his reaction to those foul promises of rape, torture and eventual murder.

"You are fucking sick Gus. Even Hell is too good for you. You can put down the fucking gun. No need to shoot my Alexandria. I will do what you tell me to do," said my Master as he looked down at me tearing up with a sincere look of apology.

I nodded that I understood. We were going to have to follow Gus's instructions until we could get him distracted enough to lose that gun. Otherwise, we were going to die before shooting a single scene of this horrific home sex tape. I had to trust my Master, and he had to trust me.

Gus laughed. "Wonderful. Okay sweetheart, you take these handcuff keys and you let your Master go. Be careful, you keep yours on. Master pretty Boyd, you let her uncuff you then you throw those cuffs and those keys back or your little toy gets broke, got that?"

228

My Master nodded while shooting terrified looks at me. I just took a deep breath and nodded back. We were ready to play our roles as rapist and victim. This was an act we had done many times without a gun pointed at our heads. Who could have known that the violent psychotic beginning of our relationship would come in handy someday? I was not sure I was ready to get back on the sex wagon yet, but thanks to the gun, I was going to have to try. The video recorder was an added stressor. I decided it would just have to be ignored for now.

I took a deep breath and saw my Master do the same as the handcuff keys slid across the floor. I maneuvered my hands to pick them up. My Master and I stood back to back while I clumsily managed to unlock his left wrist. He then took the key and undid his right, then as Gus ordered slid them back to the chuckling Gus.

While the Pig Monster reached down to collect his items my Master grabbed then pulled me into a tight hug. "I will be as gentle as I can be, forgive me. Remember how much I love you," he whispered into my ear.

I nodded very slightly that I understood. My Master immediately began kissing me deeply to hide his real reason for the embrace. I returned his kiss hoping Gus had not caught his offering an apology for his future attack on my unit in advance. It may not have helped the fear I felt, but it did offer me comfort that my Master would do his best to avoid injuring me where he could.

"Whoa there Master pretty Boyd. Too romantic for this film. You stop that kissy facing right now. Push that girl to her knees and make her blow you. I want to see some deep throating here, make that girl fear you. She fights you or pukes, you know what to do. Hit her or I will shoot her myself." Gus chimed out sounding thrilled while positioned himself and his video recorder to catch every single bit of our rape session.

I need not go into too many details here. You have already learned that Master Boyd and I were normally rather violent in our carnal congress. My Master followed Gus's demands to the letter. I had no problem behaving as if upset, traumatized and afraid. The traumatic rapes I had endured in May at the hands of the prison guard made this taped assault difficult to manage.

Master Boyd had some difficulty at first achieving interest due to the cruel atmosphere, stress of Gus barking orders at us both, the camera, and guilt at having to be harsh toward his lover. He did have an addiction for violent coupling with me, but not like this. In our private sex life, he and I had an understanding that I was faking my fear of him. Master Boyd always believed my behavior was an act while he was forcing sex.

This time the rape was very real. He was aware I didn't want him to do what he was being ordered to do to me. He also realized I was terrified. This was too brutal even for his blood. Master Boyd had to pause and try to relax many times, due to all the above. I did my very best to assure him with my eyes or by silently mouthing words of encouragement when I could, despite my own horror at this situation.

Somehow, we both were managing to get through the discomfort, indignity, and true pain caused by Gus's acting as a director while holding us at gunpoint. No other act of carnal congress between us would ever be as harsh, violent, nor unpleasant as that one was during our big break into video.

I was forced to endure my clothing being ripped from my unit, rough fondling, physical abuse, painful deepthroating, brutal vaginal penetration, and eventually good old-fashioned sodomy.

The last one had been the object of severe contention between my Master and I in the past. He had learned a painful lesson from Gothic Barbie. Thanks to her vicious service for service empathy lesson he had sworn to never engage in dry sodomy against my unit again. Unfortunately, Gus did not provide my Master, or me, with any decency, privacy nor lubricant during this horrid sexual act.

To make good on his promise to me as Gothic Barbie), when Gus ordered him to perform this foul act, he cleverly applied a natural lubricant while the piggy cameraman was distracted trying to get a better vantage.

PS: *If you don't know what my Master did to make this act less a burden than you are simply going to have to guess. There are just some things I would rather not spell out for you.*

Just know, he did what he could to provide some mercy during this horrible indignity. While his engaging me this way was still very painful, he did his absolute best to be as gentle as possible. This often resulted in his getting yelled at by our director for not being rough enough.

My Master was commanded at various points to slap, bite, scratch, grope or choke me. When he tried to refuse, Gus would threaten to take his place to show him how to do it correctly. Master Boyd wisely would immediately follow the orders realizing it was him or Gus. He was not going to stand for allowing Gus to harm me at will. He did his best to make it look painful without using his full strength.

I didn't have any problems with my job of yelling, begging, crying, and screaming. I even attempted to struggle against, and retreat from my Master's advances during some of the more heinous demands which were barked out by Gus. It was not a pleasant experience trust me. I knew my Master had no choice, but that didn't make it less painful to endure.

I got through it by reminding myself that it was my Master Boyd. He had Simon's Key. That meant he had the right to engage me anyway he desired even though this was not what he wanted. No matter what, I have to say it was better my beloved Master abuse me any day he wanted than the foul Gus.

Master Boyd and I worked together through the entire coupling. There was no doubt it appeared to be a full-on violent rape of the worst kind. Gus was led to believe I had been severely traumatized by Master Boyd's sexual congress with my unit. Little did he know my Master and I had already been through this nightmare during his early acute cycles. We had worked out the horror of it once before. We both knew we would work it out again. Our love was strong enough to handle most anything by this point.

As my Master reached his climax, after Gus finally demanded he finish, Gus was already trying to find somewhere to lay his video recorder to capture his own rape of my unit. He tossed the cuffs at me demanding I re-cuff my panting, worn out, but sexually satisfied Master.

I am sure, if he had been given the choice, he would have preferred to obtain his rights under any other circumstances than those that day. To be fair, he had waited over a year to engage in his sexual addiction. I got the impression, at that point, he wouldn't have turned down fucking me in the center of Hell to get his fix. The only devil here was in the details.

I walked over to him as he readjusted his clothing. He looked at the floor appearing angered and horrified by what he had just done to me. I had been crying a bit but I flashed him a bitter smile then a quick wink. Master Boyd mouthed 'I'm so sorry baby' then turned around to be re-cuffed.

I began to put on his cuffs as I sniffled and shuddered truly traumatized by the foul sexual attack I had just endured. Despite my horror at the act, Master Boyd had made me love him even more. I was deeply touched by his amazing display of kindness and gentleness – and he was compared to what he could have been – when he knew I could never blame him for anything he was ordered to do. How could I? To deny Gus's demands meant one or both of us would be injured, even killed.

Master Boyd stood there allowing me to apply the metal bracelets to his wrists. I closed the last cuff and brace myself for Gus's foul attack. I was beyond frightened, especially now that I had gone through such a rough re-introduction to sex. I did my best to reminded myself that Master Boyd could be trusted. I just had to have faith that my Master would not let me suffer long. I had to believe that he would find a way to stop Gus from hurting me like he already had done before.

Gus grinned while balancing his video camera on a shelf aimed to the area where I stood, "You stay right there sweetheart. Don't move a muscle. You two are fucking beautiful. Master pretty Boyd, you are an animal. I am surprised she can even stand up after that. You did a great job partner. My turn. Let me to show you how to really tear up a piece of ass. Now Master pretty Boyd, you stay over there in your corner and watch how a real man fucks. If you try any funny business I promise you she won't survive for the next shoot." Gus started to walk toward me undoing his pants pulling out his own prop for the next scene.

I shot a look of fear and caution towards my now angering Master. He nodded while looking at the floor to contain his urge to attack Gus prematurely. This had to go as we planned or all was lost. My Master and I would have to suffer a moment, like it or not.

"Master pretty Boyd sit down. I am watching you buddy. You will watch me too. Bitch on your knees, you are not done yet, you whore." He grabbed my shoulders and pushed me to a kneel while keeping his eyes on my Master who had backed off and sat down as commanded.

Gus grabbed the back of my head and forced his dick down my throat just as he did in Baltimore. He pinched my nose while deep throating me, cutting off my air and forcing me to gag violently. I had already endured this bullshit with my Master only a short time before. My stomach was agitated and my gag reflex primed for exactly what I hoped would happen.

When Gus allowed me a breath of air after forcing himself for the fifth thrust, I vomited so viciously that it nearly sent me face first to the floor. I was careful to aim my stomach acid bath directly at the Pig Monster's shoes. Gus let out a yell of anger as my hot unit fluid began to run into his shoes. For a moment he forgot to keep his eyes on my Master.

Master Boyd had focused his attention on his handcuff trick and did his best to ignore the scene of his One and Only being orally raped by the foul Gus. His resolve to follow our plan worked beautifully. When he saw my regurgitated onto Gus's footwear, he saw his chance to strike.

My Master came out of the corner holding his chain like a garrote. I felt my Master brush past me just as he wrapped his chain around the Pig Monster's neck. Gus let out a cry of surprise. Gus never even saw his doom coming.

Master Boyd quickly dodged behind the Pig Monster while he pulled the slack from the makeshift noose. Gus's tongue popped out and his eyes bugged while my Master put all his strength into cutting off the prison guard's air supply.

I retreated to the wall as the two huge men struggled. Master Boyd held on while Gus did his best to buck him off. He clawed at the chain wildly, his face first turning red, then a shade of grey blue. I watched as the initially violent thrashing of Gus began to slowly weaken, until finally the brute fell to his knees barely able to reach his arms toward his neck any longer.

Master Boyd didn't let up even as Gus started to make a gurgling sound in his throat. "I hope you can hear me, you twat. Are you enjoying being choked? You seem to love doing that to little girls. Isn't so much fun when you take on someone big enough to fight back now is it?" My Master started to laugh maniacally while Gus's eyes became dull, he stopped struggling as his unit went limp.

I stood there against the wall still coughing from Gus's forced deep throating. I watched the Pig Monster hit the floor face first as Master Boyd let him fall forward out of his chain. My Master was still laughing. I joined his merriment in amusement at the bizarre scene of him standing over that unconscious pig. We were both near madness with anxiety driven mirth.

Master Boyd reached down and rolled Gus to his back, "Baby, I am going to get the keys and let us out of our chains. Then we have to decide what to do with him." He started rifling through his clothing looking for the answer to our freedom.

I sighed as I sat down against the wall knowing something Master Boyd did not. "Master, Julia has the keys not Gus."

My Master's eyes went wide. "What? No, it can't be. Gus has to have the keys." He frantically pawed through the prison guards clothing.

I nodded. "It can be, and it is Master. I saw her put them into her purse while you and Pig Monster here were exchanging insults last night." I pointed at Gus.

Master Boyd looked up at me appearing terrified. He pulled his chain hard trying in vain to reach the video camera and the gun Gus had positioned before coming to submit me to his foul desires. Try as he might they were too far to grab. He sat down and ran his hands through his hair while I removed my cuffs and joined him.

"Shit, just shit. How the fuck are we going to catch that stupid bitch. She is going to come here, see Gus laid out, then either shoot us both or call the cops. God damn it Alexandria. That fucking recorder has me on it looking like I am raping the hell out of you. If she grabs it and leaves us here I am cooked." Master Boyd appeared to be working himself into a frenzy.

I shook my head. "Master, you have a fucking chain around your neck. They will hear Gus ordering you to do those things. No one will believe you are raping me. You look like you were a hostage too. Plus I will tell them you had to do it. I won't say you raped me." I knew that it was also possible that anyone who saw that tape may think Master Boyd and Gus were working together.

My Master shook his head. "No one will believe you. You know better. That video will show you crying and begging and me. Oh God, I can't even think about what I did." He covered his face with both of his hands while pulling his knees to his chest in complete despair.

I realized painfully that there would be some questions asked about his choking the prison guard down, along with my own very real performance of terror. I was just as frightened about what Julia might do as he was. I couldn't have them put my Master away over something he was forced to do.

Despite my own misgivings, I did my best to sound like everything was fine. He was starting to panic. Anxiety at that point would only cause us both to misstep. This was no time to lose our heads.

I suddenly got an idea "Master, when do you think Gus will wake up?" I glared at the big would be killer whose eyes were oddly half open as was his mouth.

My Master groaned "Not for a very long time Alexandria."

I shook my head, "How can You be so sure Master? He could get up and attack again, anytime right?"

He uncovered his face and shot a disgusted look at the heap of flesh called Gus. "Trust me baby, he isn't going to be a problem. Why?"

I smiled wickedly. "Think Master. What if we took off his pants and propped him up? I could hang around him so when Julia comes in, I can drop my head into his lap. She will thing he is getting a blow job. You can pretend to be handcuffed and out cold on the floor. When she comes close enough, we grab her. But if Gus wakes up, we are fucked."

Master Boyd's face broke into a smile while he got up and pulled me into a tight hug. "My God Alexandria, you are fucking brilliant. That could work. Julia will be pissed Gus started without her."

I chuckled. "Okay help me get him set up and then we had better take our places. Time for our next scene Mister Hollywood. Can you dig it?"

My Master ran toward Gus and started dragging the big Monster toward the wall. "I will dig it with his shovel. Come on baby, light, camera, action." He sung out while I aided him propping Gus against the wall.

We pulled down his pants to his knees and backed up to try to gage if Julia would fall for his being alert. I shook my head feeling a bit confused.

"Master, we need to open his eyes all the way and push his tongue in somehow. He looks kind of dead, not excited." I pursed my lips trying to figure out how to get his gaze to look more natural.

Master Boyd shook his head. "Doesn't matter. Julia will be so pissed she won't even notice. All she will see is the video recorder and you with your head bobbing. She will buy it. I know she will."

I sighed. "Okay, well then you lay over there on your side so she can't see you are uncuffed. She will think he uncuffed me because I am so small. When you think she is close enough, grab her."

He laid down as far as his chain would allow him to go and be on the floor comfortably. I sat down next to Gus. He had not moved a muscle. Master Boyd had knocked his block off for sure. I glared at the Pig Monster wondering how many puppies, pigs, girls' other things he had hurt in his life.

"Should've stayed in Baltimore motherfucker," I growled as I pushed his shoulder.

Gus's head slumped forward from my mild push. I raised an eyebrow. Something was wrong here. I reached out and grabbed the prison guard's wrist. His flesh was cool. I dropped his hand rapidly then flashed a look at Master Boyd who was laying in the floor staring at Gus with hate in his eyes.

"Master, uhm, Gus isn't going to wake up, is he," I asked suddenly realizing the extremely serious situation heaped against the wall.

Master Boyd shifted his gaze to me. "I told you he is not going to be a problem anymore." His face was stone cold as were his words.

I nodded. "Good. Julia should be here any moment, Master. When she gets here, you grab her but let me handle it from there. We get the key and then send them both back to where they belong, deal?" I tore my sight from his face looking toward the floor.

My Master let out his breath. "Are you absolutely sure? They could return to end us. You realize that I hope."

I sighed. "Yeah, I do and yeah I am positive. They will just let them go again. They are never going to stop. We have to deal with that for the rest of our lives." I looked back at the slumped Gus.

"It's not fair I know. We didn't ask for this bullshit, but we are doing the right thing sending them back. You trusted me, now I am trusting you," he said while glaring at Gus once again.

"I won't let Julia get you. You didn't let Gus get me. Protect and defend works both ways, Master." I looked up into his eyes smiling with bitterness.

He nodded. "I love you, Alexandria. No matter what happens just like I told you earlier. If they get us then find me in prison or the Summerlands. If it is prison, bring cigarettes for my boyfriend that is a directive."

I chuckled. "I remember that directive to bring smokes for your boyfriends in prison."

Master Boyd laughed hard. "I said it was a directive to bring smokes for my boyfriend, not boyfriends. Shit baby, you make me sound like a slut." He wore a look of righteous indignation on his face as if I truly had questioned his virtues.

I looked up startled by his inappropriate humor given our dire circumstances but couldn't help but laugh too. "Okay Master, I just want you to know I don't share. I am a jealous kind of wife. You must not give him your heart. That belongs to me."

Master Boyd snickered crazily. "I will be sure to tell him that. I am sure that won't be an issue for him since my ass is all he will be interested in."

I smiled wickedly. "Well, you are safe there too. I seem to recall I made that mine too. Tell him that also has my name on it." I winked, which made both of us laugh hard.

We finally settled down from our dark humored conversation. At least another hour or perhaps two passed before we heard Julia's car pull up. I shot a nervous look at my Master. He motioned me to take my place as he laid down appearing to be out cold on the floor. I jumped onto the foul Gus's lap with my back to the door and bent forward holding my breath trying to appear I was giving head to the still unconscious Gus.

The door came open and just as Master Boyd predicted Julia let out a gasp. "You sonofabitch. I told you to wait on me. I wanted to watch." She started walking towards us.

She looked at the floor. "What the fuck Gus. You knocked out the eye candy? I wanted to try him out. Shit, asshole, I notice you left your little piece alert though didn't you." She walked just past my Master.

Master Boyd jumped up and before the horrid Julia could even yelp, he grabbed her tightly by the waist. "Why Julia, no need to be upset. I am awake just for you baby. Still want to try me out? I promise I can give you something that is just to die for." He giggled wildly as Julia began to struggle uselessly in his grip.

"Let me go, Boyd. Gus, get this fucking loon off me," Julia yelled while Master Boyd pushed Julia to her knees.

I stopped faking the blow job and turned around to glare at Julia. "Hi Mistress, I missed you. How is old Sheryl and Earl doing? Did you remember to give Daisy and the boys a kiss for me?" I smiled as I got off the Pig Monster's lap.

Julia's face fell as Gus slumped to the left then fell to the floor without any attempt to catch himself.

I looked back while giggling, then shot my Master an evil smile. "Ah, looks like you broke my toy Master. Now what am I supposed to do?" I stomped my foot appearing to pout.

Master Boyd smiled widely. "Oops, sorry about that baby. Tell you what, I bet Julia would love to play. Wouldn't you Julia?" He grabbed the back of her head by her hair holding it tightly.

"Oh my God, you killed Gus. Holy shit, no please Boyd. Alexandria, I will do anything, just don't hurt me. I swear I didn't know Gus was going to, I didn't. He just said he

243

wanted a sex slave. I had no idea. You have to believe me," cried out Julia as she scratched at my Master's hand holding here tightly by her locks.

My Master and I began to howl with laughter at her bullshit lies. I knelt so I could look her in the face.

"Okay, here is the deal. You give us the keys, get in your fucking car, take Gus with you and never come back. Do you understand? Otherwise, we will beat those keys out of you, chain you both up and let you starve to death." I glared at her angrily.

She nodded. "Yeah, here, take the keys. Please, just let me go." She reached into her purse and threw the padlock keys at me.

I stood up and unlocked my Master first. I removed his chain then unlocked my own doing the same. I looked back at the slumped prison guard.

"You know what? I think we will leave you two love birds alone together after all. What do you think, Master?" He stood there with a look of insanity in his eyes to match my own.

"I think it would be cruel to split up this perfect match. We are crazy but not mean baby. I vote we keep them together as a pair." Master Boyd giggled.

I nodded. "Well there you have it, Julia. We all agree, all of us, that you and Gus were just meant to be a match." I grabbed my chain off the floor and wrapped it around her neck padlocking it into place.

Once she was chained in, Master Boyd pushed her head forward letting go of her hair. She sprawled face first into the floor. I kicked her butt making her roll and yelp.

"Okay, seems you two have everything you could ever need. When you get hungry you can just lie and say you are full. If you need to piss, tell yourself you already did. If you miss your family, don't worry I am sure the lie you told them before you came out here to kidnap my Master and me should sustain them for years to come. After all, you are a terrific liar Julia. You are a fucking professional. See you in hell darling." I followed behind my Master as he grabbed the video recorder and gun headed for the door.

"You fucking loons. Go ahead and leave me here. Earl will be out tomorrow. He will let me go and I will tell the cops you killed Gus. I will ruin Boyd. Alexandria, when he is gone I will come and get you and your daughter. I will make you watch me put her on the streets sucking dick for crack," Julia yelled out as we went through the door.

Our brother the sun shown in our faces as we hugged each other tightly. My Master pulled me into a deep kiss running his hands all over my unit. I moaned out feeling passion for the first time since Harbor View ended Psycho's shard.

My Master pulled back panting out full of lust. "We still have several days of vacation left. What do you say we go to our secret place? I have a shovel and a fast car." He groped my bottom pulling me close to his unit.

I felt his interest in me begging for a coupling. "You are speaking my language, Master. I believe I owe you something illegal and unnatural. Let me go handle the illegal and meet me in the car for the unnatural." I engaged him into another wanton kiss.

"We can't leave them in the shed you know. Let's drop them off far from here, then we can finally get the vacation we have been trying to take for a couple years now." My Master groaned out appearing to be in some pain at having to push off his desires for a bit longer while we dealt with the nefarious Julia and Gus.

I let him go and walked back into the shed followed by my Master. Julia was over by Gus crying appearing very angry.

"You fucking killed him. You monsters. You will pay. They will fry you for it," Julie said while she came running at me.

I backhanded her knocking her to her ass just as she got into my range. "Shut the fuck up, asshole. We have already fried bitch. Many times, we both have done years of time in prisons as well. You came after us because of that fact, remember? You wanted people no one cares about, the expendable and exploitable. Guess what?" I started to laugh maniacally.

Master Boyd looked at me smiling. "I know what. When no one cares about you, you care about no one." He winked at Julia who was still on her ass rubbing her face while he went to drag Gus to her car.

Julia glared at Master Boyd then looked back at me. "You let me go or I will fuck both of you over. You don't know who I know. I have been running with the meanest of the mean on the streets you know. I know people who will do worse to you than Gus ever thought to do. You don't know who I can call, what I can do," she growled.

I reared back my leg then kicked her in the temple with all my strength sending her ass right to the void.

"You can bleed Julia, that is what you can do," I said while chuckling as I unlocked her chain and drug her by her ankles following behind my Master and Gus.

We handcuffed the psychopathic couple and Master Boyd loaded them in the back seat. I got into Julia's car while he followed me in the Chevelle. I took the interstate and drove for four hours right into the darkness.

Finally, I found a nice rest stop just moments from the state border. I parked their car, leaving the keys in the ignition. I then jumped into my Master's Chevelle that had parked next to me. We waved goodbye to Julia and Gus and drove back to Wheatly without stopping, right to our secret camping spot.

His tent was still in surprisingly good shape considering the more than yearlong abandonment of our camp. He and I got out and stretched our legs. My Master got the shovel that Gus had beamed him with out of his trunk smiling.

"We need to bury the chain, video camera, that other stuff, and Vis queen. We can burn the tape after we are done digging. Can't have Julia or Gus getting the cops all stirred up right? No evidence, their word against ours." He laughed as he began to walk to pick a spot to break the ground.

I laughed happily. "They won't be telling anyone shit Master. ..Plus, they'd have to explain why they were here in the first place."

My Master plunged the shovel into the dirt with a loud grunt. "Yep, that is true, but no need to help them is there? You want to help or just watch? I would like you to save your strength. I have something in mind for you later. Your hands can be put to better use." He smiled while stomping the shovel into the ground a second time.

I feigned innocence. "Well Romeo, I will be happy to help. No need for you to get all sweaty without me. I believe you have done enough of that for a lifetime. I am your partner am I not? Equal service for equal service." I walked over and took my place waiting for my turn to aid him in this task.

It took us all night to dig a hole deep enough to satisfy my Master that no one would ever find the evidence of our kidnapping and struggle. Once all the offending items had been buried, we quickly started a medium sized campfire.

The early morning mist rose from the woods all around us as my Master threw the rape tape into the flames. I gazed at him adoringly as he watched the southern element engulf the film of his enforced violence and my terror. He had never looked so handsome before. He saw me looking at him as if her were a rock star.

"Do you hear the music of the morning," he said while returning my look of love.

I nodded. "I do Master. It is calling us."

He put out his hand. "Then dance with me beautiful. We can't deny the morning music."

I giggled while we began our schizophrenic trance dancing. He circled me removing his shirt. I laughed as he tossed it into the fire. He grinned as I tore off my shirt and did the same. Master Boyd took my hand and spun around me as he undid his pants. I followed suit. Within moments we were sky clad while the flames made short work of our tainted clothing. The last items into the fire were our boots and socks.

My Master wasted no time in our rhythmic waltz to call in my promise to grant him his promised rights. This time I was not afraid, and he was a gentle, generous lover. That morning he reminded me how wonderful sex can truly be.

In his arms, actions, and kiss, I reclaimed all that Gus and Doctor Baker's cruel medications and ECTs had stolen from me. Master Boyd patiently, lovingly and with great finesse guided me back to the place of my lost sex drive and access to my orgasmic ability.

After he reached his climax he cuddled into my embrace. We held each other tightly on the fine needle filled ground still coupled, sweating, panting, and smiling. Silently, we rejoiced that at long last we had found our love for each other again. We had spent nearly two years lost in the darkness of psychotic hell, unable to recover our residuals in unison.

Our brother the sun rose to find two schizophrenics snoozing, naked, next to a dying fire, and a freshly dug hole that was six feet deep. My perfect mirror had created a submissive of secrets just as he had always been the Master of them.

For the next four days we conversed, coupled, cuddled, and enjoyed each other's company in every way. Master Boyd was now a satisfied Master and I was returning from the abyss of intellectual disability and madness faster each day.

NOTE: *My memory was still incredibly unstable but my ability to read, write, and comprehend at a college level had nearly returned to pre-stroke levels. I would require a full five years to achieve as much recovery as I would ever have.*

Many things were different about me after the brain accident. I would never, to this day, experience the fullness of the emotional memories of the Psycho shard. Her memories were within my Looper but they feel like they belong to someone else if that makes sense. I also would never recover the aggressive nature of her shard. Alexandria is a peaceful, thoughtful, calm, more likely to walk away than fight shard. However, she can and will fight back if cornered, but only if.

Simon was damaged severely and would never recover his ability to see or hear the real without my aid. Master

Boyd was the key to helping him collect a tiny bit of comfort in his new hellish existence. It was incredibly sad to know that I would never be able to touch, hold, or even hug my Simon like Psycho could. But sadly that is what happened.

Simon's connection to me was significantly and permanently affected by the stroke. He became trapped within my head, back in the unit like he wanted, but separated from the others. Think of it as losing your unit and becoming a ghost who's trapped in a shattered brain. He can only see and hear the world of the real if I focus and allow him.

He uses me like a window now and is forever trapped in a hell I can't even imagine thanks to Doctor Baker's cruelty. I didn't die like the other's did, but I found my own kind of death non-the-less. If I lose any more of my connection to Simon then I am broken for good. What does that mean? Well, no worries as I will explain all that later.

For now, just accept that he and I can no longer feel each other in any way. He can talk to and see me, but not you, not unless I let him look through. Weird? Welcome to schizophrenia beauties.

We had burned all our clothing. The bugs in the South showed no mercy or discretion in chewing on our naked units. By the end of the fourth day, we decided to pack it up and head home to attend our many itchy bites and scratches.

While I helped my Master roll up our tent and collect our discarded items from our last vacation here in December 1997, he began to act strangely, appearing mildly upset. I let

251

this odd behavior go for a bit but finally had to know if I had offended him or was he concerned about something.

Master Boyd shook his head. "No baby, you did nothing wrong. It is just, well it was here when I was fifteen that I first saw the static and transmissions. I was right here in fact in this very spot when I started to get sick, you know, the onset of schizophrenia." He sat down while looking into the sky.

I walked over and sat on his lap fondling Simon's key that hung around his neck. "Was yours like mine? Dude pushed me off the Darlin bridge when the static came for me and I knocked you over in the hallway at the high school trying to run away from it. I can remember that now." I frowned recalling Master Boyd standing at the door with Mary the day Stephanie and I beat up Kelly and her bully goons now so many years ago.

MASTER BOYD TELLS THE STORY
OF HIS ONSET OF SCHIZOPHRENIA
IN 1981, AGE 15

He nodded. "Well sort of like that. I had been feeling funny for weeks. Light was too bright, noises were just too loud, color was painful to look at directly. I remember I started hiding in closets and out here to get away from all the, you know, movement. I just couldn't handle it anymore for some reason. I was out here hiding out in a tent like this one. I guess Dennis was looking for me, but I didn't want to see anyone. I thought maybe something was wrong with me. I feared they would all sense it and, I don't know, hate me or

252

something? Anyway, I heard God speak to me from the sky for the first time that day. I was looking into the clouds trying to actually see him when this light or lightning or whatever came crashing out of the heavens hitting me right in the head. It hurt like hell. I fell down and tried to get away but the static blinded me. I was scared to death while God told me that I was a sinner and the only way I could get to heaven now was to die right away. I didn't want to go to hell you know, but I didn't want to die either. I spent days listening to God talk about how awful I was, and how Dennis and the kids at school would tear me apart because I was so evil. Then Bastard showed up out of nowhere. He told me not to kill myself, but he was like a total stranger to me at the time. I though he was some creep who lived in the woods. Finally, I couldn't take it anymore. I got on the bicycle I rode out here and headed for Wheatly. When I got to town, I dumped the bike and stood on the sidewalk while I waited for the lunch traffic to get going. God was ragging me the whole time saying that I needed to just step out in front of a truck, and all would be forgiven. I was afraid but I did what he told me to do. A truck was barreling down the street. I jumped in front of it. He swerved and somehow missed. God flipped out calling me a loser because I fucked up getting killed. I mean who does that? I panicked and tried to jump in front of every car I saw coming. It caused this big scene, and someone called the cops on me. Dennis showed up and chased me down. I was freaking out, begging him to kill me, and giggling like you that day at the high school you were talking about. Do you remember that horrible giggling?" Master Boyd looked at me with curiosity.

I nodded. "Yeah and I remember you holding me while Dennis slapped the shit out of me. Then you stuffed me into the squad car. I thought you hated me. You were glaring at me and told Dennis you couldn't take anymore, to get me to the white cell. You looked angry." I narrowed my eyes at him realizing he already had a crush on me by that time as this was months after the barb wire incident, I had always wondered.

He shook his head and chuckled. "I wasn't angry, and I sure didn't hate you. I was in love with you, silly. Watching you get taken down like I did was hard. I didn't know you were sick too until that day you turned around in the hallway asking if I could see the static. I was so startled I didn't know what to do. I hadn't met anyone else who could, not a girl anyway. I mean when I went through that whole giggling thing Dennis hauled me to the Snake Pit. They put me in a rubber room with a jacket. I was more scared than ever. They sprayed me down with hoses and took me to the shock shop. You know, the whole scene. They told me I had schizophrenia, but I didn't even know what that was. I just knew that after that, everyone called me loony, crazy or whacko. I didn't feel like me anymore. I was someone else, something else. Lost I guess is the right word for it. Bastard and God kept me company since I couldn't handle being around my friends anymore. They didn't make any sense to me as if they spoke another language. No one liked me anymore. I didn't like me anymore. I spent a lot of time here in our secret place lonely, afraid and wishing I could die. Then that spring, I met Maddie and you know the rest of that story. She never treated me differently like everyone else did.

She didn't mind that I had a Bastard and did a lot of equations and could see the static and codes. Maddie didn't understand me, but she didn't judge me either. I thought she was the answer to my being all alone, but then she died. God told me that until I found my One and Only, I would be cursed to be alone. Then I found you and now I have you. Maddie wasn't the one made for me. I just thought she was. It was you all along. God was right now that you are here everything always works out right."

I smiled. "Guess God was right for a change. I suppose it is time for our collaring Master. I know you did that for Psycho, but I am not her. Simon says I can't go much longer without my collar being on the unit. It is not good for us."

Master Boyd smiled back. "I am ready if you are. I was only waiting till you were strong enough to serve again. If you are sure then let's go home and do this right this time. I can't keep chasing down shards to recollar ever damned couple of years. This time, I won't fuck it up. I will be the perfect Dominant." He jumped up, grabbed the folded tent and my hand pulling me to the Chevelle.

I looked down realizing I was naked and so was he. "Uhm Master, are we about to drive through town like this? May raise a few eyebrows you know."

Master Boyd let out a loud scoffing noise. "The town wishes it would get so damned lucky to see you naked, my beauty. No, we will take the backroads home. No need to wag any more tongues than do already about us."

We got into his black car and took the backroads from my memories that snuck us to his house when we were running from they. It always did impress me his vast knowledge of every backroad and logging trail in that huge county. Master Boyd seemed to know them all by heart.

Master Boyd and I were laughing at one of his dirty jokes as we pulled into his driveway, home at last from our partially unexpected trip. I was about to get out of the Chevelle when my Master let out a loud groan of concern.

"Shit, it's Dennis. Fuck, okay, try to act natural even though we are as natural as we can get. Fuck, just fuck. This looks bad." He shot me a look while showing irritation that Dennis had caught us driving around skyclad.

Dennis got out of the squad car squinting his eyes but keeping them focused on Master Boyd, "What in the Sam Hill are you two doing driving around on the backroads naked as jaybirds. Are you two going around the bend again? God damn it, Boyd. I am too old for this shit. You had better not be about to flip out on me."

Master Boyd looked at me appearing apologetic. "Nah, Dennis. Me and Alexandria, we went camping and well, uhm, our clothes got covered in ticks and chiggers. We took them off and tried to sneak home before anyone caught us like this." He trailed off appearing unsure if his lie was going to hold water with the old bull.

Dennis shook his head appearing disgusted. "Bullshit, you two are up to something weird no doubt. Well, anyway, get into the house and put on some fucking clothes Boyd, you too Alexandria. Carla wanted me to come by and check on you ever since that found that damned Julia Stubbs car abandoned at the rest stop in Clever. I swear Boyd you have made that woman crazy as you both are. She had some God damned premonition that Julia was coming here with that Gussy feller to get some revenge. I told the woman you were camping and fine. Julia was here for that divorce business, but did Carla listen, no. To calm her down I called over to the Baltimore cops. I come to find out that prison guard didn't show up for work and ain't no one seen Julia nor him for over five days now. They found her car, but no Julia. Carla got scared and has been calling day and night. They have an APB out on those two monsters. Now I don't think there is a damned thing to any of this, just plain bad luck for those idiots. A damned drug dealer and a mean prison guard. Who knows what happened to them? That said, you can't be running around naked and acting like fools. Since those two are floating around somewhere, you need to watch your backs. Both of you. Maybe Carla is right and they are planning to hit you two up Boyd."

Master Boyd took Dennis's angry lecture while keeping his eyes down to the ground then said, "Thanks for checking on us Dennis and I will call Carla and calm her down for you. You need not worry about Alexandria and me. I think Julia and Gus have moved on to greener pastures. Don't you baby?" He shot me a quick look that plead for support of his position.

I smiled at Dennis while doing my best to keep my girl parts covered for his decency sake. "Sounds about right to me, love. Dennis, I don't believe Julia and Gus will be bothering us anymore. Can you dig it Boyd?" I snickered.

Master Boyd smiled wickedly. "You know I can and so can you."

Dennis stood there looked back and forth at our faces during this very strange conversation. "Yeah, you two are out to lunch again. God damn it Boyd. I want to see your meds. And Alexandria get yours too. March into that house. We are having a come to Jesus meeting right now. This weird shit is going to stop," he growled out angrily.

I shrugged as my Master came around the car. He took my hand and pulled me in front of him, to try to hide my unit from Dennis like that mattered anymore, while we walked into the house to his room for fresh clothing. We heard Dennis let himself in slamming the door behind him loudly.

Master Boyd looked at me appearing a bit worried. Dennis never had like my Master and I dating. He believed our kind could not make a sound or lasting relationship. It seemed like on this day; he had decided to stick his nose where it definitely didn't belong.

This was a very touchy chapter to write and there are some questions I am sure many readers are asking yourself right now. I will neither confirm nor deny the answers to them other than to say unless you were there don't be so sure you know what is right, what is wrong, and what happened to those two monsters. To this day, Master Boyd and I have no idea what ever became of them.

Chapter 96: Ring Around the Collar
The D/s Power Couple
Master Boyd and submissive Alexandria

We are about to accept a collar once again from the Master of Secrets, the Master who should never have been and always was.

The Dominate is almost three years into his reign. His time has been marked by rape, stalking, double collars, severe psychosis, torture, inpatient treatments, kidnappings, suicide attempts, disappearances of the Psycho shard plus two ex-Masters and buried secrets. He has four years left to go.

Ready to chase your tail and get nowhere fast? Sure you are. Sometimes in life we like to sit around and pontificate where we went wrong. The trouble with focusing on the past is all you ever get is behind. For this chapter grab your bolt cutters, a good pair of shoes, and ear plugs. You don't need to listen, damn it. Since when did that become a habit of ours anyway? Okay, you start circling, and so will we, oh look and here comes Master Boyd with a permanent ring around the collar.

"Well you see, she is worth more dead than alive. Someone should cash in on her loony ass, may as well be family, right? I have a fail proof plan, and no way it can be tracked back to us since it will look like an accident. I just need one little thing. Trust me we are doing the Lord's work. She is nothing but a nasty sinner. So, are you in or

--Interim Master Mary trying to talk future Mistress Linda into aiding her in the murder of Alexandria, December 2000.

Master Boyd and I hurried to get our clothing on. I aided him in buttoning his shirt when I noticed his hands shaking. His nervousness at the appearance of Dennis made me pause. I had to confess I could not recall a lot of my memories, but it did seem to me that my Master had not been afraid of Dennis in the past. I did recall he was my Master's guardian, he and Carla. I started to wonder if something happened between the two that I was unaware of since my inpatient treatment or kidnapping.

Master Boyd shot me a stern look as I finished putting on his boots. "Look Alexandria, no matter what Dennis says you keep quiet. This is my battle not yours. Dennis doesn't understand and that is just too damned bad for him. That said, don't let his conversation get to you. I want you to ignore his bullshit, that is a directive." He stroked my cheek but was still trembling.

I narrowed my eyes. "Master, I will mind your directive, but I need to know, are we in trouble over them finding Julia's car? Maybe we should have sunk it in a lake?"

My Master shook his head then looked to the floor sheepishly. "It has nothing to do with those two monsters. He only brought it up to find a reason to bitch at me some more. Baby, Dennis is super pissed about my being your guardian. He has been trying to talk me into handing you off to Mary or anyone else. That is not going to happen. I am your Master. You are my One and Only. Nobody can take care of you like I can. Dennis will get over this or he can kiss my ass. I just don't want you getting upset. He may say a bunch of shit and that is all it is. He doesn't know. Let's go get this mess over so we can get to that collaring of yours. I think we both need bath service." He chuckled while scratching one of his hundreds of bug bites.

I nodded but still believed Dennis was simply too angry for it to be over the guardianship issue. I had been gone over a year. Dennis had made the discovery of Master Boyd's control over my treatment and care when I first went into Harbor View.

"Why would he still be this angry over old news?" I wondered.

I still had not acquired all my memories yet. I realized in the past I may have known more about the complex relationship between these two men. For that moment I admit I was mostly lost. I tried not to stress over it. I would just have to listen to what the Old Bull had to say to determine how serious his beef, and what the real problem could be.

We walked out into the living room to find Dennis sitting in the recliner near the door. He was leaned forward on his knees. I noticed a bottle of Dr. Pepper sitting next to him on the coffee table. He always brought a bottle of that soda when he was gossiping or going to do a lot of yelling. His throat got dry I guess? He certainly didn't look happy, nor did he look up at us as we walked by him. I felt a chill run up my spine. I really hate yelling. It makes me nervous.

I followed my Master to the couch and sat down next to him. Master Boyd immediately pulled me over to his lap cuddling me close to his chest while wrapping his long arms around my unit. This strange overprotective behavior had developed after my brain accident.

In the early stages when my mind was weak, I was quite childish and frightened as I should have been. My Master really enjoyed my immature and intense affections while playing with Simon's key. He told me on the vacation he felt like when I acted like this he was completely loved.

Gus's cruelty and rape had stopped my interest in seeking shelter in Master Boyd's embrace or anyone else's for that matter. He had managed to regain it while we were being held hostage in the shed. My Master found a great deal of pleasure in it despite our deplorable conditions.

So much so, that even once we had escaped to safety, he had ordered I engage in it. The entire camping trip he had practically cradled my insane ass. I had allowed it by doing as he asked without a fight. I had assumed it was a good way to re-bond with my Master that didn't include screwing our brains out every five minutes. Yeah, he was that bad.

However, his insisting I behave this way in front of Dennis or anyone was unacceptable. I thought about refusing him this infantile public display of affection but decided it was not in my best interest to start an argument right that moment. I did my best to ignore it. I told myself it was only a normal reaction to both my disappearance and the stress of our brush with death during the kidnapping and other nasty shit while in that shed. This excuse seemed plausible on the surface, but deep down, I knew something more was going on here.

The whole scene was disturbing. There is simply no other way to describe it. I had known Master Boyd for well over thirteen years. His behaviors were weird that day even for him. Dennis raised an eyebrow over my being pulled onto a lap and held like a baby to his chest. I almost moaned in psychological torment at the look on his face. Master Boyd was asking for it no doubt.

Dennis took a deep breath then cleared his throat. "Boyd, Alexandria, I want you two to end this relationship now. Boyd you need to give her Guardianship back to Mary before you get her hurt worse than she already has been. Look at her boy. She is like a little baby. If her inpatient had been handled right, well things maybe would have gone different. I know you love her. If you do you will listen to me. She needs more help than you can give her Boyd. End this and move on with your life. For land's sake let her move on with her life too." He looked at my Master appearing stern but also with pity.

Master Boyd shook his head violently. "Dennis stay out of my love life and my business with Alexandria. You don't have the right to stick your nose in and you know it. In fact, I am offended you come here now and raise hell talking about had her inpatient been handled right. You sure as shit weren't interested in Alexandria back when you used her to trap me into Well's Hospital did you," he growled out sounding intensely irritated.

I hide my face in his chest for real this time. I could tell by the way he inflected that Dennis was just about to set him off. My Master's temper was epic, and he had become notorious in those towns for his fits of rage since our arrest during the car chase.

Dennis could handle him, I hoped, but I was in no hurry to see the two old friends get into headbutting over me. I was caught in the middle, right where I didn't want to be.

Dennis snorted. "Boyd, damn it, we have been over and over that. You didn't tell me you had her guardianship. You kept that a secret. I thought Mary would handle it. Had I fucking known I would have put her right next to you in that rubber room and kicked your ass the second the two of you got out. You have no business being anyone's guardian especially one of your own. You can't care for yourself. Look what happened. This is all your fault. I told you to let her go. Now I must worry some assholes from another state are going to run off with her and kill you to get her. Carla is riding my butt day and night to get you to marry a normal girl. I am too old for this shit, Boyd." He had started to raise his voice when making his points.

My Master took a deep breath. "Carla can mind her business too. Neither of you understand us. Stop trying to. And stop trying to treat me like a normal, Dennis. Fuck, I am like Alexandria. We are perfect for each other. No other woman will do. You and Carla want me to be alone all my life so you can keep me quiet. I know what you are fucking doing. Not going to happen." He too was starting to heat up.

I reached around Master Boyd's waist and squeezed hoping he would calm down. He immediately increased his grip around my unit. He was hanging on as if Dennis were going to try to pull us apart and toss me out the front door. That scared me a great deal.

I began to tremble. It was possible that is exactly what Dennis planned to do. I had no one else to hold my collar. I couldn't afford to be without one with my desperate situation and recovering mind.

My Master felt my terror rising. "You are scaring my Alexandria, Dennis."

Dennis scoffed. "She should be scared. You already let her get her brains baked, kidnapped, raped, and God only know what the hell else you are doing to that poor thing behind closed doors. I don't even want to imagine it. Alexandria is not the woman she was. Boyd, she is messed up. What is wrong with you? You don't fool around with someone who has been through the shit she has. That is sick," he yelled while turning red in the face.

I felt my Master wince with each accusation, especially those regarding his own interests in me. "It is not like that Dennis…" my Master began to say but was interrupted by Dennis.

"Oh? You have her in your God damned lap. I know you Boyd. That girl isn't getting any rest from duties meant for a wife. She is not your wife, Boyd. She is married to Timmy. You have another man's woman in your house and bed. Plus, the girl is touched, ravaged, and retarded to boot. Enough of this shit. People are talking, Boyd. It has to stop. Where is her fucking collar? Call Sheryl and tell that hard ass bitch to do her job." Dennis was starting to pop out the veins on his forehead at this point.

Master Boyd almost blew a gasket hearing those words while I reeled from them. I had no idea I was married to someone else. I really had believed my Master when he said we were married. I didn't even know who Timmy was. I had no memory of him.

I did recall that Sheryl had tossed my collar, but I didn't remember that Dennis didn't know that. I looked up at my Master confused, unsure what to say or do. He looked back at me appearing apologetic.

Master Boyd shot an angry look back at Dennis. "I mean it Dennis, stay out of this. It is not your business," he yelled back.

Dennis stood up appearing ready to slap my Master in the face. "I already called Sheryl and told her to come do her fucking job, Boyd. I knew you wouldn't. I think you are trying to take that collar for yourself if you haven't already. Boyd, that is not okay. If I find out you are planning to do that, or already have, so help me I will send you off to the Snake Pit. I will commit your ass. You will not be a cop after that. You will be stuck with whatever Carla and I decide to give you. Don't push me Boyd. You let Sheryl have Alexandria and let things get back to normal around her."

My Master almost fell off the couch as did I. "You did what? You sonofabitch. Sheryl tossed the fucking collar. Shit, just shit. You are trying to bring back that asshole down on my house. How dare you go behind my back. You don't know shit about the collar. You had no right. And who the fuck do you think you are threatening me? I cannot believe you are so hell bent to keep me unhappy and under your thumb. Get the fuck out of my house, Dennis. I will petition the courts for a new guardian. You are released. Now you never have to worry or be upset again with my loony ass," he yelled out in extreme anger, and hurt, as he put his face into my neck appearing beyond upset.

Dennis's mouth dropped open. "Boyd, it ain't like that. I didn't mean for it to get this far. Look, tell you what, lets both just cool off a little." Master Boyd interrupted him.

"Out. Get the fuck out of my house. I mean it. Fire me if you want. Fuck this shit. I am finally happy. I don't care anymore." He looked up from my neck spitting out the words.

Dennis nodded. "Oh, okay, yeah I hear you Boyd. I am not going to fire you. You come back tomorrow night. Cool off and we can talk on shift. Don't do anything stupid until then, promise me?" He was looking at his boots and hitching his pants nervously.

Master Boyd just shook his head with a weird mad smile on his face. "I wasn't the one doing anything stupid. That is on you. Go home. I am done with this conversation. Bring it up again and I will file for another guardian." I held my breath waiting to see what Dennis was going to say or do now.

The Old Bull looked at my Master hard. "I am not going to let you threaten me either son. We will drop this whole thing for now. I think you heard me. I certainly heard you. Alexandria talk some sense into him if you can understand any of this. Damn, I wish you hadn't gotten messed up like that. I sure could use your help with Boyd now." He looked at my frightened face with extreme pity.

My Master sucked in his breath still smiling like a madman. "Leave her out of this. Bye Dennis, you know your way out." He pointed at the door.

Dennis nodded then turned and left slamming the door behind him. Master Boyd and I sat in silence listening to the squad car start up and pull out of the drive. He stroked the back of my head and snuggled his own into my face. I listened to his heart still racing as if in terror.

I finally looked up at him. "Who is Timmy? Why did you lie to me? Am I another man's wife, Master? Is he the father of the children?"

My Master frowned. "Think Alexandria. Timmy is a scumbag. I didn't tell you because you needed a real husband, not that thief. Honey, remember he is the one you beat up before Harbor View. The golf club?"

I closed my eyes and saw the mean boy standing in the hallway next to Master Julie. The black Skylark, a trip to California, the winter in Darlin, the suicide cliff and dilapidated trailer, and Master Anita. She wanted babies. Yes, I recalled that prick.

I opened my eyes and looked at my Master. "Yeah, you are right. He is a liar. He is the father of the children. He was the only choice to escape Master Julie and Debbie."

Master Boyd sighed. "He was not the only choice. I asked you to marry me before that idiot fooled you into making a child with him. You turned me down. Told me to get a decent girl. You were a decent girl baby, the only girl for me. Those should have been my children." He shook his head laughing bitterly.

I nodded. "Except you have schizophrenia Master. I knew that already. Simon forbade me making a child with you. He didn't want Psycho babies like Victoria wanted." I felt I may start crying realizing our disease prevented a better union than was made with me and Timmy.

He winced at those words. "I always forget that. I guess God made sure I couldn't pass on my bad blood to an innocent baby. He fixed you before we messed up, I messed up I mean. I will have to be happy helping you raise the ones you have. They may be Voss, but they are still not one of us. I can see they are not sick with our illness. One day we will marry, but not now, not while you wear that collar."

My eyes went wide with shock. "What? You are planning to get rid of my collar? You can't, that is not Your right."

He chuckled. "Someday it will be, but you are right. Timmy would come after the kids if you tried to divorce him right now, especially after Harbor View, you know. He would try to take custody no doubt. Mary said his kinfolks were sniffing around while you were away. That is not okay. You will have to stay married for a bit, maybe till they are eighteen. I can see that pretty clearly. When the kids are grown up, and you are free we will discuss marriage again. Until then, collar it is. I will have to be satisfied being your Master and fiancé. We don't need that paper to tell the world we are one heart." He leaned in and kissed me deeply.

I felt myself giving into his embrace like butter on a hot stove. I realized I no longer wanted to be separated from this man in anyway. He had completely gained my trust, heart, and admiration. He had certainly gone a long way to earn it too. From standing up to protect me during the car chase to his ending the terror of Gus and Julia, he had proven his faithfulness, loyalty, and pure love. He was even willing to stand up to Dennis, his oldest friend and Guardian, to protect what was his. I was ready to follow him for all my life, right to our graves.

He pulled back from his kiss looking deep into my eyes. "It is time to collar you Alexandria and set the mirror. I have worked for many weeks to understand Simon's rules and why they exist. I have reworked Psycho's rules to make them work better for my Alexandria. I don't want to ever lose you or your collar, but in case something ever happens to me I need to know you are better protected. I will give them to you now. Show them to Simon and if he approves, meet me in the puppy's room in two hours for the collaring. Once you submit, we will begin the mirroring together. It is time to clear out Julie forever. I am getting up and going to the shed. I will leave you be until the appointed time."

I smiled "And if I don't submit?"

He growled playfully. "If you don't, I will have to shoot you baby. Simple. If I can't have you no one will. I told you all that the first time remember. Now get off and let me get those Key rules." He bit my neck lightly letting me know he was kidding as he pushed my unit off him.

I giggled. "You would not shoot me, Master. Your hand would fall off from all the masturbation you'd have to do all by yourself."

Master Boyd stood up while faking a hateful glare. "Oh no I wouldn't. I would just stuff you and stick you in my bed forever. You know that is what schizophrenics do. Haven't you ever watched Psycho?" He laughed at his bit of dark humor.

I narrowed my eyes. "I never met her Master but you did. Are you like Simon and miss her? Do you wish I were her?" I ignored his joke.

He shook his head while grabbing the tablet with the proposed new key rules. "No, I loved Psycho there is no doubt, but that said, I love you much more. You are everything she was not, and better than she could ever hope to be. More than anything else you are all mine. Psycho was tired baby. She had been hurt by so many, but you are a new slate. A chance to make it all better. I am the luckiest man on Earth. Not just because you are beautiful or smart, but because you are truly my One and Only. You love me the way I love you. Psycho never could. Her heart was already broken when I got to her. I sure as shit didn't help that by being a total asshole. This time, it will be right. No more mistakes. See you in two hours baby. Good luck with Simon." He gave me a quick kiss then handed me his reworked rules for Simon's approval.

I took the notepad and watched him walk out the back door. I felt a chill run down my spine with the memory of Gus knocking him in the head with a shovel. We had not gotten that checked out. I wondered briefly if that was wise. I then looked at my Master's proposal. I called Simon to witness the first collaring procedure of the shard Alexandria.

Simon came through the door and sat in the recliner where Dennis had just been only minutes before. He was rubbing his head and had been crying again.

"What Alexandria? You called me?" His red eyes looked at me appearing to plead for mercy.

I nodded. "Master Boyd wants you to look over his new rules for your Key. He wants to collar me immediately, but he needs your approval first. I cannot submit without it." I opened my mind's eye so he could see what I held in my hand.

Simon gasped. "Alexandria, Master Boyd is a genius. I can see through two instead of one if the key and collar are fully bonded with his first rule. It is not a cure to my injury, but it is a bit of relief. I can move through you both that way. I won't be trapped anymore."

I smiled. "Then you approve of rule one: The submission must be approved by Simon first and Alexandria must be willing." I grabbed the pen off the coffee table and put an approved next to the rule.

Simon continued to read out loud. "Rule two: Special Services of the collar can be denied if Alexandria does not find the Master in a coherent state, dangerous, diseased, cheating, abusive, or otherwise undesirable as deemed by Alexandria. If the Master forces this service, it is a crime and the collar is tossed." He looked at me appearing surprised.

I nodded. "I agree to that. It should have been a rule in the first fucking place. Had it been Psycho's life would have been easier. Think June, Tammy, Gus, and Leanne."

He just stared at me still in shock. "Yeah and Master Boyd Alexandria. He was psychotic at the time."

I giggled. "That is why he made the rule silly. He is giving me the right to tell him no and protecting me from nasty ass people in my future. They can no longer exploit me using sex with that rule. Will you approve it?"

He snorted. "Of course I fucking will. Next to rule one, smartest thing I have ever heard."

The third rule floored us both. Not because it was new. It was one of the old rules, but to see it set down by this Master was a shock: "Alexandria cannot marry a Master."

We looked at each other unsure why he would want to keep this restriction. However, we both agreed that a double collar with a vanilla twist was unacceptable. Simon readily approved rule number three.

The other rules on Master Boyd's lists were all designed like the first three: my protection from horrible exploitation at the hands of a Keyholder. He thought of every possible way I had been abused by the rules before. Breaking any of them resulted in automatic toss of the Collar. They included but were not limited to:

· All leashes were abolished unless being used to court a new Master.

· No immediate family or spouses would ever be eligible for the Key after one had held it.

· I could not be asked to do anything illegal or made to lie to protect the Master from the law.

· Special Services of the collar are offered one time a day. Full service (anything/anytime) only provided at the will of Alexandria. No Master can enforce Full service and if granted can be retracted at her discretion without explanation.

· The Master shall be the official Guardian or no submission granted.

· Failure to provide equal service will result in denial of any service or all service without argument until corrections are made to the Keyholder. If corrections are made more than three times on same issue then loss of a service for good or a collar toss if severe.

· Alexandria will not offer Special Services this will include thudding. The Master must request them. Only Alexandria can choose to honor or ignore the request. She will not be required to flirt, beg, or come on to any holder of Simon's Key even if the Master commands it.

· Alexandria will not pay a Keyholder for any service. Taking her paycheck is theft. To do this will result in immediate dismissal.

· If the collar is sold, Alexandria will have the right to deny the sale. No refunds are to be granted or acknowledged. Slavery is a crime, and to do this without consulting Alexandria can result in her right to file a charge for human trafficking.

· To poach the collar is a crime called human trafficking. It is to be reported to the police immediately.

· The identity of the Keyholder and Alexandria's relationship to them is to be dealt with during collaring. No changes can be made after the initial agreements are made.

· Protection and defense of the collar and Key is the reason for this submission. To fail at this in any way can result in Alexandria's walking away without it being a betrayal of her collar. She can and will determine if this rule has been adequately fulfilled. Definition of this rule is hers exclusively and cannot be dictated by a Master.

They were stronger, more inclusive, and wiser than Psycho had ever known. Unlike her rules, then written by Julie and Doctor Commisso, these rules were written by a Master who loved and valued me for more than what he could squeeze from my unit. My continued good health and wellbeing was the only thing he was interested in obtaining. His rules spoke loud and clear of someone who wanted my survival, rather than just controlling exploitation.

NOTE: *Simon and I approved all Master Boyd's rules. He was pleased with the changes and believed this new beginning would offer him some control over the unit that had been destroyed by the seizure accident. Without rule number one he couldn't even set a mirror any longer thanks to his weakened position of being trapped in dead brain tissue.*

Understand that prior to Doctor Baker's experiments Simon was a separate entity that was trapped outside the unit. Since he was on the outside he could interact, touch, and even fight or punish us. That made his voice powerful. None of us wanted to fool with an angry Simon who could knock us the fuck out.

When his pathway of projection was carpet bombed by the ECT machine and eventual stroke, he was no longer able to get out. He was forever trapped in a tiny part of the frontal lobe surrounded by dead brain matter. The easiest way to understand this is his train tracks to the outside world were basically destroyed.

This prevents Simon from seeing, hearing, or feeling the outside world, the world of the real. He is still separate but cannot project outward. He tells me it is like being in a desert with no scenery. Just endless sand and sky. He is alone and only can hear me speaking to him like a voice inside his head.

I can still see and hear him but barely, like a ghost, unless there is a strong Keyholder. If the Master is doing the job correctly the connection is stronger and I can interact with Simon more easily. If it is weak, I can only hear him, with one exception, psychosis. If I am severely psychotic Simon comes through loud and clear and is not see through.

Interestingly, he can also hear and see a Master in good standing (past or present). He can and does verify or deny a Keyholder's requests. He cannot hear or see anyone else unless I allow him to see and hear them, which only rarely happens. The reasons are unclear but that is brain damage for you.

He can also rock the unit or knock me over when incredibly angry but nothing more. When we dance, I can see him but no longer touch him. He can see himself through my eyes but can only see me through my own reflection in a mirror.

Understand Simon is still not a part of us. He is a stranger trapped in an alien mind, thanks to that nasty shit

Doctor Baker pulled. His connection is so weak now we often worry that in time we will lose him.

So far so good, but we take no more chances. If this connection is broken then so are we. Master Boyd understood that. His rules were stricter and unbreakable to prevent anyone from being able to traumatize us further and use the collar as their excuse. For that I am forever thankful.

I walked into Ma Cherie's room with fifteen minutes left on my two-hour consideration time. I sat down next to her playpen and smiled while thinking of how much fun she and Seine were likely having. I was ready to get the collaring over with so we could go hang out with Mary, Seine, his little woman, and the kids. I was still giggling with my memories of how frightened Seine was of Ma Cherie on their first meeting when Master Boyd walked through the door.

I saw the collar in his hand, and he had an odd look on his face. I furrowed my brow as he closed the door behind him. Something told me there was much more to this than I had ever experienced with past collarings.

My Master turned around looking me over still appearing strange. "Well? Did Simon approve?"

I nodded while I stood up. "Yeah, he likes the changes, Master. He said the submission can proceed. He approves You as continued holder of his Key."

Master Boyd's look softened a bit. "That is great news, but one thing. I won't wait any more until 2006. I am either Master now or forget it."

I almost fell over. "Huh? You said what? You are Master. I don't understand?"

He shook his head. "Simon said no male Master's until 2006. That is five and a half years away. I won't wait that long to assume my rightful place. I will collar you today and you will be mine exclusive and at my discretion or this won't be happening." He threw the collar to the floor appearing disgusted at my response.

I looked around for Simon unsure what was going on. "Master, I didn't see anything about a taboo on male Keyholders on the rules he approved. I told you he approved you as Keyholder. I don't see anyone else in this room, nor do I know of any other bids for the collar."

Master Boyd glared at me. "Dennis said he if finds out I am the Master he will have me committed. I am in a lot of trouble. If I don't collar you, then you get sick. If I do collar you, I get sent away. Simon approves me now but before he said not until 2006. I won't chance giving up everything I have, including you, until I am sure you are going to be mine and only mine."

Simon arrived behind Master Boyd through the door. He was still holding his head. I stood there shocked. I couldn't recall ever seeing a Master and Simon in the same room at the same time. My mouth flew open and my eyes went wide in awe.

"Tell him to find an interim that will act as a fake out for Dennis, like we planned before but this time the Master is in name only. Only minimal service provided and no special services. Hell pay them to take the credit if you must." Simon moaned out appearing to be in much pain.

I nodded but my surprise at seeing Simon at a collaring was still quite evident. "Uhm, Master, Simon says you are to be the only Master but you can choose a fake with almost no service offered to keep Dennis from suspecting you. He says it is the only way to protect and defend you in return for your equal service."

Master Boyd looked behind him. "He is behind me, isn't he? That's who you are looking at isn't it? That could work to solve this problem. Yes, very smart actually. Okay I agree but no special services and I pick the fake," he said over his shoulder.

Simon could hear him. "Tell Master Boyd we agree to these terms." My old railroad man was smiling again appearing to be happy with the sudden notice that he could hear another voice other than my own for the first time in more than half a year.

I nodded. "Yes, we agree with your proposal Master. Simon can hear you. He warns to be incredibly careful who you choose. I cannot serve two Masters."

Master Boyd smiled. "Nor would I have you do something so stupid. I have someone in mind. Now time to come and kneel. Alexandria you are about to belong to me and only me forever."

I walked over to him while he picked up the collar and pulled out Simon's Key from under his shirt. "There is no such thing as forever Master. There is now and yesterday. Don't make promises that are not yours to make."

He scoffed. "I will never toss the collar nor lose it. I wrote the rules myself. You will be my mirror. You are my One and Only. There is nothing on Earth that can separate us once I bond my Key to your circle of silver." He opened the heavy neck bracelet in preparation.

I knelt before him looking at the ground. "Simon's Key, Master, not yours. I belong to Simon. You are enacting his will. Forget that and you're doomed." I warned as the first tears began to form behind my eyes in frustration at my inability to survive without the indignity of submission to another.

Master Boyd began his promises to his collar and to Simon. He didn't falter and again ordered monogamy, and the title Master Boyd. He didn't order chastity and included my right to refuse any fake Master's commands. He added strangely I was to never leave his sight without telling him exactly where I was going and how long I would be away. Master Boyd requested all services be provided him if I deemed him worthy of it in equal service for equal service.

He swore to serve, respect, obey, adore, love, protect and defend my collar and Simon's Key to his death, even if he was for any reason rendered no longer the reigning Master.

I raised an eyebrow over that last statement but decided to let it go. I was so despaired at that point I decided to ask about it later.

At that moment, I just wanted this nightmare over. A collaring always remind me I am helpless, disabled and at the mercy of another's decision to be kind or cruel. It is a total loss of power and will that I must replay each time a Keyholder fails or tosses, and by this time, I had done it twenty-three times. You have to include Debbie, Julie and Master Boyd twice. I was really tired of the failure always being wrapped around my neck.

Simon oddly didn't leave when we began the promises. I was terribly confused by this unusual behavior of my lost inner self. He had never attended one before, except Debbie's because he had not been split off back then. I tried to ignore his standing there watching behind Master Boyd. It was more than uncomfortable for some reason.

I made all my promises without forgetting any of the brand-new rules. I swore to honor, love, adore, obey, defend, protect, and serve without resentment or hesitation.

Master Boyd who had started out appearing harsh and stern was smiling wider with each word I said. He knew we were approaching the finalization of our contract in a D/s partnership.

As I finished my reciting of the warnings, the tears broke out heavily. My Master then knew he had reached his hilt of power. He didn't hesitate even a moment after my last words to lock the collar back around my neck and bond Simon's Key.

I could barely breath as I heard the lock snap shut, followed by the weight of metal on my shoulders. Alexandria was now officially owned by her first Master ever, the schizophrenic cop Boyd Simmons.

NOTE: My Master wanted my first collaring and he had hoped my last if I would have seen it his way to be done by the letter. He was to be my first Master, the foundation of my original mirror. All my future mirrors would pivot around what he was granted full privilege to create in his own image. This was an honor that my Master took seriously. Psycho had been mothered in by Master Julie, her base mirror.

Had Psycho's pivot mirror, Master Julie, been so conscientious as Master Boyd had been maybe she would not have died in November 1999. As it was Psycho's shard lasted for thirteen years. The Alexandria shard is about to celebrate her twentieth. Say what you will about Master Boyd, but one thing you must do is give him credit where credit is due. His creation was SOUND. Even if he is crazier than I am.

I was really wailing as my Master stepped back to admire his new acquisition. "No need to cry baby. I won't fail you this time. I have a fail proof plane to protect you if anyone ever tries to hurt you again. I will prove I am the right one for this job. Normally we would consummate the collaring right away, but this time, let's go visit Mary and

283

the kids first. I intend to enjoy my special services all night, so I think maybe it would be best to wait."

I nodded. "As You wish Master. However, I thought only I can offer full service?" I tried to wipe up my tears so Mary and the children wouldn't know I had been crying.

He laughed. "You are going to deny full service to me?"

I scoffed. "I believe that is my right, Master. Your rules remember." He helped me to my feet then pulled me into a tight embraced.

"Okay, then I am respectfully requesting full service be granted to me always. I can't make you but that would please me to know I have my rights whenever I like." He kissed my forehead.

I winced. "And if I say no to your request Master, then what will you do? Retaliate?"

He shook his head. "No baby. If once a day is all I get. so be it. You shouldn't be crying at the collaring, you know. You are the real Master here. I am your slave, not the other way around. I am only here to do what you want me to do or let me do. You wear my collar and I wear your leash." He laughed at that true statement.

I nodded. "Full service is granted. You said the right words Master. You understand I can revoke it if you abuse it because it is mine not yours to begin with." I hugged him back tightly glad that at long last someone finally got the reality of the Collar and Key delusion.

That afternoon and night went beautifully. As a well-organized D/s couple we were able to enjoy Mary, the kids and the pups without any fighting, misunderstandings, or missteps. We brought both Seine and Ma Cherie home with us that night. Seine was like my Master regarding his own One and Only, he couldn't stand to have her out of his sight.

Master Boyd had always liked and respected Seine despite the fur baby's dislike of him. They would never truly be buds but with Ma Chérie around he was far too busy to consider biting my Master like he had always wanted to. We settled the canine pair into their special room and even took a bit of time to play with them both.

Once everyone was winding down, I noticed the look in my Master's blue eyes. I knew he was ready to call in his rights. I pretended to be afraid when he made a sudden rush at me. I even begged and kicked as he lifted me over his shoulder dragging me out of the spare room headed for his own. It was all an act. I was aware he was merely demonstrating his dominance. This time I was anything but frightened by his surface aggressive behavior.

That night I reaffirmed that he may have been my dominant in most realms, but not in the bedroom. There I outmatched him in every way. I had accepted him as my lover as well as my guardian and Master. I no longer held back, nor was I unwilling to meet his needs. I also expected and demanded he meet my own. He had bragged he would call his rights all night.

I made sure he kept that promise. By morning it was him begging to be let out of my embrace. At one point early that morning he tried to break free of my amorous advances. He ran but I tripped him. I laughed manically as he whined and kicked while I drug him back by his ankles to the bedroom. He had requested full service. I made sure he got it. Careful what you ask for I always say.

NOTE: *Once Master Boyd had consummated the collared me, I should have been able to say, and we still live together today happily. After all, he was a perfect Master until the very end. He never tossed, traded, sold, or lost his Key. He kept all his promises. So, why the hell is he not the Master today?*

Ah, well the answer to that question had already started the day of this story. You just must read between the lines. Remember what I always say: Nothing is ever what it seems in the world behind the shattered looking glass.

It would take another three-and-one-half years before I would have to say goodbye to this amazing Keyholder. I can tell you there were many reasons this union failed, but the biggest one was the mother of madness, schizophrenia and all its problems.

It has been said that our kind cannot exist as a couple. Master Boyd and I would not be an exception to this sad rule of thumb. I will spend time, and four more Interim Masters, explaining the various and complex reasons this seemingly loving D/s relationship fell apart.

In the end, I would like to ask all of you to try not to judge Master Boyd too harshly. He was, and still to this day is, the second greatest Master of them all. Unlike all the others, it was not really his fault his collar was forfeited. There is no doubt he still loves me with all his heart. After all, I am still his One and Only (a primary delusion never goes away) and 'God only makes one for each of us.'

That said, we are cursed in an unholy and unworkable union pure and simple. There is no cure for what ails us, nor will there be one in our lifetime. I think all of you will agree it wasn't even the disease itself that ended us for good. It was the way society views those like us. What does that mean? Well keep reading, you will soon understand.

So, I will tell the story best as I can and let all of you decide what really lies beneath the destruction of Master Boyd's reign.

That day Master Boyd had to return to his job as Dennis's partner. I didn't envy my Master having to sit with an angry old bull all night. It was obvious that they were not seeing eye to eye anymore on most things.

I was still unfit to care for my children full time thanks to my memory slips and moments of catatonic like trances along with random Grand Mal seizures that had become very common after the brain fail.

However, my Master decided to leave me with Mary while he worked for my own safety. He drove me to her house along with my fur buddies after I got him ready for his first day back to work. He sat there looking at me nervously before letting me get out to go inside.

"Baby, I don't want you to leave her house, even to go to the mailbox okay? Stay where Mary can see you always, that is a directive. You are still unwell. I will call at lunch break to check on you." He stroked my cheek looking at me with love in his eyes.

I nodded. "I will be okay Master. Julia and Gus are gone now. Doctor Baker is gone too. I am in residual. There is nothing to worry about anymore." I smiled at him while kissing the hand he stroked me with.

He smiled back. "Yeah, you are right. I am worried for no reason. Get inside and I will see you in the morning."

Me and the fur babies got out and waved as he pulled out. Mary was waiting on the porch. It was going to be a fun night with my family and my Maiden. I was just so happy to finally be home, safe and with a strong Master who loved me. If only I had a better grip on reality things may have been different.

Mary and I were making dinner for the kids when the phone rang. I assumed it was Master Boyd calling on his lunch break. I told Mary I would answer and she nodded while turning the potatoes.

"Hello?" I was making faces at my son while waiting to hear my Master's voice.

"Ah Psycho. Nice to hear from you. How are you feeling," said a woman's voice.

I narrowed my eyes. "Who is this? I am not Psycho. I am Alexandria." I was irritated immediately by the gall of this female.

The woman giggled. "Okay, whatever. We both know you are Psycho. It is Sheryl, you loon. Don't you remember your old boss? So, you ready to come back to work or what?"

I almost passed out. "Sheryl, fuck off." I slammed down the phone feeling my heart racing in my chest.

Mary came running. "You okay Mother? What happened? Who was that." She looked at the phone like it would bite her.

I shook my head trying to catch my breath. "Sheryl, the idiot who sent Julia to kidnap me. Shit, just shit. How the fuck did she know your number? Or that I was here?" I looked at my Maiden in confusion.

Mary looked at the floor. "Damn Mother, that was my fault. She called here earlier. When you were missing, I called your old office to see if they had heard from you and left my number. Then she called here a lot while you were gone. I kept her posted, I didn't know you didn't want to hear from her. She called earlier today and asked about you. I thought she is the Master? She said she is. She isn't?"

I almost died right there. "Uhm no. She tossed my collar Mary. Shit she knows I am here. I got to get out of here now." I started grabbing my stuff wildly shaking in panic.

I remembered Sheryl very well and I knew she was trouble. It was maybe paranoid to think she would show up there, but then again I wasn't taking any chances after Julia and Gus. I was suffering extreme PTSD, as was Master Boyd, after the horror of Harbor View, Baltimore and the Cumberland shed. I was not thinking straight thanks to a violent panic reaction to even hearing that woman's name. Sheryl was the name of Psycho's killer. Alexandria didn't want to be next.

Mary chased after me while I grabbed my purse and kissed the kids goodbye. "Where are you going? Mother you can't just leave. Damn it. Boyd will shit a brick."

I put up my hand to shut her up. "I will walk back to Boyd's place. I am not staying here. She could be on her way, damn it." I took off toward the front door.

Mary chased me across the porch and yelled at me from the yard "Mother, stop. At least let me call Boyd."

I didn't listen as I kept trucking. Mary was without a vehicle. Ronny had borrowed her truck to do a construction job out of town. I had no time to call a cab or my Master. I had to get out and get to home base. I was sure she would never dare to come to Master Boyd's house. All I had to do is get there.

My Master lived about four miles from my Maiden. I took off walking toward the backroads. I assumed the one thing Sheryl would not know is which direction I had run if she tried to put the hurt on Mary to see where I was headed. I was that freaked out by the red headed ex-Master. Turned out, I had reason to be afraid. As I said, I knew Sheryl well.

My brother the sun was saying goodnight to the world when I heard a car speeding up behind me. I stepped into the ditch and kept walking. The backroads were not well traveled but people did live along them. I thought someone was headed home.

Until I heard the vehicle slowing down. I turned around to see a blue green Taurus pulling up behind me. I somehow recognized that car, but only from a dream. It stopped in the middle of the road and the driver got out.

I peer through the dim light to try to make out the shadow coming my direction. My heart began to speed up. The passenger's side door opened too. Another person got out. I didn't need to see another moment of that shit. I took off like a jackrabbit running fast as my platforms could carry me.

I didn't get far before the person who got out of the passenger's side jumped on my back sending us both face first into the gravel road. I let out a scream of terror while the dark figure rolled me to my back holding my arms to my chest.

I peer up into the face of a woman I didn't recognize. She had short curly blond hair and was much larger than me at around five seven and at least one hundred and sixty pounds. She was smiling at me and panting out of breath from her chase.

"Got her Sheryl. Bring the collar. Hey, she already has one on," yelled the woman.

I heard the name Sheryl and began to struggle with all my might. The strange female held me tight. I wasn't able to get up.

"Oh, ignore that shit. That fucking Boyd did that you can bet. I have a key for it. Paula, hold her tight girl. She is a wiry cuss. You let up she will be gone." I heard Sheryl say as she limped towards us.

"You let me go or you will be sorry. My Master will kick your ass, bitch," I yelled out turning red from the force of her weight on my unit.

Sheryl walked up staring at me with a smile on her wizened old face. "Your Master? Whatever Psycho. That asshole is crazier than you ever thought to be. No one is going to believe him. Paula, honey do me a favor and unlock that shit off her neck. I want to put mine back on." She held out a key.

Paula looked at her "I can't let go her arms Sheryl. You are going to have to do it yourself sister. I am not getting punched by this loon. Not even to get my job back."

I suddenly remembered Paula. She had been fired over Missy Links. She was the case worker who allowed that poor girl to be molested by her Uncle for years. I really began to fight once I recalled her. This bag of shit was up to her old tricks. The last thing the world needed was her ass back with DCFS.

Sheryl snorted but slowly squatted next to us. "Shit, I am too old for this. Psycho, hold still you bitch. I am your

Master and you would do well to remember that. I have a cane you know. I know how to use it too. Do you recall that?" She reached out and began to unlock Master Boyd's collar.

I shook my head wildly trying to prevent her removal of my bonded circle. "I remember you are an asshole. You sold me out to Julia. You, cunt, get off of me. All of that was your fault. You are not the Master. You tossed the collar, Sheryl. No second chances," I yelled as she finished opening the lock ignoring my struggle.

Sheryl scoffed. "Oh yeah? First of all, you went to Harbor View because you are a schizophrenic idiot. I had nothing to do with that. Your Master Boyd put you there I heard. Julia, that stupid bitch double crossed me. Have you seen her? She seems to have gone missing. You know anything about that Psycho?" She removed Master Boyd's collar.

I glared at her. "Yeah, I know where she is Sheryl. Tell you what. Get your dog off me and I will take you to speak with her. You two can become reacquainted. In fact, I do believe you both should be reunited right away." I spit in her face.

Sheryl wiped my saliva off her face while taking her own smaller sleeker collar out of her purse. "Ah, now there is my girl. Vicious and full of demons. That is what I love about you Psycho. Always ready for a fight. Reminds me of me. Now hold still while I get my collar back on you." She forced her circle of silver around my unit locking it into place and showing me her key.

"Fuck you, Sheryl. I will not submit," I screamed out as she put her key into her breast pocket.

Sheryl chuckled. "You already did a long time ago Psycho. So it is done. You are mine once again. Get up Paula. Let the little loon up." Paula let go of my arms while both women stood upright.

I got up quickly and promptly punched Paula in the gut and pushed Sheryl to her ass. "Go to hell, both of you." I reached down and snatched up my Masters collar from the road and took off running into the woods before the misguided women could recover.

I could hear them chasing me through the brush while I did my best to stay ahead of the would be kidnapping DCFS workers. I simply could not believe my bad luck. After all that had already happened, I was on the run once again.

It seemed that I was never going to get away from those who would try to exploit me for their own gain.

Okay, wow, okay yeah Sheryl is back, and she brought a new friend. Gee, I wonder what happened to her other one. It is hard to believe but this happened. What happens next is even more insane. I just couldn't win for losing.

Chapter 97: Miss Direction
The Rise and Fall of Interim Rebecca
The D/s Power Couple
Master Boyd and submissive Alexandria

Well, we all thought it was a new day dawning. Too bad it was just business as usual. Once again, we find ourselves on the run from some idiot with foul intensions. Where do we find these people? Ah, you see that is the secret. They find us. One would think we have sucker tattooed on our forehead.

The D/s couple have bonded tightly. Their metal is about to be tested by all those around them. Fingers and tongues are wagging. Everyone has an opinion about what is best for the diseased pair. Pulled in one direction, then in another, the Dominant and his submissive are coming apart at the seams.

The Alpha faces the pit of the Snake, and the submissive is in the crosshairs of the red-headed harpy. Things are looking grim in this battle for control. Simon has stepped into the fray to offer a simple solution. The fake collar. Too bad the one chosen is more of a lie than the circle she wants to wield.

Get ready to rumble. Okay, you can stretch your muscles and we will tag you in as soon as we are tired. This is one hell of a beast we are slated to try to pin down. For this book you will want to grab your bolt cutters (again), your thinking caps, and oh yeah, your glasses. What you thought you saw was not what you are about to get. Sometimes, truth is stranger than fiction.

"What the fuck Alexandria. Her collar is not real damn it. Stop treating it like it matters. I am the only God damned Master."
--**Master Boyd to Alexandria after the collaring by Mistress Linda, January 2001.**

I kept running without even considering what direction I was headed. Behind me the voices of Paula and Sheryl got further and further away. I was beginning to feel secure that I had outfoxed or at least out run them.

My lungs were screaming in agony for more air. I had to stop racing even though the adrenaline rushing through me was demanding I keep going. I slowed my pace but continued crashing like an angry bear right through the brush and darkness.

I am dimwitted when scared. Okay, that would be most of the time. That night was no exception. Had I not been so frightened I would have considered the possibility of getting lost in the acres of wooded land all along that backroad. The only thought going through my shattered brains, besides this is not happening, was get away.

It didn't take long for me to realize I had no idea where I was. Fresh fear over my loss of location lend me its bony hand in my bid to keep hauling ass through the inky thickets. I had shaken my pursuers at the cost of my own safety. Nothing looked familiar. Panic was now my new Master.

I finally became overwhelmed with terror and stopped my mad dashing. My heart was pounding so loud in my ears I couldn't hear anything else. I leaned against a tree looking in every direction trying to make out anything in the dimness. I was unable to recognize a damned thing.

I sat down pulling up my legs to my chest and began to wail. It was beyond my broken mind's capacity to understand why I had ended up hopelessly lost in the woods when the day had started so peacefully. My new collar, my worthy Master was supposed to end all these nightmares, right?

Many hours passed. I didn't move for fear of falling down or worse. The dampness in the air and the nighttime creatures indicated it was in the wee hours of the morning. I was nearly asleep from extreme fatigue when I hear the voice of Master Boyd calling out to me in the shadows.

At first, I thought I was hallucinating or perhaps dreaming but I heard him call my name again, this time closer. I jumped to my feet and ran toward his voice, calling back.

"I am here. Boyd, here. Please help," I yelled at the top of my lungs as I ran into brush and smacked into small trees as I was rushing before he left me assuming I was not there.

"Alexandria? Where are you," he yelled back just a bit to my left.

I turned toward the new location. "Here, please don't leave me," I screamed nearly freaking out while trying to find him in that forest hell.

I ran right into Master Boyd just as he was about to yell out again. I had gotten close enough to follow the beam of his flashlight. He grabbed me appearing grateful, tightly embracing my unit.

"Oh Alexandria. Mary called me. She said Sheryl was coming and you ran away. Baby why didn't you call me?" He breathed out while trembling.

"Sheryl did come Master. She brought Paula with her and they held me down and put this collar on me." I grabbed his hand and shined the light on her shitty collar.

He gasped out, "What the fuck. That bitch. No. Never mind that now. Are you okay baby?" He began to shine the light up and down my unit looking for injuries.

I shook my head. "No, I am fine Master. I was scared and lost is all. How did you find me?" I grabbed his waist tightly as he began to walk using the flashlight to guide us.

He growled "Luck is how I found you Alexandria. I have been looking for hours. Mary said you told her you were coming home. I came home from work and you were not there. I went down every path and still no you. I even went to Darlin. I went back to the house to check once more and when you were not there, I yelled for you. You yelled back," he said just as we stepped out into the road in front of our house.

I scoffed. "You mean I was just across the road all this time?" I couldn't believe how stupid I was not to realize if I had gone a bit further, I would have been home.

He chuckled. "It is okay baby. It is dark and you don't know these woods. Not even when you were well, and you are not well, not yet. All that matters is that you are not hurt and are back home where you belong." He kissed the top of my head.

I walked next to him still holding his waist like he was a life rope on a steep slope. "But I am home right now. Sheryl is going to come back Master. She knew I was at Mary's. She took off your collar and brought help. What if she is going to try to do what Julia did?" I shivered at the thought of Julia and Gus.

He stopped dead in the driveway. "No, she is not going to do that to you. I won't let her. I will figure out some way to keep you safe from another attack. Right now, let's go inside and get that fucking nasty collar off and put yours back on okay?" He pulled me into a kiss.

We went inside and Master Boyd got his bolt cutters out of the shed. This time, unlike the last time he cut off one of Sheryl's collars, he put a rolled-up towel against my neck. His tool broke her collar off immediately. He didn't hesitate to take his own from my hands and re-lock it in place of the fake one. I noticed his hands were still shaking. I could sense something was very wrong, but whatever it was he was not saying.

I heard a car pulling into the driveway as my Master walked to the kitchen to throw away the broken circle of silver and replace his bolt cutters. "Master, someone is here," I yelled in near terror.

He came running back and peeked out the front window appearing concerned. "Oh shit, it is Dennis, God damn it. Okay, baby sit down on the couch and let me handle this. Don't speak, that is a directive." He pointed at the sofa and shot me a warning look.

I nodded and sat down keeping my eyes to the floor unsure what the issue was with Dennis this time. I watched Master Boyd stand by the door waiting for the old bull to knock. Dennis shot him an angry look as he came inside. He then shot another nasty glare at me.

"So, you found her did you? Where," Dennis said while hitching his pants but not taking a seat.

"In the woods. She was chased down and attacked by Sheryl, Dennis. She got away and I found her wandering and lost," Master Boyd said appearing irritated.

Dennis narrowed his eyes at me. "Sheryl? She is that collar Master thingy ain't she? Why would she attack Alexandria?"

Master Boyd snorted loudly. "I told you Dennis. Sheryl tossed the collar. She is bad news."

Dennis rubbed his handlebar mustache. "Judas Priest. I don't give a fuck, Boyd. This insanity has to stop. You took off shift over this drama? Sheryl is Alexandria's problem ain't she," he yelled out suddenly.

Master Boyd shot me another warning to be quiet look. "Alexandria is my fiancé and ward, so her problems are my problems."

Dennis nodded angrily. "Apparently so Boyd. I told you I was going to drop that discussion till we all cooled off, but I can't have you fucking taking off work every time Alexandria has a tiff with her. Whatever the fuck those idiots are that mess with the collar thingy. I see she has one on. If it ain't Sheryl than who the fuck did that? You? Better hope not boy. Do you know what I am going to do if I find out you are behind that shit?" He pointed at my Master's collar.

My Master glared at Dennis. "What would you do Dennis? I don't believe that is your fucking business. I told you to stay out of my love life."

The old bull chuckled bitterly while smiling with fury. "Oh I can't stop you two from knocking boots that is for sure. But I can end that guardianship of yours over her. I can also have your ass put away for taking advantage of a weak-minded girl by making her call you Master. You want to try me on that Boyd? With your history and your illness? She is another man's wife as it is. You add in there schizophrenic as hell, and if I am to understand correctly, just had a stroke not more than six months ago. Won't look good before the Judge would it?"

Master Boyd stood there with his eyes wide open in shock at what Dennis just said. "Seriously Dennis? You would do that to me? To Alexandria? What the hell is wrong with everyone? Damn." He walked over and sat next to me still appearing unable to wrap his mind around that threat.

Dennis shook his head. "Boyd I don't want to get nasty with you, nor Alexandria. I want you to fucking listen to me. She needs help. You are not the one to give it to her. You are missing work, tried to kill yourself, been in the God damned hospital four times now since this all started. And look at her. She isn't fairing no better. The two of you together are a nightmare. I am not going to stand for it no more. Now did you put that collar on her, Boyd?" He pointed at me again.

My Master looked at me appearing confused. "No, he didn't Dennis," I said flatly before my Master could mess up his life by admitting to what he had indeed done.

Dennis scoffed. "He didn't huh? Then who the fuck did Alexandria? Boyd said it ain't Sheryl."

Master Boyd looked at the floor, "It is Rebecca Dollar's collar, Dennis. Not that you have any business knowing. Stay out of this, I mean it."

The old bull nodded. "You think it is not my business Boyd, but you are my business. So here is how it is going to be. Rebecca can take care of her own. That is why that fucking collar thingy exists if I remember correctly. You send Alexandria to her. I am sending you out for five days training. When you get back you will transfer the Guardianship to Rebecca and that is final. Alexandria is moving out. This stops now." Dennis hitched his pants and left slamming the door behind him.

My Master let out his breath while I began to hyperventilate my own. "Master, are you tossing my collar? What did I do wrong?" I felt I was going to die right there in terror.

He shook his head and tried to pull me close, I pulled away unable to catch any oxygen. "No, baby stop, it is okay. Look, I will go to this stupid training for Dennis and you can stay with Rebecca till I get back. I can't leave you at Mary's for a bit with Sheryl running around anyway. I was going to ask Rebecca to pretend to be the fake collar. Heather told me she once had asked to be considered for it if it ever came up. This will be fine. It buys me time to deal with Dennis. You have to trust me. Remember we trust each other?" He pulled me toward him forcing me into his embrace.

"No Master, I don't like Rebecca. I remember her from Ginger's days. She is weird. Please don't make me go," I wailed out now in tears from extreme terror.

None of this was making any sense. I didn't understand why Dennis was making me leave my Master's home. I didn't understand why Sheryl was trying to recollar me. It seemed that everyone was against me suddenly, and I couldn't recall doing anything to anyone to deserve any of it.

Master Boyd held me trying to console my grief. "Baby, Dennis is upset over all the trouble we have caused in the last two years with our sickness. He will calm down once this all settles. Sheryl is a bitch. I will deal with her when I get back, okay? You can't work anymore. The doctors say, well they say you are not able to maintain a job. It is up to me to support our family. I don't want to lose you nor have you and me having to live out of dumpsters like most of our kind do. Dennis has my job in his pocket. I must play this shit for a minute till the dust settles. I am asking you to play along too. I will take you to Rebecca's this morning. I will be gone a few days. When I get back I will fix all this. I just need you to be quiet and go along with this until I can get the details worked out. Can you do that for me, or do I need to make it a directive?" He held my chin and looked into my eyes pleading with me to help him work out this serious problem with his guardian.

I nodded while tearing up. "Okay Master, as you wish. I won't go against you but do I have to serve Rebecca?"

He appeared to be thinking. "Uhm, I wouldn't think so. I will offer to pay her see if that will work. If not, you can cook and clean for her only. She is nothing more than my collar sitter. You are not to submit to her. No special services. You belong to me. She is just a fake. Do you understand?" He kissed my forehead.

I closed my eyes sighing in relief, "Thank You for Your mercy Master."

He chuckled. "Was that what you were worried about baby? I told you I am never letting you go. You are never to submit to anyone else. I just must figure out how to get Dennis off our ass before he fires me or worse. If I had another guardian, well, doesn't matter. This will work for a minute. Protecting, defending, and caring for you is my job, so you let me do what I do, and you do what I tell you."

I nodded. "Yes Master, that is the way it is supposed to work."

Master Boyd smiled. "Yes it will work too. Okay baby let's go get us both packed for a quick break. Oh, and since I will be gone for nearly a week, I would like to request special services of the collar if you would be so kind." He winked at me.

We went to his room to pull our bags for this most unexpected separation. I didn't even get his socks packed before he grabbed me by the waist and again requested special services.

I, of course, granted them without further requests. The man took his rights as if he planned to be gone for a year. His eagerness and the urgency of his lustful advances made me nervous that he didn't think he was coming back.

When I voiced that concern, he assured me he was just making sure to build up enough stamina to be away from his One and Only for so long. I wanted to believe him but after all the troubles we had over the previous twenty-four months I had difficulty finding security in his promise to return quickly.

The problem of course was not only my chronic bad luck, but a severe case of PTSD. That undertow of gloom and doom had reached painful levels since the kidnapping, rapes, and filming at the shed.

It wasn't just me suffering from this nasty flair up of an old nemesis diagnosis. Master Boyd was also showing extreme symptoms thanks to his own foul treatment at the hands of Harbor View, Julia, and Gus. Dennis couldn't have picked a worse time to lay this stress on the doorstep of two very disturbed schizophrenics.

Neither my Master nor I were finding peaceful rest due to nightmares. We also were demonstrating hyper vigilance, anger outbursts, irritability, inability to focus and/or concentrate, negative feelings about the future, distrust of others, flashbacks, fear of everyone, and random severe terror with panic attacks.

We could never tell Dennis or anyone about the situation with Gus and Julia in the Cumberland shed so we had to suffer in silence. We knew no one would believe we did what we had to do, not just in self-defense but to stop those monsters from hurting anyone else. That didn't help make the nights less dark, nor could we chase away the horrible memories in each other's arms. Like it or not, Master Boyd and I were on our own to deal with what no one should ever have to do, much less two barely functioning psychotics.

Once we had finally finished packing and lovemaking my Master had me dress him for his trip. I asked him how far he would be sent. He laughed and told me the training center was only two hours away.

That made me feel better, but I still was unhappy about having to stay with someone I barely knew. I was going to be separated from my kids and fur babies yet again as well. It seemed I was having a hell of a time just being home. For someone without a job, I sure was getting shuffled around a lot.

We got into the Chevelle to head to Wheatly proper where the long-forgotten Rebecca lived. While I watched the world go by, I remembered her. She had thrown a party after my catatonic fit during mid-summer at the Springfields. Mistress Ginger had not collared my brother Matthew, but she had only days earlier leashed me to Christopher.

FLASHBACK: *My Brillo pad bath after that nasty situation forced my Mistress to keep her hands off my girl parts. Mistress Ginger had wanted to upset Linda by coming to the party at Rebecca's house. She had pulled me into the hallway and had me employ oral congress while she screamed loudly in ecstasy. Linda had caught us of course and it had broken her heart.*

Not long after that, I had a psychotic fit that landed me in the hospital. I recalled I needed to cut out my alien tongue and rouge hands. Dennis and Master Boyd had come to stop me. I hit the future Master Boyd in the head with a chair from Rebecca's kitchen table. He must have met her that night.

I had long since forgotten the short gay masculine woman whose party had set the stage for such a nasty segment of my life. I thought of my red-headed Goddess Mistress Ginger and my lost lover/brother Matthew.

My chest began to ache, so I pushed them from my mind. Psycho's memories seemed like someone else's but when it came to Matthew, apparently Alexandria loved him too. Even almost five years later, almost to the day, I couldn't even think of his name without immediate tears and grief. I could see his larger dented collar forever entangled with my smaller one sinking to the bottom of the river.

"Baby we are here," Master Boyd's voice broke me from my trance of despairing memories.

I shook it off while looking ahead at the house from Psycho's memory. It was the same color and even had the same smell that Psycho had recorded in her Looper. I got out feeling apprehension grip me like the claw of a hawk around a mouse. Chills ran down my spine in a tap dance of tension. I felt glued to the spot. My Master saw my dismay and came around the car to hold my hand as we walked to the door to knock.

Rebecca answered appearing to have just awakened. She was rubbing her eyes and her short dark hair sticking straight up.

"Boyd, hey man what's up? Oh wait, am I under arrest?" She yawned then looked me up and down smiling.

"Holy shit, is that who I think it is? The Psycho herself. Ginger's hot little collar. Damn, are my eyes playing tricks on me," yelled out Rebecca as her grin got even wider.

Master Boyd frowned. "She isn't Ginger's anymore. She is mine. Can we come in Rebecca? And no you are not under arrest."

Rebecca's eyes went wide, and her jaw dropped. "Yours? Get out of town, no way. Boyd, wait is this a joke? Ginger is back in town ain't she? Tell that bitch good one. Where is she Psycho? In the car?" She started to chuckle.

I winced at hearing that name. "Ginger is not here Rebecca. She is gone forever." I looked at the ground grimly recalling her abandonment of my collar to Master Leslie.

Rebecca's smile melted. "Wait, what? You mean Boyd is telling the truth? Huh? No can't be. Psycho you are a, you know, submissive. Does he know that" she said to me as if Master Boyd were not standing right there holding my hand.

Master Boyd rolled his eyes. "Uhm yeah he knows that, Rebecca. I am her Master. That is my collar. So can we come in or we going to advertise this shit to your neighbors some more? Also, that is Alexandria. Stop calling her Psycho, thank you."

She nodded but appeared to be in some shock. "Oh okay Alexandria. Yeah come on in. The house is a mess. My girlfriend is out of town. Really Boyd, that is your collar? How the fuck did that happen? You're a cop, man." She looked at my neck in amazement.

Master Boyd took a seat on the very same sofa that once I had sat next to Mistress Ginger on. He pulled me onto his lap for his strange child holding PDA demonstration. I didn't fight this time as I was happy to be as close to Simon's Key as possible. I never cared much for Rebecca and didn't want to stay even a minute much less five days with her.

Rebecca closed the door and sat across from us in her old rocking chair as she had done six years earlier. She looked us over with a weird grin on her face.

"So, what can I do you for Boyd? I mean surely you didn't come see little old me to show off your lovely lady here. Lucky bastard. How the fuck did you get that collar? Did Heather sell it to you?" Rebecca said nosing into things that were not her business.

My Master scoffed. "Long story. Doesn't matter. It is mine. The reason I came is to ask for a favor. I am willing to pay you for the favor, but you must keep this all to yourself. Can you do that?"

Rebecca laughed out loud. "Depends on the favor man. You wanting to stash pot or bodies here, forget it officer. If it is not breaking the law and the pay is right I am your girl."

My Master smiled at me trying to make me feel better. "Well it is like this, there are some who are not okay with me being Alexandria's Master. You know because I am a cop like you said. I need someone to pretend to be the collar holder if asked and I need someone to keep Alexandria safe when I travel or do business. There is an old Master gunning for a re-collar. I must go out of town today for a few days. What I am saying is I am willing to pay you to keep her here in your house in secret till I get back. Then I will continue to pay you to say you are the collar holder if anyone were to ask you. Okay there it is."

Rebecca's mouth flew open again. "Really? I am sure this must be a dream. You want me to pretend to be her

Master if anyone asks and hide her in my house for a few days from a crazy ex-Master for pay?"

He nodded. "Yeah that is what I said. I will be gone till the end of the week. Will you do it? I can pay you for it, but you have to keep this all to yourself. This never happened."

Rebecca sat back in her chair smiling wide again, "Well fuck yeah I will do it. I remember her. Man, she is one hot girl. Had this whole house moaning. Sure, I want in on that. And I get paid too?"

I looked up at my Master very frightened at that statement. He saw my terror and shook his head.

"Wait a second Rebecca. Alexandria is staying here as your guest. She has her meds in her purse. You make sure she eats, takes her medication, and stays out of trouble. You lie to anyone who asks about her collar saying it is really yours, but you are not to get any services, not those kinds. She can cook or clean for you as you wish but no sex, thudding or bathing stuff. I mean it. You are getting paid to watch over her only. Those exclusive services belong to her Master, me." He frowned at her.

Rebecca scoffed. "Ah okay got it. Well, that is a lot to ask man. You better have brought your wallet."

My Master snorted. "Is that a yes?"

Rebecca nodded. "Yeah you got your sub sitter man."

He smiled. "That is great. I will pay well but you get half now and the other half when I get back. She had better be in the condition she is in right now or I wouldn't want to be you Rebecca." He reached under us and grabbed his wallet counting out some money to pay the woman.

She laughed. "You fucking pigs are alike. Quit threatening me. She will be fine man. You act like I am some crazy bitch. What you think I am going to dig a hole and bury her in the woods or something?" She reached out to take the money.

Master Boyd and I flashed a look of terror at each other. "Why would you say something horrible like that Rebecca," yelped out my Master as we both gulped feeling that statement hit a bit too close to home.

She jumped appearing startled. "Hey, just saying dude. Not going to happen. Look here, I am not going to hurt Alexandria was all I meant. Wow, you need to take a chill pill man." She snatched the money from my Master hand.

I gripped my Master around the waist in a vice hold. He felt my fear rising. It was very apparent I was upset. He asked Rebecca if we could step outside a moment and say goodbye. She waved us on not even looking up from her cash counting. Master Boyd pulled me along after him to Rebecca's front porch.

"Baby, it will be okay. I will be back at the end of the week? You can call the kids but don't tell anyone where you are. If Sheryl comes back, I won't be here to protect you. Don't leave this house. Do what you are told and behave yourself. I will call you everyday promise. I will be home to get you before you know it. Now kiss me and remember that

I love you will all my heart and soul." He pulled me into a deep kiss while groping my unit passionately.

Rebecca came to the door as we finished our goodbye. "Okay Boyd, have fun doing whatever you damned cops do. She will be fine. See you this weekend. Alexandria, get in this house before you make my neighbors jealous." She laughed while motioning me back inside.

My Master waved, then got into his car and pulled out while I went into the house. Rebecca closed the door and locked it.

21st Master: Interim (no collar and no key)
Master Rebecca – The Faker
Reign August, one day and one night

Rebecca stood there looking me over with a strange smile on her face. "Wow, Ginger's hot ass collar standing in my house alone. Never thought I'd see the day."

I kept my eyes down cast. "I am not Ginger's anymore. I belong to Master Boyd, Rebecca."

She chuckled. "Ah not true. You belong to me until the weekend sweetie. I do believe that is my collar for a few days."

I looked up in fear. "No, you are just a holder of a fake collar. Master Boyd just needed me to stay here till he gets home." I felt uneasy and dizzy, something was very wrong here.

Rebecca clicked her tongue. "Fake collar huh? Well I don't see any other Master here now? Just you and me doll face. Now I have always wondered what you did to Ginger in my hallway. I have had a lot of fantasies about it over the years, but here you are. I think that is where we will start. You show me what you did to make that hot bitch scream for God and we will find other shit to do after that." She began to walk toward me.

I backed away feeling very frightened as I realized she was much bigger than me, "Master Boyd said no special services, no submission, just cooking or cleaning. He paid you to let me stay without service like that. He said no. I say no." I stood my ground feeling it was my right to deny this weirdo her request.

Rebecca laughed. "Whatever pumpkin." She jumped forward grabbing my upper arms knocking me into the wall.

I kicked her as she began to bash my head, knocking me half silly. I was confused but continued to punch and thrash wildly. Rebecca grabbed my collar and began dragging me down the hallway. I grabbed the door frame holding on with all my might while she nearly ripped my head off.

"Alright, enough of this shit," she yelled as she pushed me backward and kicked me in the stomach.

I went down to the floor in severe agony unable to breath. Rebecca walked over and dragged me by my right upper arm with a strength I never imagined she could possess. I struggled despite my gasping for air. My lungs felt they had collapsed in my chest as she made it into her room and slammed her door behind us.

I tried to get up, but Rebecca dropped down on top of my unit holding me by my throat while she groped under my shirt and began tearing at my pants. I clawed at her hand while she squeezed out what little breath I had left.

"Stop fighting me, you bitch," Rebecca growled in a suddenly deeper voice than I had ever heard come from her before.

I struggled harder trying to buck her off my unit as she removed my pants to my knees. She quickly flipped me to my face then grabbed me around my waist. I pawed at the floor as she lifted me to her groin. Then to my utter shock I felt her forceful entry. Rebecca was a man.

In pure horror she, oops, he began to thrust harshly holding me by my waist so I couldn't get way. I did my best to crawl, but Rebecca followed while continuing his rape. I finally had enough air to scream for help, but it did no good. The Interim Rebecca reached his climax before I could even get out a raspy plea for mercy to flow out of my voice box.

Rebecca panted and laughed. "Wow! Now that was fun. A start gorgeous, but next time not so much fighting. I like to take my time you know."

"You fucking asshole. You are a man. You just raped me. I am calling the cops. Get off of me," I cried out tears flowing like rain.

He chuckled while still coupled and holding me tightly. "Yeah should've told you I guess. Funny no one ever noticed. I just like to dress like a girl, but I am all man baby. I am not even gay. I love pussy. That is a fine one you got there too. This is great. Your Master won't be back for five days. Just think of all the fun we are going to have? Then when Cindee gets home in a couple days, we can bring her in too. She is wanting to be a collar. You will teach her how to do it right. See, you'll even have a sister collar in this house. No need to tell Boyd our little secret, or anyone for that matter. Just to be sure I think you can stay right here in my room until you realize this is the way it is gonna be. You will submit to me and I will handle Boyd another day. A cop Psycho? Really? What the fuck were you thinking? Our kind don't go with cops." He slapped my backside hard making me yelp through my tears.

"Let me go, Rebecca, if that is even your fucking name. I am not your kind," I wailed out wishing for death.

He giggled. "Nah, my name is actually Robert. I guess all that time your name was really Alexandria. I like Psycho better. I will call you Psycho. Around here, a name don't really mean much anyway. And yeah you are like me, a fucking freak. In fact you are even more a freak than I ever thought to be. I know all about you nutball. Ginger had a really big mouth. Too bad I never got my cock into it. Not that I didn't try. Shit she was fine. But then I got her better half right here whenever I want. I plan to keep you too and have me a nice pair of submissives. Damn what a lucky man I am gonna be." Robert finally uncoupled and let me go.

I crawled to his closet pulling up my pants while crying loudly, "Get away from me. Help, someone help me. This is not happening," I yelled completely terrified out of my mind.

Robert snorted. "Oh yeah it is happening doll face. Now you shut that pretty mouth. Wait, you know what, I think we will just keep you quiet till you settle down. What do you say?" He got up and came at me again.

I did my best to fight him off, but he was indeed a man. I was no match while he slapped, punched, and kicked me to near unconsciousness. While I lay there near out of my mind from his cruel blows, he took off my clothing making clicking noises and comments of approval.

Robert finished eye humping my unit then picked me up throwing me onto his bed. He tied me to his headboard and put a ball gag into my mouth before I could recover any strength. I was no longer able to fight or yell for help. I glared at the bastard while he made sure all his ropes were tight and my ability to get out of them null and void.

He smiled at me. "That is much better. You just rest up doll face. I will be back later for more fun and games. When that cop of yours calls you had better play nice or before he can get back, well there won't be anything worth coming home to. You be a good girl and I will go easy. Hell, you will love it. All you need to do is stop fighting me. I am a lover not a fighter baby. You think it over and we will talk again soon." He got off his bed and left me tied there in the dark as he turned off the light and shut the door.

I lay there cursing Dennis, Boyd, Robert, Doctor Baker, Sheryl, Mary, God, and everyone. I was beyond angry. I had only just escaped the Baltimore horror only to be kidnapped and reintroduced to the finer points of rape in a shed while being filmed. I escaped only to be thrown down into a dirt road and forcibly collared by someone I believed was likely involved in all my misfortunes as of late.

If all that was not enough, I was just given over to a fucking rapist. Worst of all I was handed over like a side of beef by my own God damned Master who had paid the shithead to enact the crime. I simply was blowing a gasket.

When Robert returned to continue his abuse of me, he found out really quickly he could not remove his ball gag. I screamed, bit, and even tried to chew through the ropes. That didn't stop him from forcing himself on my bonded unit repeatedly for rest of the day, but he didn't get all he had hoped for, a blow job. I tried to bite it off.

In his anger at my refusal to submit to his interests and collar he slapped, thudded, and even bit me back. It didn't stop my struggling and thrashing against his unwelcomed lustful advances. By nightfall I was fatigued, despaired, and beaten to hell. It seemed to me Alexandria was not fairing any better than Psycho ever had.

It had to be around midnight when Robert finally came to bed. He crawled into the bed next to me and once again forced his vile sex on me. He was spent to exhaustion himself and fell asleep while in the middle of his carnal congress with my unit. I decided right there it was time to use guile to get out of this mess. I bucked his disgusting unit off mine causing him to nearly roll off the bed. He woke up and looked at me groggily.

I did my best to appear smiling despite the gag. He smiled back and yawned.

"You finally ready to submit to me, Psycho? I mean you would sure have a lot more fun if you would just give it up honey." He stretched.

I nodded and tried to make a seductive look with my eyes at him. He stopped stretching in surprise.

"Hey, do you mean it? Or are you fucking with me?" He got into my face.

I arched my back as if interested and nodded again. He saw what appeared to be an invite to violate me. He smiled widely.

"Well hell year." He removed my gag.

"Let me go Robert and let's do this collaring right. You have to untie me though or I won't submit." I smiled again seductively.

Robert narrowed his eyes. "What changed your mind? How do I know you won't just run off and get the cops? Do I look like an idiot to you?"

I laughed. "You think the cops would even believe me? Come on man. Hell, Boyd is so scared of Dennis did he not pay you to look after me and to lie too? You can't keep me tied up forever anyway. What you going to do when Boyd calls here today? So, we going to do this or what? I am really ready for that consummation of the collar. I can give you whatever you want after that." I writhed as if interested in him.

He chuckled. "Yeah I knew it. You are one of us. Not a fucking cop's submissive. Not that vanilla shit, no way. Okay girl I will untie you, but I want to do the collaring the right way. The way Cindee and I did it. Wait, you're going to train my girl too? You will love her and she is going to blow her skirt for you."

I purred. "Can't wait lover boy. The more the merrier I always say. Been a long while since I went muff diving. When I am done with Cindee, you'll be lucky to get in edgewise." I kissed at him appearing very turned on.

His hands were shaking with excitement as he began to loosen the ropes holding me hostage to his odious desires. "Fuck, I think I may nut just listening to you gorgeous."

I giggled. "Oh do go on Master Robert. Wait till you get my special head service. There is nothing I am more trained to do." I smiled diabolically.

Robert grabbed his dick. "I can't wait till you wrap those lips around this. I need that head service." He let my first arm go.

I arched my back to stretch. "Oh I think you do need my head service. It is truly to die for Master. At least one actually met God after I employed it." He released my other arm as I got onto my knees on this bed still smiling and posing in sexually suggestive ways.

He stared at me in awe. "Damn you are so beautiful. Can I get that head service before the collaring?"

I laughed loudly. "Oh I intend to give it to you right now lover boy." I stood up quickly and kicked him in his face with all the force I could muster.

He flew backward off the bed onto the floor. I jumped off right onto his sternum knocking his wind out. I then grabbed the lamp from the nightstand and hit him in the head with it. Yeah I did, so sue me. He promptly went nighty night. I stood over him naked laughing maniacally.

"How is that special head service there, Robert? I told you it is to die for." I threw the lamp on the bed and went to put on my clothes.

I mumbled and cursed while putting back on my scattered clothing items. My anger was rising again. I looked over at the unconscious Robert the rapist. I thought briefly about taking a shower but decided it was best to get out of there while he was busy counting birds in the bush.

I grabbed my purse and took back Master Boyd's money sticking it into the secret ripped place inside my bag with Julia's missing five thousand. I really needed to get out to Darlin soon and bury that. Yeah that is where it was for those who were wondering.

I walked out the door and down the sidewalk headed right for the center of the sleeping town of Wheatly. My father darkness caressed my bruised face with his soft fingers and gave me his misty kisses. I immediately felt better. I belong to my father more than Psycho ever did. He whispered his secrets into my battered ears. I closed my eyes and breathed him inside my unit. I knew he could heal my wounds like no other. Having my daddy there to hold me in his inky arms did help my pain. However, for my anger, I would need a bit more aid than even his vastness could afford me.

Ah, there up ahead was just what I needed to cure me of that most uncomfortable emotion. The old annex building. The Wheatly boys in blue now used that old cinderblock building to store their overabundance of confiscated items from the unruly townsfolk.

I did believe I owed the cops a bit of a service that night. It was after all Dennis, and Master Boyd's fault I was wandering through my father's reign with Robert's unwelcomed seed running down my inner thighs. Yeah, I would think remodeling service is the correct equal service for the one they provided to me.

I reached down and picked up several large pieces of gravel and a bottle from the side of the two laned main street. With all the strength I could pull from within I threw the first rock right into the window of the building.

Bullseye, one of the windows shattered loudly. I jumped up and down giving a thumbs up to the roar of the approving crowd inside my head. I pelted the bottle at the glass opening adjacent to the one now bleeding shards of glass.

Another explosion echoed into the blackness. I bowed to my adoring audience as they screamed for more. I spun on my toes while throwing another rock. My fans howled in delight as the next window collapsed from my aim. I smiled and courtesy while blowing kisses to those amazing folks who had come to watch me destroy, errr, redecorate the annex building for my police friends.

The squad car pulled up flashing its blue and red lights while I hurled my fourth rock right into the remaining window. It appeared to be raining glass in the reflection of the police vehicle's headlights.

Jeers and boos from my audience filled my ears. The fuzz had come to end our service, but we were not done damn it. I turned to angrily face the offending cop who dared to interrupt our show.

"Alexandria, what in the Sam Hill are you doing," I heard Dennis yell out from his position behind the squad car door.

I spun around smiling happily. "Why I am loving you Dennis. The way you love me. Don't you like my work? You know it really hurts when someone you trusted fucks you over for no apparent reason." I tossed yet another rock that bounced off the cinder block wall.

The crowd hissed in my ears. "A swing and a miss, Dennis. Did you see that damned wall get in my way." I giggled at that obvious statement.

"Alexandria, honey. What is going on? Look, you need to stop throwing those rocks. You are getting yourself into a lot of trouble here. What would Rebecca say," Dennis called out keeping his distance due to my rock ammo.

I laughed maniacally. "You mean Robert? Oh my, what would he say? Not much Dennis. He doesn't have any fucking teeth anymore. Hard to speak without fucking teeth. Tell you what, since you seem to give a shit about what Robert would say, call him. Ask him how his dick got into my unit while you are at it, oh wait, I remember now, silly me. You put it there, Dennis. Thank you. Just what I fucking needed." I threw another rock into another of the windows, shattering it into smithereens.

Dennis groaned. "Alexandria, what are you talking about. Do I need to call Boyd? Is that what this is about? Stop throwing rocks at the windows, damn it."

I spun around to smile at Dennis with tears running down my face as I walked into his headlights. I heard him and Linda, who was driving, gasp at the sight.

"Why don't you call him, Dennis? Go ahead. Is that what this is about? Yeah, you fucked me over Dennis. This is your fault. You made him send me away. Robert broke my face because you broke my heart. Now I broke your windows. Fair is fair, my friend." I bowed then saluted as I spun back and threw another rock at the building.

Linda yelled out, "Alexandria, please stop this. You need help. Let us help you. Who did this to you?" She sounded concerned.

I laughed. "All of you did it to me, Linda. So fuck off. No worries, I got this." I threw yet another rock.

Dennis decided I was out of ammo. "Alexandria, that is it, you're coming in. Now get over here in the squad car. Don't make me take you down girl."

I smiled as I took a deep breath. "Tag, you're it Dennis." I took off running down the street fast as my platforms could carry me.

Dennis came flying up fast as greased lightening while Linda jumped into the car to give chase down the street. This time I gave the old bull a run of his money. I bobbed, weaved, and even elbowed him off me once before he finally knocked my ass to the ground.

I just giggled and coughed while gasping for air as Dennis cuffed me. He grabbed my upper arm cursing the day I was born barely able to breathe himself.

"God damn it. What is going on with you? Shit. Just shit. You are going to have to pay for those windows, if the judge don't send you off to jail for it too I will be shocked." Dennis growled as he stuffed me into the backseat of the police vehicle.

"So the fuck what, Dennis? Then your precious Carla will be happy, won't she? With me down river she can have Boyd all back to her little old self. So, can you? What is your problem? This should be a happy day for you. Since you want me the fuck gone so bad. Well, all you had to do was ask. Shit, no sense in beating up the bush, oops. I mean raping the bush, oops I mean one in the hand is better than two in the bush. Shit, guess I just have bush on the brain. I am just not any better than old pervy Robert. He has been enlightened. You could say he has seen the light." I was beyond giggling at my stress driven insane speech pattern.

Dennis looked at Linda as they drove me to the station for booking. "She sounds nuts but Linda she ain't sounding retarded. I thought she was retarded?"

I sputtered as I howled at that statement. "Oh I am retarded alright Dennis. Look where I am. Anyone who stays in this town is fucking retarded. Lucky me, I am stupid and crazy." I fell over in my seat really laughing at that truism.

Linda and Dennis took my giggling ass into the station. You could have knocked every officer over with a feather when they saw who was being brought through the door. Like the bad old days, their very own Psycho was in cuffs, being hauled into the intake room.

Even shy Keith scratched his head looking around for the infamous Boyd who was supposed to be keeping his loony on a leash. I had not been arrested for mischief since he collared me in 1997. Everyone knew that was thanks to the schizophrenic cop's loving care. Everyone but Carla and Dennis.

As Linda had me stand against the wall and spread them I loudly announced I was ready for all the cops to come and check out the goods. I yelled next and then demanded Linda hand out numbers. I was beyond foul in my descriptions of what she might find up my skirt.

"Mother, what has gotten into you. You have not pulled this shit since you were a kid. Aren't you getting too old for it," said Linda beyond confused by my regressive behavior.

I giggled. "Ah not old Linda, ripe. Robert got into me darling. Let's go ahead and let everyone else get in there too. May as well do it all at once so I can get it over with. I am tired of this trickling shit." I smiled at her then blew her a kiss.

Linda shook her head. "Dennis is calling the hospital. They are sending someone over with a shot you know. Mother, I thought, I just assumed you got better pills. I just can't stand seeing you like this. Boyd will be upset too."

I nodded. "You bet he is. But he ain't here, now is he? Tell that doc to hurry with the shot please. It is always much more fun to masturbate with my Prince around. Hey, sneak in later and I will let you watch the show." I winked at her while laughing.

Linda crossed her arms. "You need to stop that shit now. Who the fuck is Robert? Did that asshole beat you up like this? We need to file a report on him if he did. Can you be rational for a moment so I can do that?"

I frowned suddenly. "Rebecca is Robert, Linda. Your old friend is a man darling. Did you know he was packing a loaded gun? Well, welcome to my nightmare babe." I rolled my eyes as I began to cry just as rapidly as I had been giggling.

Linda stood there appearing confused. "Wait, did you say Rebecca, Rebecca Dollar is armed? She beat you up?"

I groaned. "Fuck, Rebecca is a man, damn it. His name is Robert. God damn, his gun is his cock. Do I need to draw a picture for you too," I yelled out now furious as my tears dried up quickly.

Linda almost fell to the floor. "Rebecca is Robert? Holy shit. Dennis, Dennis! Fuck me, stay here Mother. Dennis, God damn it," She ran from the room.

I got off the wall and began to sing a song about a Mexican cat named El Gato. Linda returned with a jail uniform. I was dressed in orange then cuffed and hauled over to the ER for a rape kit and photographs.

Quick note: *That is always a fun way to spend the night by the way. Just got raped and now you get treated to another bunch of strangers poking and prodding your violated parts. What is even better is all the questions and answer sessions after. And drawing the pictures so you can prove what that fucking DNA they just pulled from you already said.*

Best of all is the parting gift the rapist leaves you, besides the PTSD and nightmares. It is the six months of testing for STD's and the fear that this time you will not be lucky. I was lucky again, but the fear was enough to keep me stressed as they all have been over the years, just saying.

Dennis and Randell left the hospital to pick up Robert. He had of course split town. In time they did catch him. He got probation for is crime. I got a lot of nice embarrassing photos, questioned like a criminal, and the indignity of having to be raped again. Rape kits are just like rape if you have never had the pleasure of one.

In the end, he took a plea bargain to avoid public scrutiny. Lucky me, I got to take that for him. The freak schizophrenic) raped by what at that time was viewed as a freak (man who dressed like a woman) Nice huh? Welcome to the legal system ladies. At least he got probation for his crimes. More than any of the others ever did.

PS: I did knock out all his front teeth though, yay me.

I was taken back to the jail nice and comfy. My shot of Prince Val was my consolation prize for the violence of the day and night. My Master was called and told I was arrested but not told about the stress that caused my anger outburst.

No one wanted to be the one to break that news to my already overwhelmed fiancé. They all knew about Gus in Baltimore. Dennis forbade anyone from telling him about the rapes. He thought it might send Master Boyd over the edge and cause him to leave the session.

Since My Guardian was stuck in a training session, I was a guest of the white cell for the week. In all honesty, that was my plan. I committed a petty crime to be hauled into the one place I knew I would be safe. It did get a bit out of hand, but hey, I was freaking out. Breaking a few windows was not a major crime. I would not even get jail time for it but who knew those windows could be so expensive?

Quick note: *Restitution and a year probation were what I got. You know the same that old Robert got for raping me in the first place. Yeah, you read that right, a whole year of probation. Makes sense. I mean beating up a girl, tying her to your bed and raping her repeatedly is bad unless you do it to someone who doesn't matter. Had I been the fucking prom queen, or a town father's daughter things would have been different, just saying. Oh well, sucks to be me doesn't it?*

When Friday night finally arrived I was laying in my cot trying to trace the dots of dead flies on the ceiling with my mind for the thousandth time. Not a lot to do in jail, you know, when the door opened. I turned my head to see Master Boyd standing there looking angered.

I smiled bitterly as I recalled seeing him in this very cell back in May 1997, when he was the rapist instead of about to find out about another.

"Breaking out the windows in the annex building, Alexandria? Really? What are you like fifteen?" He crossed his arms while standing at the door.

I rolled my eyes "Gosh Master are you planning to ground me?"

Master Boyd sighed. "You were supposed to stay at Rebecca's. You have made a lot of trouble. I have no idea what I can do to fix this shit now. Dennis is hot and now he is threatening my job if I take you home. I guess a directive don't mean shit. Not with you."

I looked at the floor. "Uhm, they didn't tell you did they Master." I felt a cold chill run down my spine.

He snorted. "Yeah they told me you were breaking windows and dancing around town like a fucking loon. It sounded like you didn't even wait till I was out of town. What the fuck Alexandria." He raised his voice slightly.

I winced. "Master, You may want to sit down. I need to tell you something." I took a deep breath.

Master Boyd looked around the cell appearing irritated. "Where shall I sit my love? Your lap maybe?" He snorted again seeming very indifferent to my request.

I nodded. "You were warned Master. So, Rebecca is actually Robert."

He stood there appearing not to understand. "Huh? What the hell are you saying Alexandria? Robert? Who is Robert and what the fuck does that have to do with anything?" He scoffed.

I pulled my knees to my chest and took another deep breath. "Uhm, okay Master just going to say it. Rebecca is actually a guy named Robert. Rebecca had a cock, Master."

My Master's eyes went wide. "What did you say?"

"Rebecca had a dick, Master."

He shook his head wildly. "Okay, uhm Rebecca is kind of boyish sure, but saying she has a dick, really Alexandria. That is no excuse for…" I interrupted him here.

"Master Rebecca has a dick and he used it on me. You left me to be raped. He beat the fuck out of me and I had to file a rape charge. Do you hear me this time? I broke the windows so I could be safe in case he came back for me, or Sheryl did." I put my face into my knees and began to weep for the hundredth time since my arriving in the cell.

My Master was silent for a moment. Then I heard him pound on the door loudly.

"Keith, let me the fuck out of here. Where is Dennis? God damn it, fuck." I heard the Keith let my Master out and he stormed off to attack the old bull for withholding this information.

I looked up to see Keith's red cherub face. "Here Alexandria, for you. Please keep it. No one I have ever known could use one more." He handed me his handkerchief with a smile of pity.

I smiled back. "Stay sweet Keith. You were always my favorite, you know."

He blushed. "If you need anything, you just let me know. I am right outside the door. Ain't nobody gonna hurt you with me there." He looked down as he walked out.

I used that handkerchief too. I needed a Keith or Officer Bradley in my life. If only I didn't have to be in a white cell to find one.

My Master returned rather quickly and came rushing to my cot to hold me. He cried right along with me offering many heart felt apologies that could not undo the damage. I know he didn't do it on purpose. He had no idea Rebecca was Robert. My Master never would have left me there had he known what would happen.

Despite his ignorance of the situation it had happened when he abandoned me. His Guardian had put me into the path of danger for the second time in so many days. I was tired of being afraid, beatings, rapes, kidnappings, and cruelty in general. I was nearly thirty now and nothing was changing. I was still a murder or suicide waiting to happen. I was still spending more time in mental institutions or jail than in my home with my children. Something had to change or Alexandria would fail on a larger scale than Psycho.

My Master got ahold of his emotions and pulled my head to his chest pledging to find Robert and make him pay. He was still missing at the time and Boyd did find him as promised. He then told me I was to get my clothing. We were going home. Dennis was told that if he said a word my Master would quit on the spot. Of course it was the weekend, so it was Boyd's days off anyway.

I was given my clothing while my Master went to sign me out. He came back to find me dressed and ready to go home. We walked together to the parking lot while he told me we could talk over what happened when we got back to the house.

"Boyd wait, Dennis wants to see you for a second. He needs your signature on a report," yelled Cathy before we made it to the car.

My Master shook his head. "God damn it. I am just about to blow baby. I have had it." He gritted his teeth.

I patted his hand. "Go sign the damned thing then let's go home Maser. I've had enough of this place too but like you said, one of us has to work."

He nodded. "Okay, wait here. It will take two seconds, baby. You sure you are okay. Come back inside with me?" He pointed at the entry.

I shook my head. "Not on your life Master. Just hurry up."

I watched him walk inside turning around several times to make sure I was still standing there. I stretched my legs and paced in a short line but had to move over to let a car pass by to park in the lot.

I looked back at the door hoping to see my Master before the officer that just pulled in came by to speak to me. When I was grabbed by the arms and pulled backward. I let out a yelp just as I was smashed behind a seat into the back of a two-door car. I tried to get up and come back out and was palmed in the nose.

I fell back as the car started speeding off with me still in the back while the passenger who had grabbed me jumped in yelling to gun it. I was still seeing stars when I saw the wicked smile in the rear-view mirror of none other than the Queen Bitch Sheryl herself.

Wow, someone is not having a nice day. Can you dig it? Yeah, at this point I must confess I was ready to jump off the river bridge to find Matthew. This was one of those weeks you say what the fuck did I do to piss off the Gods. I have had some bad years but 1996 through 2001 were the worst ever. From the death of Matthew to the rape of Gus and Robert I couldn't win for losing. But guess what? We are not even close to done with the bad luck yet. So, hang in there, this ride just started, and Sheryl is the driver.

Ready to meet Master 22? Hope so cause she is just around the corner. Wait to you see this gal.

**To be continued in Book Thirteen of the
"27 Masters" series entitled
"The White Room"**

About the Author: Alexandria May Ausman

Alexandria May Ausman in her 16th year was diagnosed with Schizophrenia. She was quickly abandoned by her foster parents. While still only a teen, she was forced to battle this devastating illness alone.

Alexandria has struggled with lack of a support system, numerous psychotic episodes, exploitation, homelessness, and an uncaring mental health system.

Alexandria raised two healthy children. After obtaining her bachelor's degree in psychology she worked as a child abuse investigator and became a diagnostic psychologist while acquiring her Master's in psychology. Alexandria never forgot the experience of 'slipping through the cracks.' Her life's goal is to help people suffering abuse and/or mental illness have access to necessary services. By accident, she became a model of 'gothic attire' and the World Goth Queen.

She began writing a fictionalized account of her life experiences after a catastrophic return of psychotic symptoms. Today, Alexandria is retired, and homebound due to crippling symptoms of schizophrenia. She currently lives in Tallahassee, Florida, with her loving husband and loyal support dogs.

www.ingramcontent.com/pod-product-compliance
Lightning Source LLC
Chambersburg PA
CBHW071521260626

47170CB00002B/460